Natalia

Naofumi Iwatani

Keel

"Well, if you must call me something shorter, you can call me Natalia," the woman said.
"Is that your real name? Or an alias?"
I replied. "Which is it?"

Table of Contents

Prologue: Use of Floating Weapons

"Hah!" I caught the swift strike on my shield while looking across at my training partner—Ren. "Try harder!" I was training with Ren in the village. The reason was simple: Ren had asked for me specifically to train, but I wasn't sure why. Raphtalia would be a better choice for training with the sword, or even Eclair—especially seeing as he had the hots for her.

This was coming on top of the fact he had placed all sorts of crazy restrictions on me. For a start, rather than defend, he had asked me to try using a "sword." I used a long and thin shield that was possible to use like a blade. Then he had asked me to use Float Shield and control them like I would swords floating in the air. I was now battling Ren with Float Shield and using Change Shield to turn them into various different forms. Of course, he had also forbidden me from using skills, magic, and life force. We'd even aligned our stats to be close to each other. It seemed like a lot of hassle for a training session.

Ren dropped back a little, squatted, and rushed at me with a shout. It was still a training session, so Ren had also turned his own sword into one with only a dull edge. He had been fighting with just one sword until a moment ago, but after he stepped back, when he rushed in again, he was suddenly attacking with two. I took the incoming strikes on my shield, meeting him head-on while also sending my float shields around behind him for a pincer attack.

Ren gave a grunt in response, his eyes still fixed on me while he used one of his swords to stop one of my float shields. That was impressive—almost like he had eyes in the back of his head. Not that my attack had been difficult to read. Then I used the second float shield more sneakily, cutting it in low across the ground.

"I saw that one coming too!" Ren crowed, quickly back-stepping to avoid the float shield. His reliance on hit-and-run tactics was alive and well, but he also seemed more precise—aside from his stats—than when he'd fought Eclair. He had been training with lots of different people since then.

"Naofumi, try harder! I want you to use every possible trick in the book to attack me! You can do better than this!" Ren taunted.

"Easy for you to say," I replied. Ren seemed a lot more into this than normal. Our training had already attracted the attention of Eclair, Raphtalia, Fohl, and others from the village, who were watching from a safe distance. Eclair seemed especially interested, as though there was maybe something she could learn from our clash.

"I've been wanting to see Hero Iwatani using a sword . . . and the results are most interesting. Is that how he normally uses one?" Eclair asked, looking over at Fohl. I normally fought to protect rather than attack, which probably created a fundamental difference in my overall approach to combat.

"No. Brother's sword stance is normally more like the one used by Raphtalia, and before he would use the same kind of quick-tempo attacks as Atla while copying your techniques, Eclair. He admitted it was all a bit monkey see, monkey do, if that's the phrase—he certainly isn't fighting like that." Fohl provided an accurate analysis. He was talking about when I fought Takt. I'd totally beaten the crap out of him, basing my movements on Raphtalia and Atla after training with them for so long, while unleashing my own copies of Eclair's attacks. "I don't mean to be rude, but he doesn't look very comfortable fighting like this." That was because I was normally the one blocking the attacks, not unleashing them like Raphtalia, Atla, Fohl, Ren, or Eclair. I wouldn't be surprised if my attempts to fight looked like some crazy and pointless dance. "That said," Fohl continued, "the fighting style he's using now is also very hard to read. If you fought him only watching his movements, you'd definitely get hurt."

"Because he's normally so focused on defending us . . . he moves around us so skillfully, in order to keep us safe," Raphtalia chimed in.

"That's right, Sister," Fohl agreed.

"Hmmm. It definitely is a strange form of attack. Very interesting," Eclair observed.

"Are there any other examples of this fighting style that the Sword Hero has asked Mr. Naofumi to use?" Raphtalia asked.

"A book on martial arts I read long ago referenced it—a style of fighting using weapons floating by magic. It seems the four heroes from the past have made use of it," Eclair revealed. The little party of spectators seemed to be having fun chatting away while Ren and I hammered at each other—and Ren wasn't giving me the chance to join in the discussion.

In fact, focused intently on the training, Ren was only pushing himself harder and harder. He came at me again with a roar.

"Naofumi!" he shouted. "Why don't you use twin shields to fight two-handed?"

"Sorry to say it, but I still haven't found that skill yet," I admitted. The very idea of a combat style with a shield on each hand sounded pretty crazy to me. Even if it did offer an increase in defense, taking incoming blows on both shields felt like it would be really difficult. It might give skills like Shooting Star Wall a boost . . . I mean, I could run game-style simulations in my head all day, but I'd never get a real answer without actually trying it out.

Seeing as I could only have one shield in my hands, I wondered if that counted as a handicap. This was a completely different world from Japan, after all, with the existence of stats like a video game, so it was a mistake to take even small things for granted.

"I see . . ." Ren said, sounding a little disappointed. He tried to drop away and put some distance between us again, but with a shout I lined up my two float shields with the shield on my arm, forming a horizontal wall and then closing in on him.

A loud sound rang out as our weapons clashed, Ren grunting as he was pushed to defend with his sword. One of my float shields landed a blow, and so I slashed with the other directly behind him.

Ren proceeded to catch it on his other sword. If his plan was to keep on dodging, then my best course of action would be to press the attack with the float shields and then close in once he was busy blocking them. I just needed to take a moment to see what his response was going to be.

"Pretty nice . . . but not enough!" Ren exclaimed, swirling his swords in a wide circle that appeared to leave him completely exposed. I was ready to take advantage of that when he crossed his swords in front of himself and slashed them downward in a powerful cross. Even if I took this new attack on the float shields and tried to attack him from the side, I wasn't going to be fast enough. I didn't like it, but there were no rules saying I couldn't evade rather than guard, Shield Hero or not. In fact, I needed to try and read beyond what Ren would be expecting from me, meaning dodging something might be a nice surprise for him.

I backstepped away, avoiding Ren's descending attack, and

then placed the float shields to prevent any follow-up attacks in the spot I came down in. Ren's blades slashed down where I had been standing, one of them sticking into the ground and the other one landing on one of the shields. Ren paused for just a moment before launching a follow-up attack with a wordless roar. He circled around on the spot and came right at me, swinging his sword quickly, but without too much force behind it. I was impressed by his reflexes. This kind of breathless succession of attacks would certainly be difficult for someone not as well-versed in defense as myself. Even quick, light attacks could create an opening, after all, if enough of them were performed. I had the two float shields and the shield on my arm too—three shields in total, and he was keeping the pressure on me.

"The Sword Hero has really improved, hasn't he?" Raphtalia commented. "From a purely technical level, I'm not sure I could match him anymore."

"Indeed. Ren has impressive concentration, that's true, but I don't think he's watching anything other than Hero Iwatani. In the chaos of an actual battle, that might leave him unable to respond to unexpected attacks from the sides," Eclair said, cutting to the heart of the issue and proving again that she was an expert warrior herself. "Have you noticed the difference with Hero Iwatani? He's been glancing over here every now and then for the entire time they have been fighting. A good indicator that he's tracking his surroundings."

"Yes, I noticed. Even as he fights the Sword Hero, Mr. Naofumi is listening to us talking," Raphtalia said.

"Ren trained with the Spear Hero too, but he didn't show this level of concentration. Hero Iwatani is most impressive too, being able to push Ren to such a high level," Eclair replied. I wasn't sure it was all that impressive. This was just Ren's tendency to fixate on one thing coming out again, which I didn't consider a good thing. His intense focus on a single adversary in situations like this was an issue to be addressed, not praised. He was much stronger in one-on-one fights.

"I'm more interested in how Brother is using those floating weapons. Sister, isn't there something like this for the seven star weapons? A vassal weapon from another world is similar enough to the weapons here, correct?" Fohl inquired.

"Duel-wielding is the best I can do, I'm afraid," Raphtalia admitted.

"It's likely something that can't be copied easily. I'm pretty sure it would make me crazy, trying to pull off a trick like that. You need to use life force and magic while in a strenuous combat situation. Just thinking about it makes my head spin," Eclair said.

"I know what you mean," Raphtalia agreed.

"One thing though . . . the seven star heroes do have weapons they can make float too, correct? Like the ones I've seen Hero Iwatani use during practice," Eclair said.

"That's right . . . He used them when he borrowed the Staff from the Wisest King of Wisdom," Raphtalia recalled. "Maybe we should look for them."

"It would be wonderful if something turns up, but I can't imagine they would be easy to find," Fohl said.

"Indeed . . . they seem quite different from the holy weapons, at least in this regard," Raphtalia agreed. Both she and Fohl seemed quite disheartened by the prospect.

Back with Ren and me, he was now breathing hard after launching a succession of attacks. I wasn't going to let that opening slip past me, so I thrust my shield out—he avoided that, but I was already piling on with my float shields, slashing down at him. The biggest demand on me here was mental control of the shields, which meant I wasn't expending the same kind of stamina that Ren was.

Ren grunted and went on the defense while I slid the float shields around behind him, outside of his view. Then I quickly slashed them down at him from the air. I was waiting for the instant in which Ren's attention would be caught by the incoming shields. I was ready to circle around him and start slashing at him again. My shield made contact with his abdomen, not a heavy hit, but enough to make him gasp for air. Then Ren lowered his swords, accepted defeat, and started to breathe hard.

"Phew . . . looks like you beat me," Ren said.

"You were moving pretty well out there," I told him. "You

just need to stop concentrating quite so hard on what is immediately in front of you." Just as Eclair had already pointed out, Ren tended to elicit incredible focus in battle. Intense concentration wasn't a bad thing, but it could also excessively limit your perspective—an extremely inflexible way to fight.

"I see," Ren replied.

"Hey, we were both fighting with odd handicaps that we wouldn't normally have to deal with. I don't think a normal battle would require quite as much concentration," I said.

"No, it's important that I reflect on this," Ren asserted, not accepting the out that I allowed him. He definitely had a stoic attitude. "We don't know what kind of foes we will be facing in the days ahead. Naofumi, I hope you'll train with me again. As I improve, can you also start using magic to launch ranged attacks at me? Stone, rocks, any kind of missile would be fine," Ren asked.

"Sure, I guess," I replied noncommittally. I didn't need a flying rock taking him out, I thought to myself, spinning my float shields idly. Ren was watching them as they spun. "I guess there's something else I should say."

"What?" Ren asked.

"If you're so taken with my float shields, maybe you should use a similar skill yourself?" I suggested. I'd heard that his weapon from the Spirit Tortoise materials had included a skill that allowed him to attack with floating swords. If he could freely strike with swords in all directions over a wide area, that would be a pretty difficult assault to deal with.

"To be honest . . . I'm not that great at controlling floating weapons," Ren admitted. He quietly called up a floating sword and tried to move it around in front of himself. It looked like he was doing pretty well with it.

"Looks pretty good to me," I told him.

"Maybe when there's nothing else going on. But if I'm moving around myself or have to concentrate on attacking, the swords stop moving. I don't think I could keep moving them around so freely in battle like you do, Naofumi," Ren admitted.

"I have it easier because I'm normally just blocking stuff," I told him. All I had to do was watch the movements of my opponent and move my shields when I wanted to redirect the impact of an enemy attack. If I actually needed to attack as well, that would make things much harder for me.

"I don't think that really matters. You were using the shields skillfully in our fight just now. If I tried that, the swords would just hang in the air. Watch." Ren started to run around with his back to the float sword, showing me how it wouldn't even follow him unless he concentrated on it. "If this was two or three swords we were talking about, that would make it even harder," he said.

"Hmmm," I pondered. This was the same problem that Eclair had brought up earlier. It seemed silly for a moment that there was something I could do so easily that Ren had so much trouble with. But then again, I also had skills that Itsuki and Motoyasu couldn't really use either. "Maybe you should try training with the swords out all the time?" I suggested.

"I'll give it a try, but please don't expect too much from me. I don't think I can match you, Naofumi, or . . . a certain other someone . . ." Ren said. I'd been sensing something else going on here, and his mention of an "other someone" clinched it.

"Hey, Ren. You've been trying to fight someone else through me, haven't you?" I asked. Based on how Ren was acting, and the things he said since we started this special training, I was sure that he was trying to get me to match the movements of someone from his past.

"Yeah, that's right. I'm sorry to put this on you, but I couldn't think of anyone else who could possibly do this for me," Ren admitted.

"I had a hunch," I told him. "Is this from back in your VR game days?" Back in his own Japan, Ren had been hooked on a game set in a world very much like this one. I imagined that a boss or some other character in that game had used an attack pattern like the one he had made me copy. It had been unorthodox, but honestly, it had been good training for me too, so I wasn't complaining.

"Kind of, but also . . . not quite," Ren replied noncommittally.

"Which means?" I prompted.

"It wasn't in *Brave Star Online*, but someone I knew on the network. I wanted you to try and copy the same movements they used," Ren explained, sounding like he regretted it after the fact. I wasn't angry about it, so there was no need to be so repentant. He could really be a buzzkill sometimes.

"Ren, you were using Hero Iwatani to fight a powerful foe from your past?" Eclair asked, coming into the conversation.

"Yeah. I'm sorry for not being up front about it, but I thought Naofumi could match that same combat style," Ren admitted.

"So that's what this was about," I said. Someone spinning around floating weapons—what were they, some kind of psychic? "What kind of person are we talking about?"

"Like a combination of half your personality now and half your personality when I first met you," Ren explained.

"They sound like a real pain in the ass—but I don't know what Brother was like before," Fohl chimed in.

"Hey, Fohl?" Raphtalia cautioned. "You might want to choose your words more carefully. Mr. Naofumi is glaring at you." I had to wonder again exactly what Fohl thought of me. If I didn't like the answer, I might have to put the screws to him—like sending him off on a long journey with the overly excitable puppy Keel. Trying to keep up with all the crazy stuff she came up with could be super exhausting. She was different, but just as dumb as the filolials. She also seemed to think that

Fohl was incredibly cool, while for his part Fohl wasn't exactly sure how to act when he was around her. Putting them together sounded like a great punishment, at least for one of them.

"There wasn't a skill like float weapon in *Brave Star Online*, which is why I was able to win there," Ren continued.

"This is the same person you mentioned when you defeated me that time?" Eclair asked, to which Ren nodded. Back when Ren had still been full of himself, he'd been on the ropes in a fight with Eclair before winning by unleashing a torrent of different skills. When that happened, I did recall him saying something about beating the top player from a different game in *Brave Star Online*. It sounded like he was still carrying that victory with him—the fact he had beaten this player, but not on their home turf.

"When I think about it now, I'm sure they took it easy on me in *Brave Star Online*. Even if it's just an illusion, I want to try and match them . . . if I can," Ren explained.

"This player was that strong?" I asked. Ren nodded without hesitation.

"Back on their home turf, even now I couldn't stand a chance. I'm sure of it. They would be stronger than me in this world, for sure, because of the existence of floating weapons," he declared. That was impressive. Stronger than Ren right now meant they had to be quite the foe.

"I sure hope they don't show up among the revived at some

point," I commented snidely. This was all starting to sound like foreshadowing for something.

"I'd certainly hope not. They seemed pretty solid, personality-wise," Ren replied. We were probably talking about the strongest person Ren knew—which made me unsure how to react, being compared to them. I could get angry at his rudeness at overlapping me with someone else—or feel pride that he would place me alongside someone he respected as such a powerful rival.

It seemed most like me to just not really be that bothered.

"We're talking about someone similar to Brother? In personality too?" Fohl asked.

"Cut that out, okay?" I said. That seemed to calm him down, but there was definitely something there we should get into. I glared at him and he shook his head, begging for leniency with his eyes.

"They were involved with the operation of a large guild inside *Brave Star Online*, so they didn't have any glaring personal flaws. I never heard of any trouble surrounding them either. I guess those are other reasons I compared them to Naofumi," Ren explained. I wasn't sure about his response there—it didn't exactly sound like he was protecting me. Still, I guessed he was trying to say we were similar due to things like me managing the village. "If I got summoned as a hero, I wonder if they weren't chosen too," Ren admitted.

"Enough talk like that. It sounds like self-abasement, and if people hear a hero talking like that, it will affect morale. Anything else you have to say like that, keep it to yourself," I warned him. Ren had been like this—a real downer—ever since he had come to the village. He'd been tying himself up in such knots while we were away in Kizuna's world that he'd actually collapsed! Talk about being weak under pressure. That was clearly why he didn't want to take on too much responsibility. He didn't want to take it on and get hurt through his failure.

"I just want to become strong . . . as strong as they were," Ren finished.

"And this is how they fought," I replied. Close combat with a mixture of floating weapons—it was like fighting someone armed with multiple weapons.

"If we wanted to get even closer, I think we'd need to put you on a filolial with higher stats than me too. Of course, you'd keep the float weapons coming from every direction," Ren mused.

"My god, what kind of monster are we talking about?" I exclaimed, only half joking. I had to accredit some of this to Ren simply building this individual up in his own mind—into some kind of god of war wielding floating weapons. I was having trouble picturing them now. "Ren, I think you should stop talking about this person completely. You're starting to sound like how Motoyasu talks about Filo," I warned him. The illusory

Filo who existed in Motoyasu's head had ballooned into an angel of mercy—while the reality was a greedy feather brain who didn't think past her next meal.

"Do you think so?" Ren asked.

"Yes. You know how these things can get built up in your mind. If you actually met and fought them again, you might find them a lot weaker than before," I told him. The more I thought about the relationship between Motoyasu and Filo, the more conviction I held in my words. "In any case, if this kind of routine can help you improve, I'll help out whenever I have time. Just keep on training," I told him.

"Okay!" he replied.

"The most important thing for you to work on is being able to respond flexibly in battle. Being focused isn't a bad thing, but you need to stay aware of your surroundings," I told him.

"That's not easy for me," he admitted.

"You need to put aside your belief that you can't use float skills and continue to practice with them as often as possible. These things aren't just going to come naturally to you. Like with power-up methods, your preconceptions might be holding you back," I warned him. This rival that Ren was so fixated on used floating weapons. That might have given him a bit of a complex relating to them. It would definitely open up more attack options than using two swords at once, so getting the hang of them would provide a big advantage going forward.

"Yes, you're right, Naofumi. I'll keep on training," Ren replied.

"If you still can't get the hang of it, at least try and protect your back. Keep your swords out behind you at all times— imagining you have a tail or wings might help," I advised him. The float weapons moved around when you thought about them, so it shouldn't be that hard. It all came down to your mental strength.

"You know what? They said the same thing to me," Ren said, his eyes glazing over.

"Stop reminiscing!" I replied. It was time to put a pin in this meaningless conversation.

"Hmmm. Watching you two fight made me want to spar with you too, Hero Iwatani. A shame that Hengen Muso Style doesn't offer techniques of that type," Eclair said.

"You might be able to come up with something similar— perhaps by applying some magic," I suggested to her. Maybe some wind magic—Shildina already used that to fly around.

"Hmmm. I don't think I have suitable magic capacity, but I'll see if I can make things float by focusing my life force," Eclair pondered. Now we were getting into the realm of psychic abilities. I wondered for a moment if life force was really so versatile—but then I recalled the Wall technique that formed a barrier for an instant, or the Gather technique that could change the trajectory of incoming missiles, and decided it was quite possible. The old lady might have some ideas on creating a new technique of that kind, but there was no asking her right then because she wasn't even in the same time zone.

"Don't you think Itsuki would be the most dangerous, if he attacked with floating weapons like this?" I suggested.

"Oh . . . the Bow Hero using floating weapons?" Raphtalia said.

"Yeah, think about it. He can use bows and guns. He wouldn't even need to move them around a lot—just lock on from a distance and open fire," I said.

"When you put it like that . . . yes, that would be quite a frightening tactic," Raphtalia agreed.

"Not to mention he could also bring out loads of different instruments and create his own orchestra—but that might be harder to pull off," I continued. We had determined that if we were at the same level, Itsuki had the strongest attack power among all of the heroes, but also the weakest defense. From one perspective, it was like Itsuki and I were opposites of each other when it came to attack and defense. Of course, unlike my complete lack of attack power, Itsuki still had some defensive power, so it wasn't completely the same thing. Taken in that light, my Shield Hero predecessor, Mamoru Shirono, was likely closer to being the opposite of Itsuki.

That brought me back to facing our current situation. This wasn't an easy one to explain, but right at that moment we were living in the past of the world to which we had been summoned. A mysterious attack, likely launched by the enemy forces to which S'yne's sister and Bitch belonged, had blasted us back into the past along with my entire village. We now had no way to contact anyone left behind in the future, which included Filo, Motoyasu, Itsuki, and Rishia. Here in the past, we had entered into an alliance with Mamoru Shirono, my predecessor as Shield Hero, and the nation he was affiliated with, Siltran. As for Mamoru himself, he was blessed with stats that made me just a little jealous. He was a Shield Hero, but he was also able to attack. He had a good handle on Float Shield too, now that I thought about it. Maybe I should ask him to come train with us next time. From the perspective of Ren's future growth, that would definitely prove useful.

As I was pondering these things, something else hit me— float weapons were actually a lot like the remote-controlled ranged weapons that often appeared in mecha anime. I thought weapons like that looked so cool up on the screen and would have loved to have gotten my hands on them at the time, but once I actually did get my hands on them . . . they weren't that great, really. It made me sad to experience all this geeky stuff and not be as moved by it as I had once hoped.

It was like when you saw someone using gear you really wanted in an online game, and then when you actually got it . . . it just didn't feel as strong.

"You've got a really sad look on your face, Mr. Naofumi. In any case, I think training by using your floating shields like enemy blades is very useful. It's like training to avoid a barrage of incoming attacks," Raphtalia said. I voiced my agreement. I also didn't want to imagine the chaos of everyone in our party all attacking with a horde of floating weapons though, so maybe things were better off without too many changes. Ren, Raphtalia, and S'yne could get away with it, but once you got to people like Fohl, it would just look like some kind of joke—the Gauntlets Hero making gloves float in the air to attack with them. I was just thinking about mecha anime, and now I'm onto rocket punches! Everyone who knew me could tell when I was having one of my strange ideas, so I decided to stop that line of thinking at once.

"One thing we could try to make them more effective would be to find or create an accessory that makes them automatically attack your current target," I mused. Accessories allowed additional effects to be added over those already contained inside a weapon. One example was an accessory that allowed Glass to cause slashes through the air when she swung her fan. Something like that sounded like a practical way to make Ren's float weapons more effective.

Accessories could also enhance specific skills, and there was a wide range of them to find . . . but they weren't without their issues too. First and foremost, you could only find out what effects they offered by putting them on and trying them out. Some effects—such as extra sharpness—could be hard to determine even when you tested them. Another issue was the resilience of the accessories themselves. In some cases, using them in quick succession could break them completely. So you needed to search for the effect and handle them with care in order not to break them . . . There was a lot of additional work involved.

But since we were stuck here until we could find a way home, I actually had the time. Luckily, I'd learned how to make accessories, and Imiya—another student of the art—was here with us too. We could use the resources here in the village and the new materials we had discovered here and see if we couldn't create some fabulous new accessories.

"An interesting idea . . ." Ren said.

"It will be total luck whether we can find one or not, so don't count on me too much!" I warned him.

"That's fine. If you're going to make some accessories, I can work the forge and make weapons for everyone," Ren replied. He had apprenticed with the old guy, I recalled. "I'm not quite as skilled as my master or the other students, but I've got some blacksmith techniques that can help fill in the gap." It sounded like he'd been a quick study. Maybe it was a bit like accessory making in that half the battle was just learning the patterns to bring out the appeal of the materials. He could use life force too, meaning he could probably make some pretty powerful stuff. The forge we had added when expanding the village would get some use too. "Making weapons is pretty interesting," Ren continued. "Especially for someone like me, who has always had to rely on rare weapon drops in the past. Now I'm hoping one day to be able to make weapons that start with rare additional effects, like master does." From among the current villagers, Ren was probably one of the better ones at forging, so it certainly couldn't hurt to have him make some stuff. "Okay. Show me what you can do," I told him.

"Mr. Naofumi, I think it's time to go over to Keel and the others at the stall in Siltran. Then we need to go and meet up with Ruft and Melty at the castle, correct?" Raphtalia said.

"Huh? Yeah, it's that time already. Let's call it a day for training. Everyone back to whatever you need to be doing," I said.

Thanks to the mysterious attacks from the forces of S'yne's sister, our entire village had been moved to the past of this other world—to the corner of a country called Siltran, which in the future would become Siltvelt. That was the situation we were still trying to deal with.

Chapter One: The Siltran Situation

I gave orders for everyone to get back to work after the training exercise, and then we took a portal to the castle town in Siltran to see how things were going. "Castle town" might have sounded quite grand, but Siltran was just a small country with some pretty dated architecture. The town was also currently undergoing some serious renovation work. We'd deployed the skillful lumo therianthropes from our village in order to help out.

"Raph!" Raph-chan, who had been helping Keel and the others out, pointed in our direction—with a plate on her head, of all things—to let everyone know we were coming.

"Hey, Bubba!" Keel, in her dog form, waved at us from a stall selling food. We weren't running the stalls to make money, but rather to help out with Siltran's recovery, so the prices were set nice and low. Keel was the one drawing in the crowds, mainly using body language because she couldn't speak the Siltran language—and it seemed to be working, because the stalls were doing well. I was overseeing the cooking, so the food was good, which also had to help. We were also using defeated monsters as ingredients and welcomed people bringing in their own food.

"How's it going? Those frenzied gestures you were

bragging about actually do seem to be working," I commented. Just looking at the crowds and the smiles on their faces told me things were going well.

"You bet they are! I'm starting to pick up the lingo too! I can say 'good morning,' 'hello,' and all the good stuff!" Keel yapped, happily wagging her tail. It was hard to keep Keel down, that was for sure, and the way she eagerly interacted with everyone around her probably kept the customers entertained. She was also strong enough to fight off anyone looking to cause some trouble. I'd heard urgent circumstances could help you learn a language faster. We'd been here in the past for a while now, and she had to be exposed to the language all day long, meaning she would surely pick up some everyday phrases.

Siltran apparently used an old dialect of the demi-human nation. Other than the heroes, those who had learned the language in Siltvelt were helping Keel and the others out with translation, but sometimes they still came across words they didn't know. Even in Japan, I'd heard about differences in the language that different people couldn't understand, like the classical Japanese we learned in school.

"Bubba?" Keel inquired.

"It's nothing. Just glad how well things are going," I told her. Keel's development—her speed at learning—always seemed to outpace my expectations. In a month she might be fluent in the Siltran language.

"Me too!" she yapped happily. Then I noticed that Raph-chan was taking orders. She was a monster, supposedly removed from language completely. There were also some filolials—those capable of interacting with customers—dashing around between the stalls. They had to be useful in keeping things moving briskly along. I took a moment longer to watch the system in action.

"Ah . . ." That was when my eyes met unexpectedly with someone hiding in the shadow of a nearby pillar. It was a child called Cian, if I recalled correctly—one of the kids Mamoru looked after. A demi-human with ears like a cat. She had a bit of a shy personality, but my Shield Hero predecessor Mamoru claimed she had taken quite a shining to me.

The kids who Mamoru was looking after, like Cian, were also coming to help out at the stalls. Food supplies in Siltran were low too, and this was a place anyone could eat their fill and help the children learn some independence at the same time—two birds with one stone.

It looked like Cian was helping out by washing dishes. I didn't want to give her too much attention, and there didn't seem to be any need to go over there right now.

"Have you had any trouble here at the stalls?" I asked.

"Nothing at all. Sometimes some shifty-looking adventurer types show up, but if they make a scene, we toss them right out. And anyone looking suspicious gets the stink eye from everyone else," Keel reported. I nodded. It sounded like everything was going well.

Siltran was a nation founded by races with little prowess in combat, and among them, low levels didn't help with an aptitude for battle. I wasn't looking to generalize too much, but to say how many demi-humans and therianthropes they had here, many of them were the smaller, grass-eating types. This had led to their nation being targeted by the far larger Piensa, getting caught up in a conflict and suffering all of these damages as a result. Waves were occurring here and yet some people still wanted to wage war—I couldn't understand it. People never changed. That was the sorry lesson I was taking away from all this.

Just after we arrived, Piensa had attacked Siltran with their powerful Dragon Battalion—all in the name of world peace, of course. So we had joined forces with Mamoru and driven them back. We had faced issues with fighting strength and numbers, but I had gathered up a horde of wild monsters and crashed them into Piensa's dragons, causing massive damage and allowing us to capture their commander and force them to flee. Our experts in information warfare—Melty, Ruft, and the Shadow—had also played their part. As a result, we had won the day, and that victory now meant the situation was leaning in our direction on the whole. Piensa wasn't expected to make any big moves for a while, but I wasn't too sure about that assessment. At the very least, I hoped they would keep it in their pants until we returned to our time; then they could go at it all they liked, while we were safely in the future again.

In any case, Siltran was putting us up and so we were helping them recover while also continuing the search for a way to get home.

"Bubba, Bubba! Now you're here, will you cook for us?" Keel and the others were all looking at me with sparkling excitement in their eyes. As it turned out, I was a pretty good cook, and so everyone always wanted to eat my cooking. They loved it when I cooked for them.

"I need to go and talk with Mamoru, Melty, and the others in the castle first. If I have some time after that, I'll come and help out," I told her. This promise was met with shouts of enthusiasm. "You have to get plenty of ingredients ready for me to cook though, okay?" I continued.

"You bet! Everyone! We need to get a pile of stuff to cook!" Keel yipped. The others all shouted their agreement. Siltran was currently suffering a shortage of raw materials, including stuff for cooking. We had the village bioplants turning out vegetables, and we were defeating wild monsters to use as meat, but every day still saw shortages. It felt like our emphasis was still mainly on helping them rebuild, but of course it would've been useful for us to have some money too. We were still gathering more building materials than hard cash, but as long as restoration work continued, it was good.

The feeling I was really struggling with was that of being stuck here in the past, dragging our feet, when what we really needed to do was get back to our own time.

"Keel and the others looked so alive, didn't they?" Raphtalia said as we headed from the stalls up toward the castle.

"Keel is a ball of energy, you know that," I replied.

"That's true, but it might also be the reason she ended up tagging along this time," Raphtalia mused.

"A pretty rough bargain, if that's the reason she got dragged into all this," I replied. We often ended up leaving Keel at home. She was badly injured during the incident with the Spirit Tortoise, preventing her from visiting Kizuna's world, and we'd also left her in the village when we went to earn some cash to buy slaves at the Zeltoble coliseum. She actually did help out quite a lot, but we'd never taken her along when going out into the unknown. "The way she keeps her spirits high at all times really helps relax the tension of everyone around her. That's a big help, I admit."

"Indeed. I feel better with her around too. That is a big help," Raphtalia replied. When serious stuff was happening, panic was the biggest threat. Having party members like Filo and Keel around could certainly be an effective remedy to tension mounting too high.

As we chatted, we finally reached the castle. S'yne greeted us—the girl who was normally found directly behind me—standing in the castle courtyard, learning a new technique from R'yne, the Sewing Kit Hero from this world.

"That's it. That's the way," R'yne encouraged. This was a special technique unique to their race—the ability to sprout wings, something lost in S'yne's time. If she could get the hang of it, then she would be looking at a considerable power-up, and so she was working on it quite enthusiastically. However, just like learning life force, it was proving a difficult technique to master. R'yne herself, it seemed, was an ancestor of S'yne's. She had apparently come here from S'yne's world, which in our time had already been wiped out. This was the kind of coincidental meeting in the past that was made possible by waves that also occurred back here in the past.

What was less exciting about this situation was that R'yne seemed to have a pretty one-track mind—and that track was sex. She rarely missed a chance to drop some harassment on me and—unlike the style I was accustomed to from the likes of Sadeena—R'yne played fastball. I really had to keep an eye on her. One of her most sparkling gems had been to question whether sex with me would feel painful or not due to my lack of attack power. I was never going to forgive her for going there, that much was for sure.

"Hey, Naofumi. You here to see Mamoru?" R'yne asked.

"Yeah," I replied briefly.

"He's with Melty and Ruft, deciding on what kind of action we should take next," she replied.

"Okay," I said. That meant they would be in the castle's meeting room. No problem dropping in on them there. "R'yne. How are things going with teaching that technique to S'yne?"

"Hmmm . . . pretty good, I guess?" That pause, that spoken question mark at the end, was her clearly trying to avoid hurting S'yne's feelings. S'yne still turned away upon hearing this. I decided not to say anything. If I praised her too much, it might just end up hurting her more in the long run. "It involves taking your magic and circling it through your body as pure power, but that's easier said than done. Some people need to add a magical attribute or the wings won't pop," R'yne explained.

"There are all sorts of types of magic," I said. "I can see how it might be hard."

"Indeed. It's even harder if you don't have a complete grasp of the magic from our world," R'yne continued. I had to admit, I'd never really seen S'yne use anything resembling magic. Her sister had made a much bigger impression in that department.

"Was that magic your sister used from your world, S'yne?" I asked her. She shook her head. It seemed not—which meant S'yne's sister had also learned magic from another world. From among my crew, that would be like how Shildina had learned magic from Kizuna's world. Sadeena and I had also gained access to it by such means as using the Way of the Dragon Vein on gemstones. So there were ways it could be done.

"I do understand that it can be better to rely on weapon skills rather than casting magic," R'yne sympathized, raising her arms in an exaggerated fashion as she tried to give S'yne an out on not using much magic. "I tend to only use it for a little spice here and there." If neither of them were magic specialists, it would definitely make it harder to learn it now. It sounded like what we needed was a specialist from R'yne's world to come and help out, but whether that would even be possible, because it was long gone in our time, was another point of concern.

"Well, just do what you can," I told them. "Worst case scenario, we'll have to think up some clever twist."

"Yeah, okay. I'll do my best," S'yne said, raring to go, her attention fixed on R'yne.

"We need to keep Naofumi happy, don't we! We'll keep going!" R'yne replied cheerfully, and they started practicing again right away. We'd only get in the way if we hung around chatting any longer. I signaled Raphtalia with my eyes and we headed further into the castle.

"Is this the place?" I asked. Led by some of the castle servants, we arrived in front of the meeting room where Melty and others were having their talks. I could already hear voices from inside. I gave a light knock on the door and it fell silent inside, so I proceeded to open them.

Inside I saw Mamoru and then Melty, Ruft, and other key figures from Siltran. Everyone looked in our direction.

"Ah, Naofumi. Now you are here, I think we can really get down to business," Mamoru said.

"You've been having a nice long meeting without me from the look of it. Anything I should know about?" I asked.

"Not really," Melty retorted. "We were mainly assessing the damages from the recent fighting and checking on how recovery is going in each region."

"That's about it—along with the report on the torture of that magic user you captured, Naofumi," Ruft added.

"Dafu!" Raph-chan II added. None of that really sounded like information I wanted to hear, but I needed to hear it nonetheless. I was sure Melty and Ruft could provide a simple breakdown later if I asked them to.

Dafu-chan—that was Raph-chan II—was sitting up on Ruft's shoulder. She looked like she was helping out. Those two really did get along well.

We bickered a bit, but the truth was, Melty was the queen of Melromarc back in our time, the largest nation in the future, and Ruft was working as an aide to the rulers of that nation, Trash and Melty. Not to mention, Ruft was royalty himself as the former Heavenly Emperor of Q'ten Lo. They were both young for the positions of power they held, but they were doing fine work in key positions of authority. Even here in the past, those talents were being put to good use.

"The main issues are just coming to the table now, so you had better hear this," Melty said.

"Okay. I guess you'd better make some room for us," I replied. I looked over at Mamoru, and he was already indicating two empty seats. Raphtalia and I sat down there, next to each other.

"First things first . . . domestic recovery is going well, thanks largely to the trade you and the others from the village have been promoting, Naofumi. Public safety is also being restored," Melty reported.

"Driving off Piensa in that conflict has had a powerful ripple effect. Those who saw us as weaker nation, a nation to prey on, are having second thoughts now," Mamoru added, with some noticeable satisfaction. Siltran had been close to collapse upon our arrival, with prolific raiders from other nations coming unannounced to attack. We had observed these issues when we were conducting trade and squashed most of those who tried to cause trouble. "One of the reasons Piensa sped up their attack was because of all the agents they had been sending in to cause trouble had been captured."

"The prisoner told you that?" I asked.

"That's right," Mamoru confirmed. "The fact that Siltran had started to recover quickly was also a factor." So it was the trading, spearheaded by the filolials and Raph species, that had triggered the attack. I'd known it in my heart, but it still hurt to hear that we were to blame. It was stifling to know that another wrong move on our part could trigger further attacks.

"Having laid waste to the Piensa Dragon Battalion has really hurt them. A report from Shadow has made that clear," Melty continued.

"It seems swiftly getting those rumors out there was really effective," Ruft commented. Melty and he had made this suggestion, letting all the neighboring nations know that justice had been on the side of Siltran when they defeated Piensa. The victors wrote the history, after all. Having been forced to retreat, anything the Piensa forces had to say would only sound like sour grapes from the losing side.

"That's not to say Piensa isn't fighting back," Melty said. "They're claiming that Siltran only achieved this victory because they called in heroes from another world."

"I guess it depends on which way public opinion goes, but don't they see that spreading such information may simply be shooting themselves in the foot?" Raphtalia said.

"You think they might be going for the religious angle?" I pondered. "Getting everyone together to defeat the cowardly Siltran who has sent heroes into war?"

"That might be the case," Raphtalia replied, "but do you think their allies will accept that after such a defeat?" That was true. We could easily claim that Siltran had come together and won because of one of Mamoru's strategies, a victory for the unified people of the nation without any cooperation from us. We got our information out first, meaning some cracks had surely formed in the alliance that Piensa led. What they needed right now was trust in each other, and that meant confirming the truth—which meant they were in their own struggle, and that suited us.

"If they try to convince everyone to come together and defeat Siltran at a time like this, I don't think it will go well for them," Melty said. I had to agree—it would be the height of foolishness to try and launch another assault with all this confusing information circling in the air. The other surrounding nations had to know that too.

"Which means the wind is blowing in our direction," I said.

"It might be, just a little . . . but this has raised the issue of whether we should be getting involved in things any more than we already are. That's the issue we've been discussing with Mamoru and these others," Melty explained. Mamoru nodded, looking over at his subordinates. None of them looked that good in a scrap, to be honest, and they didn't look very comfortable here either. They were likely getting a bit carried away now that they glimpsed the chance to back a winning horse for once. This whole situation had come around due to their cooperation with us, and so the idea that maybe now we shouldn't fight was causing some friction.

"This started out as a battle that we had to resolve for

ourselves," Mamoru said. "It was a mistake to try and have you resolve it, Naofumi."

"I do see your point," I admitted. The battle had been triggered by us turning up here, and we'd helped Mamoru and his forces because our village was positioned to get caught up in the fighting. Getting involved any further probably wasn't a good idea. "What they seem likely to do in this situation is send in spies or deploy a new hero." Information was important. I could imagine a wave of spies coming in, seeking to determine the truth. The Bow Hero, who for now was siding with them, might also show his face. Why was it that the Bow Hero always seemed to play the neutral ground, the even hand of justice?

"We've been thinking about that too, but it seems pointless to have you hide now," Mamoru said.

"If word gets out that Siltran is hosting multiple heroes from another world, it should hold Piensa back and make it harder for them to sway public opinion," I said. There was no reason for us to attack them, and they already knew that attacking us would give them a bloody nose—or worse. The situation was nicely balanced to prevent any further violence.

"You need to be careful of offers trying to tempt you over to their side, or even attempts at kidnapping you," Mamoru warned.

"Indeed. You should be especially careful, Melty," I said.

"Me, kidnapped? Underestimate me at your peril! That's

a task that would at least take their Bow Hero to pull off!"
Melty exclaimed. She wasn't wrong. She had been spending a
lot of time helping Filo level up, which had boosted her own
level considerably, and she'd also undergone the physical enhancements from Fitoria . . . what was likely the same kind of
power-up method as the Whip, which had really raised her basic
abilities. Only one with the protection of the heroes would be
able to kidnap Melty; I had to agree with that. She had plenty
of protection around herself too.

"I'm protecting her too, Naofumi. No need to worry," Ruft
assured me.

"And they might come after you too, Ruft. You need to be
careful," I warned him.

"I know," he replied. Ruft had high-level illusion magic at
his command and was becoming so strong that even if he was
captured he'd probably saunter back to us before too long, having turned the tables on his captors. He was Raphtalia's cousin
and received the blessings of the Raph species. Like Keel, he
seemed to have an affinity for his therianthrope form, because
that was what he spent most of his time in. It was funny to
see Raphtalia struggling to work out how to talk to him when
he was in his demi-human form, that was for sure. During the
recent fighting he had aided me in place of Raphtalia and had
looked pretty brave doing it as he swung around a massive axe
stolen from the enemy.

"In regard to deployment of the heroes, Mamoru made it sound like the Bow Hero on their side wasn't all that keen on the idea. I think we'll be okay for a while," Melty said.

"Any chance he might switch sides completely?" I asked Mamoru, but he shook his head from side to side.

"It's not as simple as that. He has people he wants to protect too," Mamoru explained.

"Hmmm. Our guy in the future was a stick-in-the-mud as well, but we eventually convinced him," I said. Not only Itsuki, but Ren and Motoyasu too—we'd scrapped with them all, and convincing them to team up had been a pain, but things had worked out in the end.

"Whatever you may think, Naofumi, people can't just cast their affiliated kingdom aside if they have family or other people there to protect. That's exactly the tactic used everywhere to get heroes on their side," Melty told me.

"Oh boy," I replied. I knew what this was. I hadn't been caught up in it myself, but this seemed like a standard tactic for countries from other worlds in forcing heroes to work with them.

"Getting a hero to change sides would be very difficult. Think about yourself, Naofumi. Would you betray Melromarc and the people of your village to go off and join another nation?" Melty asked pointedly.

"Nope, not going to happen," I admitted.

"There you go then," she replied.

"So what you're telling me is that Melromarc was probably doing all sorts of stuff to the other three heroes in order to bind them to the nation, back in our time? I'm just hoping we don't face an enemy in the future holding one of their kids hostage, then! Could you fight that?" I asked.

"Considering the events until you met my mother . . . the Spear Hero had my sister at his side the whole time. What about the Sword Hero and Bow Hero? Who do you think they could have been with?" Melty asked.

No need to even mention Motoyasu, really. With Bitch around, anyone or anything that might threaten her position would have been wiped out or horribly hurt. Lyno was a good example. She had been put through hell right behind Motoya-su's back with him none the wiser. As for Ren and Itsuki . . . I felt they would need a closer bond than that before they started fooling around. If it looked like they were being tricked or forced into anything, I could easily see them sensing the danger and making a break for it—and if they were just propositioned normally, they would probably just turn it down.

"It could be said," Melty continued, "that we managed to make them our allies so easily for the very reason that they avoided such machinations and remained single heroes in the first place." The issue might have come up if they had shacked up with someone while they were still out of control. But I didn't really suspect them to turn on us at this point—at least I hoped not.

"I think in our case they were just a little too wild right from the start," I mused.

"Right. In fact, from among our four heroes, I think you are the one least likely to be able to leave Melromarc now, Naofumi," Melty observed. She had a point. But if Melty and Trash started acting like they could control me at will, I would have to put them in their place. But then again, there were no signs of that at the moment. In the case of the queen, we had made use of each other with a mutual understanding. In that light, she had left Melty and Trash quite the inheritance.

"In any case, luring over the Bow Hero in this time is going to be too much of a challenge," I stated.

"That's the short of it," Melty agreed. The future we knew about from this point told us that Piensa was going to eventually get wiped out, while Siltran would become Siltvelt. I wondered what that meant for the Bow Hero. There was Faubrey to consider though, which was a country that collected the bloodlines for the heroes. So maybe after the worlds were fused, the Bow Hero ended up working with them. That seemed like one possibility. He might have defected or slipped away to another nation.

Any information we had on those details was basically little more than fairy tales according to Melty and the others from the future, meaning they couldn't be trusted to represent reality. Even the reasons Piensa collapsed might not have been imparted accurately. Different materials on the same topic even said different things, such as Siltran wiping them out prior to becoming Siltvelt or that the Shield Demon King used his mighty power to eradicate them in a single night.

"The Bow Hero in this time at least seems willing to listen to reason though, right?" I said. He didn't seem as hard-headed as Itsuki had once been, for example.

"That's true. If we can present a logical argument, he may lend us an ear. Based on this defeat, I wouldn't be surprised if he cautioned Piensa about further action," Mamoru replied. We just had to hope that he had the influence inside Piensa to cool off anyone who was pissed with us for kicking their collective asses.

"If Piensa really is trying to take over the world while keeping the Bow Hero's family hostage, then we just need to bring his entire family under our control instead," I said. I gave an evil chuckle for good measure. If Piensa could do that, then we could play them at their own game.

"Oh wow . . . Naofumi, you look so alive right now. Not that I'd expect any less than this from you," Melty quipped.

"He did seem to have something weighing on his mind when I met him. If that's the case, we can make use of it ourselves," Mamoru agreed with me.

"Which means we need to wait to hear the report from Shadow," Melty said. As it turned out, Shadow had been among those who ended up getting dragged to the past with us. He had fallen in with the Raph species and picked up the techniques of the Q'ten Lo ninja, making him handy to have around when it came to gathering intel. In fact, I couldn't think of anyone better. Raphtalia and Ruft had abilities that suited them to infiltration too, but they were too important in other ways to risk on such missions.

"Mamoru, I don't think we should get any more involved than this," I concluded. "If you want to persuade the Bow Hero, you can handle that yourself."

"Okay. You've been a big help already, in so many ways. I don't expect there to be any fighting anytime soon either," Mamoru replied.

"Good. Next issue," I said.

"Let's move on to a detailed report on the recovery in each region, along with what we have learned from the robbers and spies we have captured so far. There are issues of taxation to discuss too," Melty continued. It all sounded like bags of fun, and the meeting continued for a while longer after that.

I was impressed by Melty and Ruft though, handling the running of a nation so competently at such young ages. Maybe this was also the result of watching Trash firsthand for so long. Melty had been educated since a young age to take the throne, and while Ruft was a bit more of a hothouse plant in terms of his upbringing, he was still a member of Raphtalia's family and possessed exceptional strategical thinking. Just having the two of them involved was sure to push the situation in Siltran in a far better direction. That's the impression I was left with once the overly long meeting finally ended, and then we headed away from that stuffy chamber of discussion.

The discussions, however, did not end.

"Our primary goal is to get back to our own time," Melty said, "but at the same time we need to prepare under the assumption that our enemies will be waiting for us when we return."

"I agree," I said.

"That's why I'd like for you and the others, Naofumi, to continue the trading while also getting in some fights with powerful monsters. I've set up a number of patrol routes, so if you could divide them up between the heroes . . ." Melty rattled on. I wondered for a moment if she should be making every single decision. Back home we'd get Sadeena and a crew together and go to the oceans to level up, maybe using the whip power-up method. I wondered if maybe there was something we could do with the mirror one—but the holy weapons offered better modifiers, to be honest, so the shield would be more effective in the end.

"Okay. This era is facing the issue of the waves as well, and that's something we do need to be involved with. Let's go to Keel and help out with the stalls a little, and we can decide who to take along from there," I suggested. If Ren and I were going to take two slots for the four heroes, then put in two seven star weapon or vassal weapon heroes . . . and fill out the rest with villagers, that should allow us to do some hunting without completely decimating the local ecosystem. "Experience from the sea is better, is it?" I asked Mamoru. We probably should consider some ocean time if we could get it in. But the issue was that Siltran wasn't that close to the water.

"Is that the case in the future? I don't think we've ever really felt a difference between the land and the sea," Mamoru replied. I thought about that for a moment. It sounded like there was no difference in experience here in the past. When we killed those balloon snakes, which were like a subspecies of the balloon, we'd earned a lot more experience than normal balloons. So that was true too. They didn't feel any stronger, so I'd thought maybe they had some additional experience for some reason. It was hard to compare them though, due to the snakes being a subspecies. I didn't have the mental capacity to remember everything, after all. I didn't need to get lumped in with Raphtalia and her perfect recall of everyone's names or Ruft and his perfect recall of all of Trash's strategies.

But I also remembered Ren saying that Q'ten Lo had offered more experience. Maybe there was a reason for all this. It felt like the one behind the waves—the one who assumed the name of god—had a hand in all of this. They were definitely sending in the resurrected, destroying all sorts of important materials, really causing a mess for us.

"Mamoru, if you've got the time, maybe you could join us. Raise your crew a bit? Do you want to tag along?" I asked him.

"Yeah, that sounds good. I'm looking forward to it already," Mamoru replied.

"Okay, let's go back to the stall where Keel and the others are. You haven't had any lunch yet, what with the meeting, right? So get some food too," I said.

"Off you go, Naofumi. We've got some materials we need to finish up with, so we're heading back to the castle," Melty said.

"You're no fun, Melty. You're going with 'bossy' here, Ruft?" I asked.

"Yep. I've got a lunchbox ready, so I'll be fine," Ruft replied. Of course he did. He was always well-prepared.

"Okay. I know things aren't easy for you, Melty, Ruft, but thanks for all your hard work," I told them.

"No problem. You do your bit too, Naofumi," Melty replied.

"Sure thing," I replied—even though I said it a little non-committally. And so the rest of us returned to Keel's stall and helped out with the cooking. Once I took up my spot in the kitchen, however, the seats filled up with more villagers than usual, and our overall working speed actually slowed down. That was definitely something I should have seen coming.

Chapter Two: Wagon Travel with Keel and the Gang

"Okay. I think it's time we swapped out the staff working the stalls," I said. Keel and her team were doing well with trading too, so it seemed like a good idea to hand over the stalls in the castle town to some of the others from the village. They were pretty well-established by now, and if any trouble came up, they could report to Melty or someone else in command around here. The original intent had been to support the lumos who were helping repair the buildings. After returning to the village, we needed to meet back up with the traders. Just as Melty had instructed, we had to continue to enhance ourselves to be ready for when we finally did get home.

"Bubba, Bubba! Who are you taking this time?" Keel yipped excitedly.

"Good question . . . we're planning to decide after chatting with Ren and Fohl." I turned to Raphtalia. "When that happens, though, would you like to try leading your own party? As a way to increase the units we have in the field?" I asked her.

"Huh? I mean, if that's what you want me to do, Mr. Naofumi, then I can give it a try . . . but do you think it's the best idea?" she replied.

"Bubba, can't you tell that Raphtalia wants to stay close to you?" Keel said cheekily. I wasn't expecting her to be the one to shoot the idea down.

"You say that, but if I take Raphtalia with me, I bet you guys would be all joking around among yourselves about us being on a date and getting all romantic, wouldn't you?" I retorted.

"You're only just working that out? Bubba, seriously, you can be so dense sometimes!" Keel cackled. I hadn't really paid attention to such chatter, it was true, but it sounded like it had just been business as usual for Keel and the others for a while now. "I think Raphtalia would prefer it if you actually did take her on a date!"

"Keel, please. Can you not bother Mr. Naofumi with any more of this? You might end up . . . creating the opposite of the desired effect, okay?" Raphtalia said.

"Why? This is your chance! Oh, but are you worried about Sadeena and the others at home all making their move once we get back? Don't worry, we can keep our mouths shut. Or are S'yne and the others here the problem?" Keel continued cheerfully, still completely oblivious to the mood around her. The pressure on us from everyone else was really starting to get intense recently. Melty had always been one to comment, and now we had R'yne making clever little comments about me and Raphtalia too. It was none of their business, really.

Okay then, I thought. I needed to pay Keel back a little for all this.

"I've got an idea. This time, it's me and you, Keel, out on a special date for ourselves. Raphtalia, you can gain some practice at command leading a separate unit, okay?" I asked.

"Huh? What are you talking about, Bubba?" Keel asked, shaking her head.

"Oh . . . very well. Please take care of Keel," Raphtalia said, sighing as she agreed to the idea. She seemed to have some idea of what I was planning—at least that it wasn't going to end up all flowery and romantic.

"Hold it, puppy-girl!" I grabbed Keel and tucked her under my arm so she couldn't get away. She thrashed her limbs, but it didn't do her any good. "You can't get away. Try it and I'll have to punish you," I warned her.

"Raphtalia! Save me from Bubba!" Keel pleaded.

"Keel, my dear, you've brought this on yourself," Raphtalia admonished. "You'll just have to live with the consequences."

"Raph!" Keel yipped. Was this some kind of final ploy, perhaps, or just a joke? Copying that cutie Raph-chan was not going to earn any leniency from me.

"Raph?" The real deal was tilting her head in puzzlement.

"Anyone else . . ." I asked, looking over at the cat girl, who was still watching from her hiding place. "Cian, you seem interested in what we've been doing. Do you want to come along too? Mamoru said it would be okay," I told her.

"That's right," Mamoru backed me up. "I'm going to help a

little, but I've got other things I need to do. Cian, I know you'll get along well with Naofumi."

"Sure, okay," she said, still a little timidly. She looked exactly like a frightened cat, in fact. For all her shy watching from the sidelines, I knew Cian was very interested in everything around her. She had been out trading with Mamoru in the past and already got along pretty well with Keel and the others—even though she was too shy to say much more than hello to them. But with a little more experience, she would be able to protect herself or escape if anything happened, such as an enemy attack. How to enhance her would be Mamoru's decision, of course, but there seemed to be no harm in spending some time together trading for the sake of friendship.

"Okay then. Let's head on back and decide who we're sending out with Ren and Fohl," I suggested. The others voiced their agreement—including Raph-chan—and with her up on my shoulder we took a portal back to the village.

We returned to the village, discussed the issue at hand, and decided who to send.

This time I would take Keel, Cian, Raph-chan, Imiya—who had been making accessories in the village—and someone to handle our cooking, while Chick would pull the cart. She was one of Filo's underlings. Except Cian, it felt like I had gathered major players from all the key groups in the village. After I made all the necessary substitutions, our cart had struck out for an area that we were told was remote, even for Siltran. We were headed for a village slightly removed from a rocky region where dangerous monsters were said to dwell. The wagon clattered along, moving quickly as filolial-pulled carts tended to do. With all the vibrations such speed engendered, this hardly felt like a pleasant trip out into the countryside.

"Bubba, please . . . forgive me!" Keel pleaded. We were sitting together up at the front of the wagon, with her in her dog form and still looking pretty uncomfortable. At least she was firmly seated, something that at a glance might even make her look cute—or at least well-trained. That could of course be on account of the maid-like outfit that S'yne had tailored for her to use when trading. It strangely suited her when she was in her dog form.

"What's wrong?" I asked her. "You still got something on your mind?" I simply had her sitting in front of me, but she was all flustered and bothered by it.

"I'll never be able to look Raphtalia in the eye again! Not after doing this!" Keel whined.

"I'm not sure what you expect Raphtalia to do to you, honestly," I replied. Even Raphtalia wasn't going to be jealous of something like this. She certainly wouldn't punish Keel for it or pick on her when I wasn't around. That wasn't Raphtalia's style at all. If she did, I'd lose a lot of respect for her. I had to believe Raphtalia was better than that. She'd sent Keel off on this adventure, saying it was her own doing—that hadn't looked like an act to me.

"Sure, Raphtalia herself might not say anything or might not even actually be bothered, but this isn't my place!" Keel replied. So I realized that's what this was all about. Raphtalia had understood my position too. From my perspective, being too focused on a single person could potentially cause all sorts of issues. This was a difficult issue to resolve, that was for sure.

"Keel, you seem to be keeping your distance a little?" I said. Maybe this was something like the hierarchical instincts of a dog. For Keel, Raphtalia and I were higher up in the pack order than she was, and so she might even feel a little fear at being this close to me. She normally didn't hold back at all, so I was surprised to see her looking so scared simply sitting in front of me. She'd been happy to mock me back in the village though. I needed to give her a little bit more of her own medicine first.

"What's wrong, Keel? No need to hold back. You can snuggle right up to me, come on," I said, drawing her toward me. She gave a yip as I ruffled her fur. She really did have a lovely coat, very pleasant to the touch. A different sensation from the softness of Raph-chan—a little harder, perhaps, but some would likely prefer it. She was definitely nicer to the touch than the dog my friend once let me pet. I started by stroking around her muzzle and then moved to her ears and throat. A real dog would love having its chest rubbed too, most likely, but I wondered about Keel. She was wearing her trading clothes at the moment . . . so probably best to skip it. Such attention could well be considered sexual harassment in this situation.

"Uuh . . . it feels nice to have you stroking me, Bubba, but I'm still scared of what happens next . . ." she whimpered.

"Raph?" Raph-chan was more than accustomed to me stroking her and seemed puzzled by Keel's reaction.

"Keel, don't be such a coward," Imiya said, popping her face forward. "And, Shield Hero, can you please stop teasing her quite so much?" I had to do a double take to make sure we had actually left Raphtalia behind.

"Hey, Imiya. We don't have to start right now, but I want to make some new accessories later. Can you help me out?" I asked her.

"Yes, of course. Whatever you need . . . Are you focusing on design? Or functionality? Or quality?" she asked.

"Like I said, I don't want to get too caught up in that kind of thinking. I just want to make a bunch of accessories. If possible, I'm looking to pinpoint something that will have effects when attached to heroes' weapons," I told her. That would happen with just trial and error. If there was a way to just instantly get the effect we wanted, wouldn't that be a wonderful world? If Therese were here, she definitely would have enjoyed getting involved in accessory making. "One of the reasons we're heading to our current destination is for some mining," I continued. "We need to find out what kind of minerals and gemstones you can obtain here in Siltran."

"Okay. I'll help however I can," Imiya replied. I gave her a stroke too, seeing as I was already stroking Keel. That made her gasp, flush red, and stiffen up. Of course, Imiya had a thing for me too. I couldn't keep them all straight, but I did need to be more careful about who I went around stroking.

I wondered for a moment how Raphtalia might react if I did the same thing to her. I couldn't quite imagine stroking Raphtalia as casually as this, however. I might have soothed her a little when she was smaller, but I rarely touched her anymore. It felt like I'd almost taken to stroking Raph-chan as a substitute. This left me wondering why I was able to stroke Keel and Imiya so easily.

The answer came to me quickly, but it was a bit controversial. It was because they had fur over their entire bodies. I decided I would have to stroke Raphtalia once we were reunited. That would also likely shut up everyone around us for a while.

I made it seem really natural, and I was pretty sure it wasn't rude . . . I'd been living in this other world for a while now, so I knew how things worked. Stroking children was not rude in Melromarc, I knew that much.

"Bubba! How long are you planning on stroking me for?

And where exactly are you stroking now anyway?!" Keel yipped. I'd been focusing a little too much on Imiya and my hand had slipped down to unconsciously rub at her chest. It was fluffy there, but there was no suggestion of breasts.

"Ah, sorry. That's your chest, isn't it?" I said. Keel started barking and then growling too. I guess I'd pushed things too far, as I'd feared I might—not that she was threatening me at all.

Then I noticed Cian watching us with a cold look in her eyes.

"What's up?" I asked her. "You're not ready to play along with us yet?" Cian immediately looked away from me—but continued to glance back over, as though she was interested, really.

"Bubba, pay attention to me! I'm angry with you!" Keel insisted.

"Yes, I'm listening. Hah, you say you're a boy but don't like having your chest touched," I replied.

"Bubba, that's a low blow!" she replied.

"What do you expect? Low blows are my specialty," I shot back.

"I think you specialize more in hitting back after you get hit," Imiya chimed in. She really did sound like Raphtalia now.

"Imiya! Please, swap places with me! I can't keep letting

Bubba do this to me!" Keel pleaded. Imiya could only give a wry laugh in return. I was still more interested in Cian right now. She was still keeping her distance, like a cat who wanted to play but couldn't commit yet. I wondered if I could use her innate catty instincts against her. I grabbed one of Chick's loose feathers as it floated up and then waved it around in front of Cian's face. The key was to make it look like weakened prey. Getting a cat interested in this kind of toy involved triggering their innate hunting instinct. Cian looked at the feather I was wielding, and then started to focus on it more intently. Imiya sensed what I was doing and went back inside the wagon. She was thoughtful and considerate at times like this. Keel, meanwhile, was watching with an expression that seemed completely oblivious to my intentions. I flicked the feather like it was weak and helpless prey just in front of Cian.

I saw the shift come over Cian's eyes, like a cat sinking back into her base instincts for hunting. I started to move the feather faster, adding further stimulation. It only took a moment longer and Cian leapt forward and grabbed it with both hands. She was then right in front of me.

"Ah!" In the moment Cian was about to nibble the feather, she snapped back to herself and covered her face with her hands.

"No need to be shy. We all just want to get along," I told her.

"Okay," she eventually replied, but she did seem to have loosened up a little. She was looking at me with a much more relaxed expression than before.

"Why do you want to be friends with Cian too?" Keel wondered. "You've already got Raphtalia."

"Keel, you really have mastered the art of saying too much," I chided her.

"Bubba is touching me inappropriately again!" Keel squealed.

"This isn't your chest. It's your chest plate," I explained.

"That sounds like my chest to me!" she retorted. Cian looked on and gave a chuckle. Then Chick started to squawk about something.

"Raph!" Raph-chan proceeded to take out an antidote from our things and offer it to Cian.

"Hold on a moment . . ." Imiya popped up again to explain. "She just licked one of Chick's feathers, didn't she? There might be some toxins on it, so Chick thinks she should take a little of this antidote, just in case." I'd completely forgotten that Chick was a filolial who specialized in poison. She used all the poisonous tricks: poisonous claws, poison spit, even poison magic.

"Poison, huh? I remember Filo having a phase where she wanted to spit poison too," I reminisced. "As if we didn't have enough trouble with everything coming out of her mouth already." I took the antidote from Raph-chan, mixed it with some honey on a plate so Cian could just lap it up, and then handed it to her. Cian seemed to understand that I'd made it sweeter for her and just quietly took some of it.

A moment later she'd licked the entire plate clean. It seemed she liked the taste. With Keel here too, I decided to whip up some desserts for them later.

"What do you mean about Filo's mouth?" Imiya asked.

"Right, before Filo met Melty, she had a bit of a mouth on her, and just like Keel she didn't know when to keep it shut either," I explained. The turning point for the poisonous tongue—the moment when she learned to engage her bird brain prior to her beak was when a single comment from her had triggered Motoyasu and awoken his undying love for her. It was an issue we still wrestled with. She was still a bit of a featherhead, but she wasn't without the capacity to learn too. Reflecting for a moment on her history, I realized Filo had been pretty unlucky, what with Motoyasu and the Demon Dragon too.

"You're saying I've got a poison tongue too?!" Keel exclaimed.

"In your case, you just say one thing too many. With Filo, she would really go for the throat," I explained.

"What's the difference?" Keel asked.

"Well, for example, we heard that a nation to the north of Melromarc had overthrown their king due to intense poverty in the nation but that the poverty issue had not been resolved.

What do you think Filo said?" I asked, rhetorically, before putting on my best Filo voice. "I feel so sorry for that poor king! So he really was just thinking about the people after all. Whose fault is it that you're starving now, huh?"

"Okay, that's pretty cold," Keel replied, seemingly taken aback by the venom of this birdy-burn. Filo had come a long way since then, it was true.

"There are the things you think and then the things you should actually say. It's like if you want me to make some cookies for you, but you can't bring yourself to just come out and say it. Instead you make a fuss about being hungry. Then Filo comes in at the side and says, 'Keel is only saying she's hungry because she wants cookies.' Do you see?" I asked.

"Yes, I think I get it. Is that why she wanted to use poison?" Keel asked.

"It was probably also because we were fighting the bioplants and the Dragon Zombie at the time, so poison looked like a powerful option," I pondered.

"We have both those things in the village now," Keel replied. "But Gaelion is still in the future." The bioplants were something, but then there was Gaelion and the Dragon Zombie too. From the perspective of Keel and the others who joined after we defeated them, they probably weren't all that frightening as creatures. I wasn't scared of them either, especially when it came to dragons. These were meant to be proud beasts, the standard-bearer for fantasy plastered on every book cover, so I didn't understand how things had turned out like this. The dragons here seemed like little more than eccentric oddballs.

"So Filo had a time she wanted to use poison, you see. So Chick, in a sense, could be considered the poison-wielding filolial that Filo once wanted to become," I finished.

"Ooh, hear that, Chick?" Imiya said. The filolial made a bit of an odd noise in response though. Filo was her boss, basically, so it had to be strange to hear that she actually wanted to be like her. Time to change the topic.

"Cian, do you know anything about the place we're headed to?" I asked.

"Nope," she replied.

"Mamoru doesn't take you out to places with him?" I inquired.

"We've been playing in the castle a lot recently," she responded. From what I'd seen of Mamoru with the kids, it was clear he was keeping them safe in the castle. He was using it like some kind of orphanage, almost. From the damages we'd seen that were done to the castle town, it wasn't hard to imagine the dangers of letting them outside. "He did take us out more often before, but then . . . She said. . ." Cian suddenly snapped back to herself, covering her mouth and shaking her head. It almost seemed like she thought she'd said too much, but I could only guess what she was talking about. Maybe the "she" was

Holn, R'yne, or someone like that, warning Mamoru it was too dangerous to let the kids out. Or maybe some darker reason lurked there.

"Keel," I called. Then I proceeded to unceremoniously pick her up and place her down in front of Cian. Keel quickly picked up on what I was doing and started wagging her tail and licking Cian's face.

"Cheer up, Cian! We're out on the road with Bubba today. Who knows what fun we'll have! The food is going to be great too, I promise!" she yipped and barked. She really did look exactly like an excitable puppy. Even the staunchest demi-human therianthrope would be hard-pressed not to crack a smile when confronted by this. Cian was laughing already.

"Hey, Keel, cut that out!" she giggled. The two of them descended into shared laughter, a cat and a dog playing together.

"Keel is saying that you need to enjoy this trip now that you're finally out of the castle," I explained for her. "And I agree with Keel. You need to have fun!"

"I will," Cian said.

"Do you want to sit up here?" I asked, indicating the spot that Keel had just vacated—not entirely voluntarily, of course. The view was pretty good from the front of the wagon, and it was the best spot to sit to combat motion sickness.

"No, thanks . . . too scary for me," she replied.

"Really? Then it sounds like it's your turn, Imiya," I said.

"What? Hold on?!" she exclaimed. She was standing right where I wanted her, so I picked her up and put her in front of me. Just swapping her with Keel—nothing suspicious about that. And yet Imiya stiffened up completely, just like Keel had, as soon as I put her down. Her moaning suggested she was suddenly feeling very nervous.

As our banter continued, I did have one thought: Keel and Cian weren't the normal party members for me, and they were girls too. When I looked at this objectively from the outside, it might well appear that I had chosen to head off on the hunt with a party of women. That was a severe oversight on my part. I wondered why I didn't realize it before now. It was simply the result of wanting to tease Keel a little and choosing members who could handle things optimally in our destination. I certainly hadn't been thinking about the gender of Keel or Imiya in my selections. I might face some blowback for this, but I'd just have to face the music if that happened.

Maybe this was also because I put Raphtalia in a separate unit. I'd have to make sure to bring Ruft or Fohl along with me next time. Ruft was pretty confident in his own furry coat, and he was sure to let me stroke him. He wasn't going to stiffen up like Keel or Imiya. Fohl, though . . . he might run a mile.

Our wagon proceeded to reach our destination without any real issues.

We started our trading and selling, while the slaves handling the cooking also started to sell some food. I decided to hold back Keel and deploy her a little later. We hadn't encountered many monsters on the way to the village. We showed off our wares and got ready to do a little hunting and mining. I showed the special pass that Mamoru had provided us with to the village chief, and he had given us permission to proceed further inside. Our wagon was now moving again, clattering along deeper into the mountains. Chick couldn't quite match Filo, but she was making good time nonetheless.

"Okay. We'll have some time before sundown for some hunting and mining. Keel, use that nose of yours to locate some prey. Raph-chan and Chick, you back Keel up, and Imiya, you find us some ore. There are supposed to be holes around here for mining," I said. Everyone shouted or squawked their agreement, but then Keel added an afterthought.

"Are you sure you aren't pigeonholing me a little there? Being a dog and all?" she asked.

"Whatever are you talking about?! Freaking Motoyasu has an incredible sense of smell. He could locate Filo almost anywhere," I told her.

"I'm not sure I like being compared to the Spear Hero," Keel replied. But then she did start sniffing around for monsters. We had already encountered some on the way here. There was a large flower-like one called a "wisteria nature bind" and what looked like a clump of sand called a "rosepink sandwalker." The wisteria nature bind would be a challenging one to cook with, but I probably could because it was a plant. But I didn't really do salads. The stem was a bit like burdock, but there didn't seem any reason to go out of our way to eat it. The rosepink sandwalker, meanwhile, was a magical monster, much like the balloons. The golem-like magic found in minerals could sometimes collect sand from the vicinity and become a monster. Rosepink sandwalkers could be defeated by causing a large enough impact—physically, or with magic—to the internal ore that contained their intrinsic magic. With my current party, having Imiya imbue her hand with magic and strike directly at their weak spot allowed us to quickly and safely defeat them. They looked very hard and annoying to fight normally. The ores collected from defeating them also had plenty of uses. We were definitely going to give them a try for making some accessories later.

The same principle seemed to apply here as anywhere else: the deeper we went into the mountains, the more powerful the monsters got. I really wanted to fight some that would make a good meal.

"What about me?" Cian asked. I had inquired if she wanted to stay back at the stall, but she had decided to come with us, so I brought her along. Having her in the party would earn her experience, so she really just had to hang out. But she had a look on her face like she actually wanted to make a contribution.

I realized that I didn't even know what level she was. From her external appearance, she probably hadn't received much training. Our trading was probably helping a little with that.

"Cian, we don't want to put you in danger, so just stay behind me. You can fight once you get a little stronger," I told her. She didn't look happy about it, but this seemed like the best course of action. Mamoru talked about taking care of the kids, but he certainly wasn't working on their levels.

"I can smell something coming from over here," Keel yipped, heading off after the monsters. She was really dashing along. On a rocky mountain slope we encountered a scorpion monster called a "spring green stalcorpion" and a poisonous spider called a "frosty gray spideviper." There was also a floaty eel-looking monster called a "graphite angrifo." Chick was immediately on her guard concerning the scorpion and its poison, and she started fighting that.

"Raph!" Raph-chan was helping her out. I was pretty sure they could handle it together. The graphite angrifo, meanwhile, had electricity crackling all over it and used magnetism to lift ore from the vicinity to attack. It could also slip quickly under the ground to evade our attacks. I guess I should have expected this kind of thing from the nation that would eventually become Siltvelt. Ren and Rat had told me in the past that Siltvelt had a more unique slant on monsters than nations like Faubrey and Melromarc—a larger selection of monsters using annoying attacks like poison was what that meant.

"Hold on!" Keel barked.

"Got you!" Imiya joined in, the pair of them hammering whack-a-mole style at the ground as the graphite angrifo popped its face up. Keel was using a one-handed sword and Imiya was using a hammer. I had to take a moment to appreciate the mole therianthrope Imiya whacking at a mole-like monster—it was almost comical.

Putting that aside, we were taking down monsters one after another, but they kept on pouring down from the mountains toward us. The ruckus we were creating was just calling more of them to come and have a go. I was protecting my party in order to give Keel and the others some combat experience, but I wasn't giving much in the way of orders. They needed some time in actual combat for themselves.

"Imiya, help me out! Get the one coming your way!" Keel shouted.

"I've got it!" Imiya replied. "As the source of your power, I implore you! Let the true way be revealed once more, and dig up everything around me! Drifa Earth Reverse!" She seemed to have realized there was no end to the supply of incoming monsters, and so she slammed her claws down into the ground and then ripped them upward again. In the next moment, it looked like all the earth under which the graphite angrifo was hiding just flipped up and rotated over in the air. Clumps of rock scattered all around for a moment and seemed like they were going to settle back down, but then they flew toward us instead.

"Shooting Star Wall!" I deployed a skill to protect all of my allies, stopping the incoming attacks. This was starting to get to be a bit much.

"They seem to have strong magic defenses. I can't believe they're attacking like that," Imiya said.

"I guess we can't clean these up as quickly as I hoped," I replied. As we discussed the situation, I suddenly noticed that Cian had vanished from behind me. The graphite angrifo poked its head out to see how its counterattack had worked and the next thing I heard was Cian's shout as she slashed at its throat with the knife she carried to protect herself. The graphite angrifo expired in short order, eyes popping out in surprise.

"That's what you needed, correct?" Cian asked.

"Yeah . . . I guess it is," I said. It looked like I needed to reassess my thinking on Cian's combat experience.

"Keel had its attention, and I saw it peeking out," she explained. She might have some aptitude for fighting after all. A little care and attention and she might be quite strong.

"Thanks, Cian! Bubba, we've got more incoming!" Keel shouted.

"Sure, I see them. Try and finish them yourself this time," I told her.

"Of course! Imiya, get that hammer swinging!" she yipped.

"I'm here!" Imiya replied. Each member of my current

party seemed to have a good understanding of the characteristics of each monster and was responding as required. Imiya took on a spring green stalcorpion, watching for the poison from the tail and smashing its pincers with her hammer. Then Keel slashed in to take the tail right off. They both attacked the body to finish the monster. For the frosty gray spideviper, Keel kept its attention on her while Imiya hammered at whatever she could hit—head, body—to immobilize and finish it off. As for the graphite angrifo, Keel yipped around, using her speed to leap and practically kick its head off before it could bury itself again.

Raph-chan and Chick were still fighting too. Raph-chan's tail was all fluffed up as she created illusions in the vicinity. The target monster was left snapping at empty air, chasing its tail, and then Chick slashed in with claws to finish it off. Things suddenly seemed a lot simpler than I had expected.

"Hmmm. It's all going smoothly, but still . . ." Something was tickling me. Monsters were continuing to appear, one after the other, and our transport wagon was getting pretty loaded down. "I think we've probably got all the ingredients we need—or can even carry." There were so many monsters. It had to be due to the waves, but things didn't seem any better here than in our time.

That was when a fresh horde of monsters appeared, coming down from the depths of the mountains as though lured by the smell of blood. Their leader was an "amber rose ultros," a large two-headed lion-dog beast that was growling and snarling as it came at us. Keel was the closest and I was pretty sure she could handle this new threat.

In the next moment, though, I realized Keel was breathing hard. "I need to . . . need to . . ." she gasped.

"Keel! What's wrong?" Imiya shouted. Keel continued to breathe hard, her shoulders heaving, and then she roared in rage and pumped herself up for further fighting. That was when Imiya dashed in, swinging her hammer around wildly as she headed right for the amber rose ultros. It didn't matter how much higher her level was though; such an uncontrolled attack would easily be avoided.

"Keel! What's wrong?" I shouted. She just continued to scream. She'd slipped into a complete panic! It reminded me for a moment of the trouble Raphtalia had experienced when she was smaller.

"Keel!" Imiya was still rushing in to try and offer some support, but the other monsters were all getting in the way.

"Gah! I had no idea Keel suffered from this kind of issue!" I cursed. Our formation had collapsed and so Shooting Star Wall had been stripped away. I was desperate to find a way to protect Keel and was about to give orders to Raph-chan and Chick to back her up . . . when something flitted overhead and leapt at blinding speed onto the back of the amber rose ultros.

It was Cian. A moment later she had ripped out the throat of one of the heads. The beast roared, a rain of blood spraying out around us. Keel was still shouting wildly, swinging her weapon around, and it happened to stick into the amber rose ultros's other head, finishing the beast off.

Keel was covered in blood, her shoulders heaving, while Cian landed with a cool look on her face. They were like . . . cat and dog, basically. But this was no time for fooling around.

"Retreat!" I signaled. Chick and Raph-chan returned calls of agreement. I kicked the monster corpses onto the wagon, hoping Chick was up to pulling all that weight, and then joined Raph-chan, Keel, and Cian.

"Raph!" Raph-chan was up on Imiya's shoulder, and I signaled for her to use illusion magic to direct the horde in Chick's direction.

"I did it! I got it!" Keel enthused, but she didn't seem to know what was going on and was still covered in blood. I picked her up. Chick was fighting as a backstop, slashing claws and beak expelling a toxic purple haze of magic amid the horde of monsters—a haze that was forming into a ball. Then she stepped back toward us and shifted to haikuikku to come over to us. Immediately afterward, with a loud popping sound, that purple ball exploded amid the monsters. Any monsters covered in the resulting purple liquid started to burst too, causing a fatal chain reaction among the horde. I swallowed. That was a pretty nasty attack. Chick gave a squawk in celebration of her victory. Yeah, wow. I was very impressed.

"That's Chick's biggest attack. It's called Venom Splash," Imiya offered from the sidelines. "Any monsters defeated by it become a secondary poison bomb, causing further damage to other monsters around them." A chain-reaction poison attack. That was clearly pretty powerful. "Some toxins should remain in the air for a while, so we can retreat now."

"Okay. We need to concentrate on getting Keel calm down first," I said.

"Yeah. Let's fall back," Imiya agreed. Cian nodded at the proposal too, and we all climbed into the wagon, then hurried away back down the mountain.

Chapter Three: Wave Trauma

"Okay, Keel . . . anything you want to say?" I asked her.

"Well . . ." she started. We had retreated to a safe location, and after waiting for Keel to regain her composure, I'd decided to sit her down and ask her what was going on. To reach that point, it required Imiya and Raph-chan to soothe her and for me to prepare a tincture from sedative herbs. Cian, for her part, was seated on the wagon, yawning, like she'd just finished a big job. "We won, didn't we?" Keel finally continued.

"That's not the issue here. I'm more concerned with how you charged, half crazed, at that amber rose ultros," I said.

"I took it too far! I'm sorry, Bubba!" Keel whined. I sighed. It was obvious she was trying to cover things up.

"Keel, if you don't fess up, then there's going to be trouble later . . . I shouldn't need to tell you that, should I?" I said.

"That's right, Keel," Imiya backed me up. "You really weren't yourself out there today." She was proving herself, once again, to be a lot like Raphtalia. Although Imiya was a little more soft-spoken, they both took things too seriously. Raphtalia could come on pretty hard, but that was due to me as well. I felt like I was starting to overlap Imiya and Raphtalia in all sorts of ways.

"Uh . . . but Bubba! I fought hard, didn't I?" Keel asked.

"If you mean charging into battle in a semi-crazed state, sure. Who knows what would have happened if Cian hadn't been there?" I replied. It didn't matter how high Keel's level had become; she simply wasn't as tough as someone like me. If she took a bad hit, then things might have been worse than a mere injury. "Cian, you really saved Keel's tail back there. Thanks."

"Keel has it worse than I do. I can tell even without understanding what she's saying. She's suffering from some kind of trauma," Cian replied. Mamoru had told me that Cian had lost her parents in the fighting. Keel had also suffered due to the waves and the slave hunts, and those shared experiences were probably helping them bond. I recalled that, around the time we started restoring the village, Raphtalia had been responsible for the mental care of Keel and the others. I had thought by all working together it had allowed her to overcome those issues, but it seemed some of them still remained.

"Keel, you need to understand what happened out there. The moment you saw that amber rose ultros, you just lost it and charged in blindly," I told her. She only moaned. Keel would normally just blow off past trauma with a burst of crazy energy. And this was a problem that anyone from the village could potentially face. Even if it wasn't there at the moment, wasn't on the surface yet, something could trigger it in the future. "Based on what Raphtalia told me . . ." I recalled what she had said.

The boss monster for the first wave, a cerberus, had killed not only Raphtalia's parents but also many others from her village. That meant it was highly likely the remaining villagers would fall into a panic when they saw any kind of multi-headed canine.

"I'm fine, okay? Fine!" Keel said, still trying to bluster her way through this.

"Raph?" Raph-chan said, tilting her head and moving in with concern in her voice. Keel seemed to nod in reply. "Raph!" With a puff of smoke, Raph-chan activated some illusion magic and suddenly became a pitch-black dog with three heads that were glaring down at Keel. I wondered if this was the same creature that had decimated Lurolona during the first wave. As soon as Keel saw the creature, her eyes widened, her face mixing hostility with fear, and she started to tremble on the spot.

"Raph!" Raph-chan ended the transformation and gave a hopeless little sigh.

"Keel, now do you understand?" I quietly asked her.

"Yeah, I think I do," she replied, seeming to see the issue now. I had to wonder for a moment how Raph-chan had known exactly what to turn into to trigger Keel's trauma. Maybe she had just worked from the description that Raphtalia had provided.

Putting that aside, I realized this could really be a big problem. If everyone in the village had this weakness when it came to multi-headed canines—not such a rare thing in a fantasy world—it could poke quite a hole in our defenses. Some of them probably really were close to getting over it by now, so it also seemed a bad idea to stir things up again. But on the other hand, we had no idea what might happen moving forward.

"You kept your cool, Imiya, because you didn't start out in the village, right?" I asked her.

"That's right . . ." she replied. She had still been a slave though, so she might well have her own trauma tucked away in there somewhere.

"If there is anything you think might trigger a similar event for you, Imiya, please let me know. We need to be ready for anything," I told her.

"I don't . . . don't like Melromarc soldiers very much, but I'm fine. I've got over that," she replied.

"And the reason you don't like them . . . Ah, I won't ask. No need to force yourself to remember anything you don't want to," I told her. When I was buying up the slaves from Lurolona, Raphtalia's home village, I'd caused the price of them to rise and that had led to slave hunters attacking us. Keel had fought back, and Imiya had put up a good fight too, so I had thought she was over the worst of her trauma.

"No, I really am fine. I'm over it, thanks to everyone's help. I also think . . . it might lighten the load for me if I talk about it," Imiya said, continuing even though I assured her she didn't need to. "Slave hunters came to my village . . . and killed my parents, right in front of me . . ."

"I see," I managed.

"My mom was pregnant . . . I never even knew if it would be a boy or a girl. And the soldiers just laughed as they . . ." Imiya finally did trail off.

"I can't imagine how hard that was. You did well to survive. That's enough, that really is," I told her. I stroked Imiya a little and gave her a hug. Everyone in the village was normally so hyper I tended to forget that they had all of these issues and injuries in their past. They had all lived their own difficult lives to get to this point—lives far harder than mine. All that had happened to me was being framed for something I didn't do. Seeing your parents killed right in front of you, like Imiya had . . . I couldn't even imagine that.

I wondered if thinking like this was an indicator of how much I had grown myself. There was nothing more arrogant than thinking you were the only one who was suffering. It was thanks to Raphtalia, Atla . . . and everyone else . . . that I'd managed to recover myself to the point I could worry about other people.

"Ah . . . Shield Hero . . ." I was probably hugging her too hard now, because Imiya made an embarrassed noise and curled up a bit. "You helped me find my uncle and other relatives, and I'm fine now. I'm through it," she said.

"That's fine, if that's the case. If you are hurting, you let me know," I told her.

"I'm very happy now. That's the truth, and it's thanks to you and everyone else," she replied. She gave me a smile and moved back from my arms. I felt the weight of all this pressing onto me again in that moment. I'd made up my mind to end the fighting, for the sake of everyone in the village, and that was not a light burden to bear.

"In any case. We need to ask each individual in question if they want to try and overcome their trauma or try and avoid it," I said. There was no pressing need to rip open old wounds. I wasn't a monster. Those with trauma had as much right to live as anyone. Conquest or evasion, I didn't mind which one they chose, so long as it allowed them to go forward.

"Bubba! I get it now! I want to become strong enough to protect everyone, no matter what happens! So I'm going to overcome this!" Keel said with a bark, which then became an interminably long howl. It sounded like she was up for the challenge.

"Cian, thanks for everything," Keel said, offering her hand with a smile.

"Sure thing . . ." Cian replied, still a little timidly. She also seemed to understand what the handshake meant and gently took it.

"Bubba! I think we've become super friendly with Cian!" Keel yipped.

"Yep, we sure have," I said with a smile. I was actually

amazed at how much stronger Cian was than expected. How light she was on her feet too—she'd really been a big help. I wasn't sure how Mamoru would react, but with proper training Cian could really be powerful. "We've got the materials and ingredients we needed, anyway . . . We should head back and discuss this problem at home."

"Yes . . . okay," Imiya replied. "I would have liked to mine for more minerals, but what do you think?"

"We've finished hunting. We can come and do some more mining if we can find the time later," I told her. "When we do so, we'll bring a party of lumos with us, maybe—people who can actually fight an amber rose ultros or two safely." The lumo species were good with their hands and great at digging holes; they were pretty useful all around. In a fantasy setting you would normally think demi-humans like dwarves would be better at stuff like this, but the lumos were so good I was ready to give up such preconceptions entirely. There were actual dwarves in this world, but not many here; Kizuna's world had more, if I recalled correctly. We definitely didn't have any in the village.

We returned to the nearby village, helped out with the stalls, and then returned home.

"I see . . . That sounds so terrible," Raphtalia sympathized. We had made it back to the village after dusk, ate our evening meal, and I was now explaining how Keel's trauma had resurfaced.

Those originally from Lurolona had looks on their faces like they thought it could maybe happen to them, while everyone else was looking on with gentle concern.

"Raphtalia, what about you? Do you think the same thing could happen?" I asked her.

"I think . . . I'm fine. I think so," she replied. We'd fought some monsters that impinged on that zone—karma dogs immediately came to mind.

"Raph!" Raph-chan decided to use the same litmus test, triggering some illusion magic to become the cerberus again. She instantly got a reaction from about half of the slaves from Lurolona. I looked at Raphtalia, and she was frowning a little as she looked at Raph-chan, but I couldn't tell exactly how to peg that reaction.

"Okay. A few adjustments to the illusion, and that could be a good test," Raphtalia said. Then she muttered something quietly to herself about Raph-chan having borrowed this creature from her memories. That made more sense. I had my own troubles with parasites like Gaelion and the Demon Dragon peeking into my own mind, so maybe Raph-chan could do the same thing with Raphtalia. In any case, Raphtalia wasn't having a strong reaction, so it did look like she was over it.

"How did you get over it, Raphtalia?" Keel asked Raphtalia, rubbing up to her.

"We talked about this when we first returned to the village, correct? I told you that I overcame my trauma a little at a time after Mr. Naofumi purchased me," Raphtalia replied.

"I remember . . . but I thought I was over it too, and then look what happened! So now I'm not so sure!" Keel whined. Raphtalia had a serious look on her face too.

"A difficult question," Ren chipped in, his arms folded as he tried to think of a solution.   "Trauma earned in battle can sometimes be overcome through sheer bravery," Fohl added. He had experience as a gladiator and seemed to be thinking of solutions relating to that. But the fundamental difference in the perception of combat might make that approach difficult. Even if the villagers understood this was a fight for brave warriors, that might not offer a solution to the issues in their minds. The hakuko and warriors of Siltvelt had a kind of Viking courage accompanied by muscles where their brains should be.

"I was thinking about this as we made our way back to the village," I said. "I have a question for anyone still suffering trauma." I looked over those who raised their hands in response. "I don't think overcoming this, like Raphtalia has, is the answer for everyone. I want you to think individually about how you want to handle this trauma." There had to be others with trauma similar to Keel's and all of them suffered from different symptoms.

"What if we decide to try and face it down, Bubba?" Keel asked.

"The treatment will probably involve some pretty stressful training, mixed with an application of drugs," I replied. I'd need to consult Rat on that. It wasn't her specialty, but she would probably have a better idea than me—and getting the treatment wrong could easily have the opposite of the desired effect. "It's like being boxed in by mental wounds that you thought were healed. You don't have to try and resolve them if you don't want to, and if it's too hard you can stop along the way. These kinds of issues are normally resolved by the passage of time more than anything else." We didn't want to cause any more damage—or mental breakdowns, to be honest. Everyone whom my question seemed to apply to started to think, anyway.

"Hey, Naofumi," Melty piped up as she watched the scene unfolding. "You've got your own trauma as well, haven't you? Like filolials?" I grunted. That was a painfully astute observation. The cause had been getting trampled half to death by a horde of filolials that Motoyasu brought into the village. Ruft hadn't seemed bothered by any of this until now, but as soon as he heard it, his face had started to look like that famous screaming painting. He and I shared the same trauma. Seeing a cluster of filolials together was still enough to make my eye twitch.

"If you want to overcome it or just let it be for now, you need to make your own decision and stand by it," I said.

"I get it," Keel replied. "But I want to overcome it!" She thrust her fist up into the air with this declaration. She was still in dog form though, so she looked more cute than decisive . . . but that was no reason to rain on her determination parade.

"Okay. But if your symptoms seem very bad, we may make the decision to stop treatment. Understand?" I asked.

"No worries! I'm going to overcome it, you'll see!" she replied. Many of the other trauma sufferers joined her in a shout of conviction.

"Which brings me to you, Rat. You got any ideas about how best to treat this?" I asked.

"I thought you'd get to me eventually," Rat replied.

"Of course. It's the perfect chance for you to show off what you can do. Or maybe I should be asking your ancestor, Holn, to prove how much better she is than you?" I quipped. At that moment Holn came back with Mamoru. She didn't stay here in my village all the time.

"As proactive as ever, Duke," Rat said wryly. "I've read some papers on the subject, that's about it, but if the alternative is asking Holn for help, then you can count me in."

"Meaning you do have some ideas?" I asked.

"Dream therapy might be a good solution. If that doesn't get results, we'll try something closer to what you suggested," Rat said.

"Dreams? Something like hypnosis?" I asked. I'd seen hypnosis in manga; it was a common trope.

"Not exactly. I'm talking about a treatment that uses magic,"

Rat replied. I mean, duh, of course, we were in a magical world. Why wouldn't there be mental treatments that used magic? "It mainly involves the use of illusion magic—something we aren't short on around here."

"Okay." I looked over at our main illusion magic users: Raphtalia, Ruft, and the two Raph-chans.

"What exactly do you need us to do?" Raphtalia raised her hand and asked for the bunch of them.

"Basically, you cast some illusion magic on the trauma victim while they are sleeping and direct their dreams to the moment that caused that trauma. Then you prepare a more suitable end to that nightmare for them," Rat explained. Illusion magic was definitely some convenient stuff.

"What kind of ending?" Raphtalia asked.

"You share the same injury, so surely you have some idea. The important thing is healing. The removal of the fear differs for each individual," Rat said. So taking the moment of trauma and leading it to a better conclusion . . . like defeating the cerberus, or being saved by someone, or a reunion with the departed . . . something like that. I got what she was trying to say, but that sounded pretty hard to pull off.

"You're a hero from another world yourself, aren't you? You have access to far more powerful illusion magic than other people, so give it a try," Rat suggested. Raphtalia tended to focus on physical fighting, but as a hero she also had access to some powerful Liberation-class magic. The blessing of the Demon Dragon also seemed to have unlocked restrictions she had been suffering under. This could actually be good magic practice for her.

"I'll do the best I can," she replied.

"Raphtalia, are you going to help us out with magic?" Keel asked.

"That's right," she replied kindly. "I'm not sure how much I'll be able to help, at least to start with, but I'll do everything I can."

"Okay!" Keel said happily. It sounded like Raphtalia was going to be working to heal the trauma of Keel and the others. They all trusted Raphtalia implicitly, so it sounded like a good arrangement. I just hoped it would work out.

However, this also raised a further issue for me.

"Hey, Rat. If you had this trick in your back pocket, why didn't you use it on me?" I asked her.

"You made a more than sufficient recovery without it, Duke," she replied. By sleeping huddled up with Raph-chan, perhaps! That wasn't what I was talking about! "What kind of good ending would you desire to such a dream, Duke?" Rat inquired, one eyebrow lifted. Like me turning on the filolials and driving them off? Or maybe all of them suddenly turning into Raph species? But then I'd just wake up and realize it was all a dream, which seemed unlikely to cure anything. "There's a big personal element in this kind of treatment. I didn't think it would make much difference for you, Duke, and so I didn't bother," Rat explained. I wondered why we had been facing so many issues recently that I couldn't do anything about or was completely ineffective against. I was really starting to feel useless.

"I'm not happy about that explanation," I replied, "but very well. Anyone who wants to try and overcome their trauma, please focus on your healing!" I stated. There were general shouts of agreement. And so, from that very night, Raphtalia, Ruft, and the Raph species all started conducting trauma healing experiments.

"That gives us a lead on resolving Keel's issues, anyway. Now then . . ." I muttered. It was time to address the stuff that had come up prior to when we went hunting. Luckily, we had countless witnesses all around us in that moment. I moved over toward Raphtalia, but for some reason she backed away when she saw me coming.

"What's wrong?" I asked.

"I'm not sure. There's a very unpleasant aura coming off you right now, Mr. Naofumi," Raphtalia admitted. Was that another indicator of her instincts? Or maybe some kind of fighter's premonition.

"You're imagining things," I told her.

"Not at all. That very reply you just gave me seems like

you're thinking something. If you're *not* planning something or other, you normally just tell me I'm too tense and to relax a little," she said. We did spend a lot of time together, so she could clearly read me like a book. It was a sign of the trust between us, which I liked, but I also didn't need her giving me a lot of unwanted advice.

"I'm kinda in the corner here. Everyone is on my back recently. Just give me a break!" I told her. Raphtalia immediately blushed.

"Mr. Naofumi! Just because of pressure from other people, you're going to do what, exactly?!" Raphtalia asked, adopting a light stance with her sword at the ready. I couldn't believe she was ready to fight me off! Did she dislike me that much?!

"Hey, Ren. Do you think Hero Iwatani is having some kind of manic episode? Or has the pressure from everyone around him finally become too much to bear?" Eclair pondered on the sidelines. Ren didn't seem to have an answer. Melty looked suitably aghast, Rift looked perplexed, and the Raph-chans were holding their breath. Wyndia had a cold look in her eyes.

"Bubba, now you're acting weird!" Keel barked.

"Keel! Silence!" I commanded.

"Ah, Brother's heart is in turmoil!" Fohl lamented. "Atla, what should I do for him in this situation?"

"Fohl!" I replied. "If Atla was alive she would be trying to get in on this—and you'd be looking at that with jealousy, wouldn't you?"

"Right, of course! But hold on . . . this is like the time you tried to bed me! Brother, you are manic again indeed!" Fohl blustered.

"It's nothing like that one specific time!" I replied. I was never going to live that down. I was also getting pretty pissed at the people I'd expected to be on my side here—the people who wanted this to happen—now all lining up to get in the way.

I continued to inch toward Raphtalia, almost as though I was expecting a fight.

Imiya stepped in and said, "Let me help here . . . From how the Shield Hero was acting earlier today, I think I can understand what he is going to do."

"Earlier today?" Raphtalia asked. "I did have a terrible premonition at one point. What did he do to you?!" It almost sounded like she'd developed some kind of sixth sense.

"Raph!" Raph-chan gave a hopeless shrug.

"If you hear the whole story, I think you'll understand," Imiya said, "but the more people who know the truth, the less impact this will have . . ."

"Imiya, can you tell me what the situation is? What Mr. Naofumi is thinking? Please, just tell me," Raphtalia suggested.

"Ah, okay. Here's what happened." Imiya moved over to Raphtalia and whispered quietly into her ear. Raphtalia had been standing with her face red and her sword ready to draw, but then her eyes narrowed, and she eventually changed to a look of typical mild disgust. She dropped her guard and came over, whispering in a quiet voice.

"Okay, Mr. Naofumi . . . just to confirm this, you weren't planning on doing . . . something like what Sadeena wants from you, right here with me, in front of everyone, right?" Raphtalia asked.

"No, of course not. Do you really think that's the kind of thing I'm into?" I replied. A little sex education for the masses? Only a real pervert would do that. Sure, the four holy heroes all came from different worlds, but that didn't mean we were completely without morals. Raphtalia gave a sigh of relief at hearing this. She couldn't have really thought I'd do something like that! Everyone was on my case the entire time about our relationship already. What would happen if we did something like that?

"I think I understand the situation," Raphtalia said. "What exactly did you plan on doing?"

"Just this." I reached up and stroked Raphtalia's head. It did feel different from when I stroked her before. She'd been a child back then; now she was taller, and her hair was so smooth. Raphtalia had seemed a little hesitant about this to start with, but now her cheeks were starting to flush a little. She was even leaning in toward me.

"Oh boy! Hot couple alert!" Keel was getting carried away already.

"Really . . . what are you playing at . . ." Melty seemed to have realized what was going on too, and sighed, but seemed willing to let it slide.

"Seriously. It's just some harmless stroking. Stop making it into such a big thing," I muttered.

"It's because you didn't explain yourself properly, Mr. Naofumi," Raphtalia admonished me.

"This would be pointless if I had to explain it. I thought Keel, at least, would pick up on my intentions, like Imiya did," I grated. This wasn't a case of being dumb; she was reaching Motoyasu levels of obliviousness.

I continued to stroke Raphtalia as I thought the situation over. Of course, I couldn't stroke her chest like I did with Keel. I mean, it was an option but would clearly be considered sexual harassment, and something inside me was putting the brakes on that. Stroking her chest in front of everyone would be a mistake. In Keel's case, that had been the chest plate of a dog. Totally different. Sadeena's tits—okay, I wasn't going there. Stroking her throat like I did with the Raph-chans and Imiya felt kind of wrong too. That led my eyes down to her tail. It looked like there was plenty of easy stroking down there. Raphtalia noticed where I was looking and placed her hands over her tail.

"That might be a bit much . . . You can just stroke my head, thank you," she said.

"Oh, okay," I replied. Maybe demi-humans had a thing about getting their tails stroked. It might have been worse than copping a feel of her tits.

"What I mean is . . . that kind of thing . . . would be better when we are alone . . . together, I mean, but alone . . ." Raphtalia stammered, turning redder and redder. I had seen demi-humans winding their tails together, like human lovers might hold hands, back in Siltvelt. When I had been paraded around the city on that palanquin, I recalled one such couple looking at me and getting all gooey over the Shield Hero blessing their union. I think I'd almost thrown up. Those two had their tails entwined together, and they had been demi-humans. Maybe holding tails was like holding hands then—I just didn't have a tail to do it with. A tail stroke could well be sexual harassment.

"Raph!" Raph-chan sensed that I still had more stroking to give and offered her tail toward me.

"Ah, okay. Thanks," I replied, feeling like I was left with little choice but to stroke the offered tail. The soft fluffy feel of it reminded me of how Raphtalia used to be.

"I understand what you wanted to achieve with this, Mr. Naofumi . . . so let's go home like this, shall we?" Raphtalia suggested. Incredibly, she took my hand, and the two of us headed back to our house like an intimate couple. Once we were alone in the room—though we kept our eyes peeled for Peeping Toms at the window—she also let me touch her tail a little. I hoped this would settle everyone down.

That night, before going to sleep, Keel and the others had

bothered Raphtalia over and over to try and find out what the two of us had done together. We hadn't done anything, beyond a little tail stuff, but Raphtalia managed to evade such questions.

Chapter Four: Thanks to the Assassin

It was a few days after Keel and the other villagers went into treatment.

"Hey!" Mamoru arrived at our village, with Cian in tow. Melty and Ruft were with them too.

"Huh? What's up? Something going down?" I asked.

"Yeah," Mamoru replied. "I told you about that person who looks like Raphtalia, right? We've finally pinned down her location. We'd like to take you to meet her. What do you say?" I did recall him mentioning such a person. She was likely to be an ancestor of Raphtalia. It certainly seemed worth going to meet her.

"Okay. We'll get ready and move out," I replied.

"We'll need to be careful," Mamoru warned. "She calls herself a pacifier, one here to observe the heroes. If things go badly, we could get killed."

"I know. We've got one of her descendants here with us though," I said. We'd also launched an attack on Q'ten Lo back in our time. We could handle it. "We're just looking to have a chat, but still . . ." We'd need to take a big enough party to be able to handle things if she did turn hostile. From her perspective we were an irregular entity. When we explained ourselves to her, it would be important to keep her a little confused. The fact there were two Shield Heroes should help stimulate her curiosity. That was why Mamoru and I were going together.

Ren, meanwhile, might be mistaken as a Sword Hero from a completely different world, so I'd keep him on standby in case things fell apart completely. Raphtalia and Ruft, meanwhile, were perfectly suited to providing the biggest surprise we had. Both of them had been blessed as Heavenly Emperor, after all. That could end up stirring things up instead, but there were too many possible merits not to take them along. They'd even let us resist a Sakura Destiny Sphere created by a sakura stone of destiny. Things were going to work out in our favor.

That said, we didn't want to take too many along. Just enough to put up a fight if things kicked off. Sending Shadow in to scout was also an option, but we were dealing with someone similar to Raphtalia here. We had to presume she'd be pretty good at spotting people trying to hide themselves.

"Melty, I'd like Raphtalia and Ruft to come along to negotiate, but what about you?" I asked the queen.

"Taking those two sounds like a good idea. If we are dealing with someone from the same island as Raphtalia, those two will likely be more effective than me. I'll get involved if fighting starts, but I'm happy to stay in the background at first," Melty said. It sounded like she pretty much shared my assessment. With that, we settled on obvious-but-safe party picks.

"Okay then. Let's go meet with this pacifier," I said. Obviously, we needed to search out every possible lead in terms of being able to get home, but even more than that, we needed to control any random elements that could potentially make trouble if further fighting started.

"Raph!" said Raph-chan.

"Dafu!" added Raph-chan II. They both seemed to want to come along.

"I'm not sure taking the Raph-chans along would be conducive to smooth negotiations," Raphtalia said.

"But even if they go well, she's going to see the Raph-chans at some point, which could ruin everything," I replied. Trying to hide things that you couldn't hide was a bad idea. If we did get along with this pacifier lady, we had to imagine what would happen if she came to our village. Showing her our hand to start with, hiding nothing, would make a better impression of us too. If we explained everything, we might be able to avoid a confrontation. We could at least explain the Raph species, preventing a breakdown of things later. They could also be useful to confuse and disorient her. When I recalled how Raphtalia had reacted when she first saw Raph-chan, it convinced me that it could work.

"Do you think we'll be able to make this work?" Raphtalia wondered.

"We have to," I replied. With that, the decision was made

for me. Mamoru, Raphtalia, Ruft, and the two Raph-chans would act as the main diplomatic unit. A second unit of Ren, Fohl, and some others would be stationed a short distance away, ready to rush in if we needed more numbers.

"Fohl, thank you," Cian said, showing no reservation in talking with him. She had wanted to stay close to Mamoru, and so we'd added her to Fohl's unit.

"Sure, you're welcome," he replied, knitting his eyes a bit. She normally wasn't that friendly, but she was closer to Fohl than me already. Fohl seemed to have noticed it himself, because he was tilting his head in puzzlement. S'yne and R'yne could leap over whenever they were needed, so they'd be keeping tabs on things with us while also continuing their training at Mamoru's castle. I was happy with that—R'yne had a big mouth, so we didn't need her chipping in with unwanted comments in the middle of important discussions. The price for mocking me sexually was a high one, she was going to learn.

I proposed that idea to Mamoru, and he agreed at once. The pacifier didn't seem to like R'yne much either. I always seemed to pick up party members who made delicate things more complicated with their presence—like the killer whale sisters. But I really couldn't knock Sadeena; she was great at pretty much everything she tried. She was adept at keeping things casual while really seeing through to the truth of an individual. That was something R'yne definitely didn't have.

Anyway. That seemed like a good setup.

With that, we used one of Mamoru's movement skills to travel over to the country where the current Heavenly Emperor was to be found. We proceeded to enter what looked like another castle town. Of course, we had the permits required, which Mamoru displayed at the gate. We made our way inside, wearing light robes and keeping our faces concealed.

"Don't make too much of a commotion, if you can help it," Mamoru stated. "This nation is strong enough to fend off Piensa."

"Okay. It's a powerful place then." I wasn't sure exactly what Mamoru was getting at, but I guessed it meant they had a lot of authority.

"They have remained neutral in regard to the conflict between Siltran and Piensa," Mamoru continued.

"Maybe they just want to pick over the bones once you're done," I said.

"I'm sure that's true. They are very strict about the flow of their people to other nations, however, and their politics are super corrupt too. But that doesn't change how strong they are, of course," Mamoru explained. I looked around the place he had led us too. It did all have a lonely . . . suppressed air to it. All the towns I visited in this other world looked like pretty crappy places to live. Keeping the peace in a fantasy world was no easy task.

As I pondered these thoughts, people started running from the direction we were headed in. Then there came a loud noise from somewhere up ahead.

"Dafu!" Dafu-chan—Raph-chan II—was immediately pointing in that direction.

"Move!" Mamoru shouted, dashing ahead.

"Okay!" I headed after him, along with the rest of the party.

"Dafu!" Dafu-chan was using the spear we found in the filolial sanctuary to fly through the air like a witch on a broom. I was a little bemused by the sight, but it also looked like loads of fun.

"Raph, raph!" Raph-chan was waving a paw. It was cute and soothing, but I also needed to maintain a certain level of tension for what was about to happen. Dafu-chan flew off in the direction of the noise, toward the castle, from which smoke was already rising. This felt like something I'd seen before somewhere.

We used our high-level abilities to force our way through the castle gate—the command structure among the defenders in chaos—and tried to work out what was going on. There was smoke rising from the plaza directly inside the gates. We heard the deafening roar of some monster or other.

"Whatever is the meaning of all this?!" The speaker was a woman who looked like Raphtalia, but with short hair, dressed in a miko outfit, and held a hammer in her hands. Dafu-chan was there too. The third occupant was a fox monster, with nine tails and everything, dying with a spear lodged through its face. The corpse looked familiar. It looked like the fox that had been with Takt. The colors on the fur looked brighter on this one though. Maybe I was just imagining things. "You would kill first and ask questions later?" the woman asked.

"Dafu!" Dafu-chan replied, with a bit of an uncomfortable expression on her face.

"Not to mention the vibrations I sense from your power . . ." the woman muttered.

"Dafu?" Dafu-chan inquired. A moment later the spear that Dafu-chan was holding started to shudder and then shattered into nothing. A gentle light floated up into the air, and it went into Dafu-chan. Fragments of that light also fell onto the short-haired version of Raphtalia.

"I see," she said. "The weapon destroyed the curse and then sacrificed itself. Its task is completed."

"Dafu," Dafu-chan affirmed. It almost sounded like the two of them were hearing something we weren't privy to.

"Very well . . . but who are you exactly?" she asked again, with more composure this time. In that same moment, what looked like a Chinese dragon flew down into the smoldering plaza to float at the side of the woman who looked like Raphtalia. I wondered exactly who they were. From the look of them, it was clear they were the ones we were here to see. When I considered the traditions of Q'ten Lo, wearing the miko getup suggested she was the Heavenly Emperor from this time, no doubt about it.

Then she noticed us and looked over in our direction.

"Okay, sorry about this. She's one of my monsters . . . but the thing is . . . her spear flew off on its own, pretty much," I tried to explain, taking a step forward. The girl looked at Mamoru and then raised her hammer, brow furrowed with caution.

"You are the Shield Hero. What are you doing here? Are you planning to use this chaos to your own advantage?" she asked.

"Nothing of the sort. We have something we would like to discuss with you, the one who calls herself the pacifier, and so we came to see you. I'd like to ask you about the cause of all of this commotion, actually," Mamoru replied. He kept his guard down, speaking softly, displaying no hostile intent.

"This is part of my work as pacifier. I was simply seeking to locate and remove another monster that harms the people and infests this nation," she replied.

"Very well . . . if that's the case. What exactly was your plan next though? Things seem a little chaotic here," Mamoru pointed out.

"I was going to explain what I was doing to the king and then ride off with my friend here. But we are talking about a person who has been tricked by this beast, of course, so he might not accept what I have to say," she said. Just from hearing her brief explanation, I figured she sounded pretty disorganized. I wondered if this really was the Heavenly Emperor from this time. It looked like she had smashed the fox with her hammer, knocking him through the floor of the upper level.

"How's that all working out?" I asked. Even as I did, a kingly-looking—and angry-looking—fellow just happened to show up. He was handsome enough and had black hair.

"You scum! How dare you! My wife!" the king spluttered.

"You had to know your wife, this foul beast you see before you, was poisoning this nation! You are the one who has been fooled here," the Heavenly Emperor replied.

"Silence! You've taken my wife from me, a crime that deserves a thousand deaths—no! I'll torture you until you split apart, then kill your entire family too!" the king raged. He proceeded to give the order to his men to attack the Heavenly Emperor. From the look of it, her plan had been about as well-planned as I'd thought.

"How sad. No wonder you let this monster into your bed. You are worth no better than that. A king who thinks so little of his country isn't worthy to sit on its throne," the floating dragon retorted. I'd seen similar creatures before, of course—like Gaelion and the Demon Dragon. We were in the past now though. This one probably had some Dragon Emperor fragments of its own.

"Hold a moment!" the Heavenly Emperor shouted, but the dragon ignored her, sucking in a deep breath, then blowing pressurized water directly at the king. With a gurgling, spluttering cry, the king was blown away. Not only was it a pretty grim sight to behold, but now we were party to regicide. I wondered how this was going to shake out.

"They've killed the king too?!" The gathered guards and ministers seemed pretty surprised, but half of them looked pretty happy about this turn of events. It looked like the king hadn't been especially well-liked. I could imagine this might be what Melromarc could have turned into in the future if Bitch had become queen. How well someone was liked really comes to light once they died. When the previous queen of Melromarc died, the guards had been wracked with grief.

"I think we had better move along. Agreed?" I asked the Heavenly Emperor. She nodded. She looked like she had worked up a bit of a sweat. We proceeded to make a run for it. "We need to get out of here before we get caught up in this!" Considering the situation, we—that is, Mamoru—were definitely complicit in this. Even if we did just happen to show up at the right (wrong?) moment, no one who mattered was going to believe that it was a coincidence.

"You're right," Mamoru agreed. If word got around that the Shield Hero was trying to destroy this nation, that could cause trouble for me too. Best to just make a run for it.

"I can't keep up with all of this," Raphtalia said.

"Raph!" Raph-chan chirped.

"I think I'm getting a feel for how things work," Ruft said. "You should have a better idea than me, Raphtalia."

"I do. I just don't want to," Raphtalia replied. The two of them were running along behind us. Raphtalia and the other illusion magic users were aiding in our escape, of course, and we proceeded to exit the castle town completely.

As it turned out, the removal of the problematic king and his queen actually resolved many of the issues the nation faced, such as heavy taxation. The people suddenly found a far brighter future awaiting them. Their deaths were said to have been from an unidentified assassin. Anyway, the nine-tailed fox made me think of a certain stylized ninja as it ran through the streets.

The nation had been insanely corrupt. At the end of the day, most people seemed grateful to the "assassin," and that kept it from becoming a larger problem for us.

We left the castle behind us as we reached some nearby woodlands. Checking to make sure no one was following, we caught our breath.

"How sad," the Heavenly Emperor said, breathing hard. "I never expected the outside world to be quite this corrupt."

"That's just how things are," I replied bleakly. "Clinging to strange ideals will only disappoint you." Looking back over my personal history, I realized finding politics that weren't corrupt was definitely the hardest task in this world. I took a moment to consider things back at home though. If you believed the TV or the Internet, it was pretty much the same everywhere.

"I don't know who you are, but you have a bitter outlook," the Heavenly Emperor replied. She looked over at us, her brows knitting together as she tilted her head. "I have to say though . . ." She seemed especially interested in Raphtalia. Of course, that was why we'd brought her along.

"We're here to explain about these people you see before you," Mamoru said. "Please, don't treat us like you treated that king back there."

"Just what do you think a pacifier does? I am highly intrigued by those wearing clothing from my home nation, but I'm not going to attack without due cause," she replied. Recent evidence seemed to suggest otherwise, but I held my tongue. Powerful people tended to take direct action—and her saying "without due cause" was telling me she very well would attack if we gave her any reason. "You, then. Why are you wearing clothing native to my homeland? Why do you look so much like me?" she asked Raphtalia. "Could it be a certain alchemist has tried to make a copy of me . . . but I don't see her here today." A certain alchemist? She was talking about Holn. She had been getting into all sorts of things recently, but I hadn't talked to her much myself. She hadn't been with Mamoru today either. Off with Rat again somewhere, probably.

"Well, about that . . ." Raphtalia started.

"Hold a moment. I sense that you have received the blessing of the Heavenly Emperor. That means you aren't some pale copy. This other one has also experienced the ritual," said the dragon that was wound around the Heavenly Emperor. The dragon was getting a read on Raphtalia and Ruft. And while that was happening, the Heavenly Emperor turned her gaze on me and my shield.

"The Shield Spirit implement . . . I sense other holy weapons too—and resistance to the sakura stone of destiny," she pondered. Having seen all of that so quickly, she might be better at this than Raphtalia and those in my party. "You're going to explain all of this, correct?" she asked.

"Mamoru literally just said that's what we're here to do," I reminded her. "How long are you planning to keep this high-and-mighty act up for, oh lady Heavenly Emperor? You're a pacifier in name, perhaps, but you just look like a girl spoiling for a fight to me. Don't forget what Mamoru is here for." Maybe she was trying to cow us into a submissive position for the upcoming talks. She looked at me with a slightly pissed-off expression.

"Huh. You got one over on us there, I admit," the dragon acquiesced. "He's right. Simply having authority is nothing to boast about," the dragon murmured, cautioning the Heavenly Emperor. She still looked a little upset but managed to take a deep breath and calm herself down a little.

"Tell me why you are here, then. What have you come so politely to report to me?" the Heavenly Emperor asked.

"Okay, here we go . . . This is going to sound a little crazy, but we're actually here from the distant future of this world—from the time of the next series of waves. I'm the Shield Hero from the future and these are my allies," I explained. The Heavenly Emperor opened her eyes wide upon hearing this and then started to digest it at once.

"I see . . . That's an interesting one. The Shield Hero from the future . . ." she pondered.

"Excuse me a moment," the dragon said, moving toward me and gently stroking the gemstone on my shield, then checking Raphtalia and the others before swirling around in the air in front of me. This was definitely a new one for me. I'd seen other dragons, but not one so Chinese-styled before. For a moment I was reminded of when we were caught up in the whirlpool in Q'ten Lo.

"I like the aura you are giving off, I must admit. If you really are the future Shield Hero, then that's a pleasant development for us," the dragon said.

"Why is it that monsters—and even dragons—seem to take such a liking to you, Mr. Naofumi?" Raphtalia interjected from the sidelines.

"If you mean they like to walk all over me, sure. I'm not giving off some kind of strange pheromones, am I?" I said, shaking my head at whatever curse my body was suffering from. Gaelion was bad enough, but the Demon Dragon was the worst. The way she acted gave me all sorts of uncomfortable ideas. I had to hope this new dragon wasn't going to earn the name Demon Dragon II. Just to test the waters, I tickled it under the chin in a spot where the scales looked like they grew backward. I didn't care if I upset the beast. I just wanted to try something.

"Oh, wow . . . what's happening here?" the dragon enthused. "Ooh? That feels good? What is this?!" I immediately regretted my action and stopped. But it was too late—I saw a new fire appear in the dragon's eyes already. "What new territory is this? Can you stroke me some more there? I had no idea such a thing could feel so good!"

"Could this be the proof of R'yne's theory that you can't cause pain?" Mamoru started, but I gave him an intense glare to silence him. There was no need to bring sex into this again! Meanwhile, Raphtalia and the Heavenly Emperor were looking at me with the exact same look in their eyes—mild hopelessness, bordering on disgust.

"This one is fun! I like him!" the dragon stated.

"I'm not having fun!" I replied.

"You're so popular, Naofumi!" Ruft said.

"You can keep this kind of popularity," I shot back.

"I'm still trying to see if your story checks out," the

Heavenly Emperor said with a sigh. "Everything seems like it's in line, and the target awareness of the spirits in your weapons has not been disassociated—meaning you don't seem to be using them for personal purposes." The Heavenly Emperor had been on her guard from the moment we showed up, but she finally dropped her defenses. "To top it all off, it seems you have already stolen my dragon away from me."

"No one is stealing anything," the dragon replied. "They have just caught my interest. I had no idea that being stroked here would make me feel this way."

"It sounds like something has been stolen to me," she replied archly. "Now, about your claim of having come from the future, perhaps you can explain that?"

"Sure thing, if you've got the time." I proceeded to tell the Heavenly Emperor about how the attack from S'yne's sister's forces had sent our entire village back in time, then how we had met up with Mamoru and were now working alongside him.

"I see. I think I understand. That would also explain why I am sensing two Shield Spirits. You have other spirits too, don't you?" she asked me.

"You have keen senses. That's right. The Mirror vassal weapon from a completely different world to this one is also lending me its power," I told her. The effects of that seemed to be unlocking things with a mixture of shield and mirror elements—things like a Mirror Shield.

"If multiple spirits are willing to lend you their power, that means you are both trusted and powerful. Not the kind of individual even a pacifier may engage without due consideration," the Heavenly Emperor said.

"The Book Spirit and Mirror Spirit practically fought over him," Raphtalia added, a little cheekily.

"I see," the Heavenly Emperor said. "You are quite blessed, if that is the case." I didn't deny it, but that had been more about returning a favor for having helped them out. "The heroes in the future seem to get all the favors," she continued, giving Mamoru a pointed look. I wondered for a moment why she seemed too hard on him—and then remembered the conflict with the Bow Hero.

"I wouldn't exactly put it like that," I replied. Those who had summoned me certainly hadn't done me a favor.

"My thanks for finding me to report all of this," the Heavenly Emperor said. "Otherwise, it could have caused quite the misunderstanding later. I didn't expect to find the future Heavenly Emperors of Q'ten Lo here, after all."

"That's why we've come to you," I said, seeing my moment. "Do you have any idea how we could resolve our time-based problem? We're really just looking to get back to our own time."

"I regret to tell you that my knowledge as a pacifier is somewhat incomplete. I have no idea how to resolve a situation such as the one you describe," the Heavenly Emperor admitted, her brow furrowing a little as she replied.

"Ah, one thing," Raphtalia said, stepping in. "It might be wise to introduce yourself to Mr. Naofumi as quickly as possible. Otherwise, he will give you a strange nickname, and those never seem to go away," she cautioned.

"I see no reason to share my name. Just call me 'Heavenly Emperor from the past.' I'm fine with that," she replied.

"I think that might be too on the nose—and long too," Raphtalia said.

"Well, if you must call me something shorter, you can call me Natalia," the woman said.

"Is that your real name? Or an alias?" I replied. "Which is it?" She hadn't thought for too long before tossing that name out. It sounded pretty made-up to me. Her chosen name was a lot like Raphtalia's name too—I was worried about getting them mixed up. The name itself felt like a combination of my name and Raphtalia's. Raphtalia herself was making a pretty strange face.

"We have more important things to discuss," Natalia said. "I don't know of any technique for traveling through time, but we may find some hints if we look into the traditions of the past."

"Traditions, huh," I said.

"Every region has its own legends. Searching around might turn up some weapons or other useful things too. So it's not a bad idea," Mamoru said calmly. The issue was whether or not we had the time for it. We had access to copying weapons, and yet we hadn't exactly been looking around for famous weapons of the past to copy and obtain. If we found a sword stuck in a plinth somewhere (the old classic), we only needed Ren to grip the handle and copy it, which would boost our attack power considerably.

Then I realized why I'd never given this much thought. There wasn't going to be legendary shields stuck into plinths. I glanced over at Raphtalia.

"The powerful gear used by the heroes of the past, and their allies, can reasonably be expected to still be around somewhere," she added. Maybe it was something like that high-energy intensive weapon copied from the four holy weapons that the high priest of the Church of the Three Heroes had used. We also had the ones from the monsters that the past Heavenly Emperor had sealed away in Q'ten Lo; after that, almost all of our gear was stuff made for us by the old guy or his master. Maybe all the better gear had been lost over time. It seemed like there was not much of a tradition of passing things down to future generations in this world.

Considered in that light, though, maybe this was also the work of the one who assumed the name of god—our enemy, and the one behind the resurrected. A little treasure hunting back here in the past might turn up the goods.

"After all of this, I still have one question . . ." Natalia said.

"Raph!" Raph-chan exclaimed as Natalia picked her up.

"Just what is this creature?" Natalia asked.

"Raph-chan is a familiar who was created from Raphtalia's hair. She's one of my favorites," I said.

"What a bizarre creature. I can't believe the spirits allowed for its existence," Natalia stated.

"I agree," Raphtalia replied. "There are so many of them back in the village."

"I will need to observe all of this some more. It would be best to find a way to get you all back to your time as quickly as possible—or maybe just execute you here," Natalia pondered.

"Hold on. You can't do that to a hero over personal issues," the dragon chided Natalia. She clicked her tongue in mild annoyance, and I narrowed my eyes at the relationship between them. It seemed like the dragon was in charge.

"You haven't finished your introductions yet," I said. "Who is this? A Dragon Emperor?" A dragon who could speak the human tongue was, in my experience, a Dragon Emperor, but I wasn't sure on the logistics.

"That is probably how one would classify me. I am the pacifier's guardian dragon. As for my name . . . in Q'ten Lo they call me the Water Dragon," he replied. That gave me pause. This was the object of Sadeena and Shildina's worship just showing up out of the blue. In the future, it had stayed hidden the whole time.

"Will that mantle eventually be passed on to a younger dragon? Anything like that?" I asked.

"Not so long as I live," the dragon replied.

"If you make it to the future, then, you're going to allow us to enter Q'ten Lo. You also stay under the sea and just maintain a barrier around the place," I told him.

"Interesting. It sounds like even Q'ten Lo will suffer tribulations. What might have caused me to summon heroes?" the dragon pondered. I was still wondering if Sadeena and Shildina would be bowing and scraping if they were here.

"What is the Water Dragon doing here anyway? What's going on over in Q'ten Lo?" I asked. I'd thought the dragon would be deep under the water, keeping the barrier going even during this time period. Maybe this was some kind of copy—a minion the main dragon had shared a core with.

"The tides do not make entry into that land easily, and we have a barrier up too. I see no reason at the moment for such heavy security. But I presume something in the future is preventing me from moving around," the Water Dragon said. We'd already come across numerous differences between the past and the future of this world, and there were the dealings of the resurrected to consider too. The dragon was likely defending against something related to them. "In any case, as I'm sure you are aware, I'm the dragon responsible for defending the Shield World. I am a kind of Emperor Dragon, but I'm not interested in fighting over fragments. I'm sure the Bow Guardian Dragon feels the same way," the Water Dragon said. It sounded like he thought we knew what the hell he was talking about.

"What are you talking about?" I asked. We didn't know anything about a "Bow Guardian Dragon." It sounded like another dragon guarding some secretive nation somewhere. I really didn't want to have to take another pain-in-the-ass field trip, if we could help it.

"I see. Their nation is harder to reach than even Q'ten Lo, that is true, so I can understand why you might have trouble finding it," the Water Dragon said.

"We shouldn't say anything more," Natalia chipped in. "They wouldn't want us sending unwanted guests their way."

"It sounds like there are multiple nations with pacifiers," I said. Based on what we'd seen in Kizuna's world, something in our world had likely wiped them out too. More information was normally better, but in this case, I wasn't sure we needed to know this stuff.

"Having heard your situation, I should probably explain a little," Natalia offered. "As I'm sure you are at least aware, pacifiers are the ones who punish the users of the spirit implements—what you called holy or vassal weapons—if they step off the true path. We can punish anyone who causes issues, so be careful not to cross me."

"No problem. We have those among our allies who have the same purpose as you," I replied.

"I'm sure you do. I was dispatched because voices from the spirits reached the altar in Q'ten Lo, informing us that a hero had potentially stepped from the path," Natalia continued. "With the global issues we are facing due to the waves, it isn't possible to casually kill the holder of a holy weapon at the moment, but that won't stop me if they are on some kind of rampage. Mamoru, you understand this, correct?" Dispatched after hearing the spirits at the altar . . . I recalled hearing something like that in the castle at Q'ten Lo, but I hadn't actually been there to see it for myself. I presumed the "altar" was the spot with the dragon hourglass—I couldn't recall much of anything else being there.

"Of course. But at the moment, should we be more fixated on doing something about the waves . . . and Piensa too?" he replied.

"I have no intention to get involved in your conflicts, but I do think it's the height of foolishness that you choose to fight them at the moment," Natalia replied. I completely agreed with her, but she was allowed to hold such an opinion because she was on the outside.

"Dafu! Dafu, dafu!" Dafu-chan said, almost as though she was chiding Natalia for something.

"This creature is saying you need to take these talks more seriously," the Water Dragon said. "Allowing heroes to deploy into human warfare must never be allowed."

"That's true . . . but we can't just charge in there and take out the leader either, can we? I'm reflecting on today already, believe me," Natalia replied. She sounded more reasonable than I might have expected. I'd almost thought she'd paint us as fools who could never understand her. "Still, I face another creature who seems eager to speak her mind. Just who are you?" At that, Dafu-chan fell silent again. "In any case, you're telling me that this world has already fused with another at some point in the future, right? I don't want to believe it, of course . . ."

"We don't know the details of exactly what happened or what's happening to us here. I'd like to believe we've come to a different world with a similar history, to be honest," I told her.

"I am going to need to observe your base of operations. You don't mind if I accompany you there, right?" Natalia asked.

"If you launch into an attack the moment you locate our base, we're going to put you down hard," I warned her.

"You have access to the sakura stone of destiny, so I understand how hard defeating you would be. So long as the spirits are cooperating with you of their own volition, it would be difficult for me to bring down punishment on you, so you may rest easy on that score." Natalia proceeded to let the Water Dragon wind up around her again and she finally dropped her guard completely. It sounded like she wanted to come with us. I wasn't quite sure what to make of her yet, but she seemed a bit more intense than Raphtalia and Ruft.

We met up with Ren and the others, still waiting on standby in the vicinity, and then we all headed back to the village.

Chapter Five: Genetic Modification

Suddenly dumping our new visitor smack-dab in the village could stir things up in all sorts of ways, so I asked Mamoru to portal us close by and then we headed in on foot from there.

"I have to admit," Natalia commented, looking at Ren with a frown, "having the Sword Hero hanging around so casually is strange for me. To me, he's a hero from a completely different world."

"Not sure what you want me to do about that . . ." Ren said, a little confused.

"No, nothing, of course. This is just something I'm having trouble accepting for myself. The spirits do not seem especially perturbed by it," Natalia commented. This was currently the world of the Shield and Bow. That meant the holder of the sword holy weapon was—strictly speaking—her enemy, and not someone she would want to hang out with. Travel between worlds should be impossible without the permission of the holy weapons, and normally if a pacifier discovered you, it would lead to immediate—and likely permanent—ejection. Even more than that, the holy weapon heroes were the foundation pillars of the world itself, so there was normally no need to send them off to other worlds. I had only reached Kizuna's world due to the unexpected accident of stealing the energy of the Spirit Tortoise and because I had the permission of the four holy spirits, including the Shield Spirit. That was an indicator of the faith I had earned, perhaps. Things had only really worked out because I asked for help from our four holy spirits, and the spirits of the Katana and Mirror, and the other vassal weapons. Natalia seemed to be clearly sensing that I wasn't using the holy weapons for my own personal ends.

I wondered what kind of ability that was. Was it derived from the sakura stone of destiny in some way? I looked over at Raphtalia. Perhaps this was a good opportunity for her to get some training in with her ancestor, like S'yne was doing.

"Say, Mr. Naofumi . . . I'm not quite sure what you are expecting from me, but please wait until Natalia has settled in before asking anything of her," Raphtalia suggested.

"I'm so happy to have met you, Natalia!" Ruft said, beaming. Natalia, however, was looking at Ruft with a look of confusion on her face.

"You seem to be the same race as me . . . and have an atmosphere about you that almost feels familiar . . . Just who are you?" she asked.

"Who do you think?" Ruft said with a laugh, pointing at himself as Natalia puzzled over his appearance. "I love looking like this!" He knew how cute he was, and he loved looking like that. The reason it didn't get on my nerves was probably because of how clear it was he loved it.

"I can't say I like it very much," Natalia admitted. "It is like that horrible alchemist has performed some foul human experiment on some poor creature with the capacity for speech." She had to be talking about Holn again. Natalia really didn't seem to like her.

"Oh, really? He gained that ability by performing a class-up with the aid of the Raph species, which originated from my own hair. If anyone is to blame here, it's Mr. Naofumi," Raphtalia said.

"I only let it happen because it's what he wanted," I replied.

"It's like you've taken the dragon blessing and applied it in your own unique manner. A very interesting technique," the Water Dragon mused, also looking at Ruft.

"You're the Water Dragon, aren't you? I've heard about you from Shildina in the future. Please continue to aid our world," Ruft said.

"Hmmm. You are well-spoken too. I think you have a bright future. Natalia, maybe we could arrange something like this for your offspring?" the Water Dragon suggested.

"Are you trying to make me mad?" Natalia replied, veins popping out on her forehead. But her anger rolled off the Water Dragon's back like water off a water dragon.

"What's the relationship between you two, anyway? I know you are Heavenly Emperor and Water Dragon, but is this like you're the ruler of Q'ten Lo and its guardian dragon off on an

adventure together? Where does the miko priestess fit into it?"
I asked. It was like Sadeena and Shildina weren't even required.
Maybe it was for the best that they hadn't been pulled back here
with us.

"The priestess who supports me? She is in charge in Q'ten
Lo at the moment. To explain this in simple terms: we are conducting our mission while I train the young Heavenly Emperor
in all sorts of important things. Of course, we do understand
the gravity of the current times too," the Water Dragon explained. So he was along to keep the young Heavenly Emperor
from going off the leash.

"So you are shoring up your defenses at home while keeping tabs on the heroes in the nations outside?" I asked.

"That's largely correct. The previous Heavenly Emperor is
still resident in Q'ten Lo too. It would not be a fatal blow to our
nation if anything were to happen to the one you see here," the
Water Dragon added. Sending the Heavenly Emperor out into
the world while also educating her—it seemed like a lot to do at
once, but it also sounded like Q'ten Lo was handling business
pretty well back here in the past. "There are all sorts of nasty
things causing trouble in the world. They are too much for the
heroes to handle alone, so we've been defeating and sealing
them away too."

"Okay. That makes sense," I replied. There were ruins with
monsters sealed inside all over Siltvelt—and the rest of this

world, to be honest. Documents on them suggested that people from Q'ten Lo had come and sealed the contents away. "Why are you sealing them though?" This seemed like a good chance to ask. "Wouldn't it be better to finish them off completely?"

"I see that even that information has not reached the future," the Water Dragon said. "They have an anti-wave effect that can reduce the effects of the waves when things are most dire. There's a reason for us sealing them like that," the Water Dragon revealed.

"Wow, okay. So that's why we found all those monsters sealed away in Q'ten Lo," I replied. Natalia tilted her head at that, clearly puzzled. "When we were there, we fought all sorts of different sealed monsters. They had names like . . . the Sealed Orochi, stuff like that. Loads of them," I told her. I knew it would cause an unusual status effect, but I got Ren to bring out the cursed Ama-no-Murakumo Sword. He put it away again immediately, but he looked lightheaded from just that exposure.

"I sense a terrible curse from that weapon," the Water Dragon stated. "But there is some light mixed in with that too."

"That reminds me, what's happening with that countdown on that weapon?" I asked.

"It's still gradually coming down, but I've no idea what it means," Ren replied. "We'll just have to give it more time." It had been quite a while already since he registered the weapon! I just had to hope it would eventually change into a powerful weapon for him—or, at least, that it wasn't some countdown to death.

"There should never be the need to create so many separate seals in Q'ten Lo," Natalia said. "I presume you have no idea what magic was used, right?"

"The awareness of things in this time and our time seems to be pretty different," I said. There was too much we didn't know. I hoped we could uncover the truth back here in the past. Just getting home didn't sound like it would be enough anymore. I also wanted to find information that would help us with our fight back in the future. We weren't ones to just roll over and give up, no matter what happened.

We continued to discuss the current situation and eventually reached the village. Imiya spotted me and came right over.

"Shield Hero," she said.

"What's up? Anything happen while we were gone?" I asked.

"Nothing major . . . I mean, this might be a very small thing, but it's time to depart on our trading and Keel hasn't shown up yet, so I was looking around for her," Imiya explained.

"Keel?" I asked.

"She's normally the first one ready to go," Fohl said, also sounding concerned.

"That dog? She's probably off playing somewhere and just forgot the time," Mamoru suggested.

"I hope that's all it is," I replied. Then I noticed Natalia looking intently at Fohl.

"I've been wondering about you too," she finally asked. "You have a vassal weapon from another world, don't you? Are those gauntlets? Gloves?"

"My name is Fohl. These are gauntlets . . . and I'm the Gauntlet Seven Star Hero," he replied.

"Hmmm. I've seen your race before, I'm sure . . . Are you a demi-human from another world?" the Water Dragon asked, also looking Fohl over. I saw where this was going. If the hakuko weren't around prior to the merging of the worlds, maybe they were a race from the world of the sword and spear.

"I know you're Raphtalia's ancestor, but you do look so much like her. At a distance I'm not sure I could tell you apart," Fohl commented.

"The difference in the hairstyles helps out," I noted. They weren't identical, but even their clothing was similar. I guessed it was being related that made them look so similar. "Anyway, so you say Keel is missing?" I asked, getting back on track.

"That's right," Imiya replied.

"Where do you think Keel could have gone off to at such an important time?" Raphtalia asked.

"I don't want to say it, but maybe Piensa dognapped her. That would really suck right now. She's tough too, so they wouldn't have taken her easily," I said. She also definitely would have made a noise about it. If there was one thing we had in the village, it was noise-makers—the filolials especially.

"But with her trauma resurfacing, they might have caught her off guard," Raphtalia said. She wasn't wrong.

"Please, Shield Hero. Can you help search for her?" Imiya pleaded. Strictly speaking, Keel was my slave and had a slave seal. No one other than me could check on it. That was why Fohl and Imiya had come to me.

I called up the slave seal item under my status and pinged Keel's current location.

"Okay, she's not far away at all. That way," I pointed. A marker was displayed for me, indicating roughly how far away she was. The main issue with this system was that strong magical magnetic fields or an interference would stop it from working properly.

This was just another problem, in a long line of problems. I was starting to get sick of it. Pacifier Natalia came to check things out and this happened, right away. I wondered if a few harsh words with Keel might be warranted later.

We proceeded into the village. Natalia was unable to stop herself from looking around.

"What's that house there? Is it made from plants?" she asked. "You do have access to some strange magic in the future."

"That's a camping plant, created by modifying bioplants

using the abilities of the shield. I've been told you don't have bioplants in this time period," I commented.

"You do have all sorts of strange stuff here," Natalia stated. "To me, they either look like items washed in from another world or the work of that evil alchemist." From among the stuff that did come from other worlds, the text on it was often corrupted and unable to be used. But the bioplants had functioned normally even in Kizuna's world. We didn't have a handle on exactly how any of that stuff worked, but maybe it made sense if you considered everything that looked out of place to be coming from another world.

"They grow quickly once planted, but they also mutate easily. We've obtained the skills to modify them safely before they almost caused a major disaster. Once we became able to modify them, though, as you can see, they're pretty convenient plants. They even make great houses," I said.

"I'll admit that seems convenient, but still . . ." Natalia replied, unconvinced.

"I understand how you feel," Raphtalia said, stepping in. "This is the village I grew up in, but once Mr. Naofumi started to modify it, things have changed a lot from how they started."

"The heroes do have a tendency to change the environment around them in all sorts of ways . . . and that's difficult, because it isn't always a bad thing. It seems all ages suffer some of the same problems," Natalia mused. She seemed to be getting along well with Raphtalia. That was definitely preferable to the tension hanging over everything. I was just about to mention it when Natalia stopped still and narrowed her eyes.

"How do you have sakura lumina trees here?" she asked.

"Those were tricky, I'll admit," I said. "We had to work with the bioplants closely. It was a pain to get them to take root."

"You've even defiled the sakura lumina?" Natalia said, her voice starting to tremble.

"Ah, this looks bad! Naofumi!" Ren shouted. Both he and Mamoru had concern on their faces.

"Well, I find this most interesting, don't you?" the Water Dragon said, clearly trying to placate Natalia. "Taking those unfettered trees and putting them to use like this, we should probably be impressed before we get angry, no?"

"This is a different matter entirely!" Natalia seethed. "You expect me to just sit back and accept such heresy?"

"You're the only one calling it that. Didn't you notice it the moment we entered this village?" the Water Dragon asked. "Can't you feel the consent emanating from the trees themselves? They have agreed to this transplant."

"Huh?" Natalia said.

"Raph!" Raph-chan pointed at the biggest of the sakura lumina in the village and then indicated for Natalia to join her by it. Natalia moved over and placed her hand on its trunk.

The light of the sakura lumina flickered and swelled up for just a moment.

Natalia came back over, a frown on her face and a sigh on her lips. She seemed pretty versatile. I hoped Raphtalia could also learn a lot of things, just like her. That would be useful in the future.

"The sakura lumina are surely lending everyone here their strength for the sake of the world," the Water Dragon said. "Based on the reactions from them I sense here, the sakura lumina themselves have not been altered a significant amount," the dragon continued. I recalled, during our takedown of Q'ten Lo, Gaelion had received information about control of the sakura lumina from the Water Dragon via a fragment. That suggested that the Water Dragon was probably well-versed in the ways of the sakura lumina. "They also function as a barrier. And it feels like maybe that was exploited somehow," the Water Dragon continued. Holn had said something similar. That might well be a clue as to how we ended up here.

"I understand that the sakura lumina are lending you their strength, but I don't like it," Natalia admitted.

"Such stubbornness will not aid you in the times ahead," the Water Dragon chided. It sounded like we were out of the woods on this issue, anyway.

"I understand how you feel," Raphtalia sympathized.

"That only makes the pain keener," Natalia replied.

The two of them were becoming fast friends. If having me as some kind of bad boss they could rail against together helped things go smoothly, I was happy to play that role.

"Mr. Naofumi, if you want to get Natalia on our side more easily, it might be easiest to feed her," Raphtalia suggested. I could feel she was becoming more and more shrewd. That was useful in many ways, but it also made it harder to pull the wool over her eyes concerning certain things.

"Not planning on a platter of poison, are you?" Natalia quipped.

"No need to worry about that with Mr. Naofumi," Raphtalia assured her.

"Okay. That sounds like something to look forward to," the Water Dragon said.

"The future Shield Hero has a way of getting people on his side, doesn't he?" Natalia said.

"That's one way of putting it," Raphtalia said. The Q'ten Lo connection seemed to really be bringing the pair of them closer together. It felt like I needed to change the subject.

"Hey, shouldn't we be looking for Keel right now? I could just trigger her slave seal to get her over here . . ." I said as we continued to track her.

"Oh, Duke. You've got quite a crowd with you today," Rat said as we arrived in front of her lab. She was the representative scientist of our village, and it looked like she was just coming back from giving the monsters a checkup. Wyndia was with her too.

"I heard you were going with the Sword Hero to meet with the Heavenly Emperor from this time period," Wyndia said, looking over at Natalia and the Water Dragon—more the Water Dragon.

"You're one who has received the love of dragons," the Water Dragon said. "I'm the Water Dragon, a guardian and an Emperor Dragon."

"A guardian dragon? Nice to meet you," Wyndia replied. She was being surprisingly polite. So this was her response to meeting such a gentlemanly dragon. Ren had a complex look on his face.

"We've made a connection with them. They've come to visit our village, but now we've lost Keel, so we're looking around for her," I explained.

"Understood, but what brings you to our lab?" Rat asked.

"It seems Keel is up ahead, in there," I told her.

"She is? What's she doing in there?" Rat pondered.

"Keel?" Wyndia pondered. "That reminds me . . . just before you left, Shield Hero . . . I saw her talking with the one who might be Rat's ancestor." That was Holn, then. Holn and Keel having a conversation—I couldn't see what that could be about. Natalia was looking silently, intently at Mamoru and then gave us all a bit of a suspicious look.

"Mamoru?" Cian asked, sounding nervous.

"Shield Hero. From that reaction, it seems you have some idea what is going on?" Natalia said.

"Dafu!" Dafu-chan seemed to think so too. I wasn't surprised to see the two of them working together already.

"It's Holn we're talking about! I can't keep her under control!" Mamoru replied.

"I'm sure you can't. She calls herself an evil alchemist, so you're unlikely to be able to control her," Natalia agreed.

"That's all it took to convince you?" I said, unable to keep from commenting. Holn seemed to be very well known. I'd thought she was capable, but maybe she was just dangerous. Raphtalia grabbed my arm and shook me.

"What's the meaning of all this?! Keel is in danger! Mr. Naofumi! We have to find her!" Raphtalia said.

"I'm surprised you haven't taken action, Natalia," I said.

"I would love to," Natalia admitted, "but the Whip vassal weapon has taken a real shining to her. She's taking a firm stance against the waves too, so for now I'm just watching the situation. There are some things she is good at." The Whip Spirit was one I was never going to understand! It had let Takt own it in the past—our past, the future—and seemed to have a pretty crazy personality. Takt had likely been binding it against its will though. Maybe it worked on the same principle as the Staff seven star weapon that Trash liked so much.

"I have to ask . . . You can't even punish someone who's as completely off the rails as her? Then what can you do?" I asked, shaking my head and looking at her almost with pity in my eyes. She looked aside, sweat gathering on her brow.

"I've got all sorts of my own issues to deal with, okay?" Natalia replied. "Stop looking at me like that or I'll hammer some of the terror of the Heavenly Emperor into you!"

"What a pitiful sight this is," the Water Dragon said, shaking his head. Her position of authority was definitely slipping in our eyes, but she was also starting to feel even more like Raphtalia, and so I was starting to like her more too.

"Dafu!" said Dafu-chan, pointing over at the lab. It looked like she wanted us to stop bantering around and go inside.

"Yes, you're right," I said. "This could be the excuse you need to punish her at last, Natalia. Just don't kill her, okay?"

". . . Okay," Natalia finally said. We still needed Holn alive, which put us in a frustrating position for dealing with her. We entered the lab to continue the search for Keel.

We advanced through the structure, smoothly arriving in front of Rat's main lab. The signal from Keel was coming from the room ahead, from the look of it. The marker was a little lower down than I was expecting.

"She's in the next room . . . I think," I told the others.

"Is something going on?" Raphtalia asked.

"I'm not sure. It's definitely strange," I replied. Raphtalia gave a sigh. Rat kept on checking the pipes running through the place. That looked suspicious too. "Is there some kind of security device up ahead?" I asked her.

"You helped build the place, Duke. There's nothing of the sort . . . that I know of." Yet Rat definitely looked even more anxious than usual.

"There's no sign of her favorite monster," Wyndia explained. "You can normally tell what it is doing through the pipes when we return." I recalled what Wyndia was talking about. It was about that strange monster Rat kept here. I wasn't even sure what kind of monster it was, but I knew they were talking about that thing in the big test tube. And it sounded like that thing moved around through all these pipes! I'd heard Rat call it "Mikey," if I remembered correctly.

"Mikey is my friend! He can't do a thing right, but he works so hard anyway!" Rat said.

"Okay, okay," I replied. "What the hell is he anyway?" It was a monster prized by an alchemist who loved monsters and who had been chased out of Faubrey. I knew that much. That suggested something pretty important—or insane. He had been in the tubes in order to recover from a serious injury, if I recalled correctly. It might be a completely new, original monster created by Rat. Maybe once it got out it would prove to be as strong as the Spirit Tortoise and proceed to go on a rampage.

"When I was chased out of Faubrey, the forces siding with Takt accused me of heresy, gathered all my monsters together, and killed them. He's the only one I was able to save, and even then, he was in a bad state," Rat revealed. She had been a pretty skilled alchemist even when she was in Faubrey, apparently, but she'd lost everything thanks to Takt. And Mikey was her one remnant from that time—a creature that looked like a bunch of muscle fibers floating inside a flask. At a glance he looked like just a ball of fur. The fluid he was suspended in looked expensive too. I wondered if she was making it using the bio-plant. "It's one of my goals to make him into the most powerful monster ever," Rat said. She'd told me something like that when she first came to the village. She told me about proving that monsters could help fight the waves too. That was the dream she had placed on Mikey's shoulders.

"If you level him up and perform a class change, wouldn't he just get stronger normally?" I asked. Maybe that was arrogant of me. This world functioned a lot like a video game, which meant I focused on raising levels rather than making physical improvements. Raphtalia and the others trained a lot, but that was about creating a proper foundation. There was some suggestion that training like that at a low level made further growth smoother. In any case, now we had determined the power-up method for the Whip. Rat could have just come to us.

"Wouldn't that be lovely?" Rat said smarmily. "After all

the measures I've taken to extend his life, there are all sorts of complex issues to deal with! His body can't even accept experience at the moment." Wow. That sounded pretty serious. Rather than enhance him, it sounded like she needed to provide medical treatment. "I had been gathering things from Gaelion and other sources, and once the treatment was ready, I was going to let him back out into the world."

"I'm thinking the world might end before you get that far," I told her. To say she had been branded a heretic, her research style was slow and steady. She was beyond just being methodical. Rat worked so slowly even Holn was on her back about it. I guessed this also came from the trauma of her experiences with Takt. From everything I had seen of her so far, she sought to preserve life and hadn't descended to the level of human experimentation.

"I'm actually making good progress!" she fired back.

"I'm sure you are," I soothed her, not in the least bit patronizingly.

"I have to say . . . you don't seem especially concerned. This sounds like some pretty risky research," Raphtalia said.

"Raphtalia," I replied, "our enemies, including those coming from the waves, will use whatever dirty tricks they can to try and defeat us. If we decide even this level of activity is beyond the pale, we might end up losing a battle that could have been won."

"I don't like to hear that," Natalia said, sounding a little distraught herself. "That's probably one of the reasons the Whip Spirit likes that researcher so much, though I hate to admit it."

"You'll wear yourself out if you keep so much tension in your shoulders," Ruft said cheerfully. "We need to relax and just do whatever we can." He was really growing up fast.

"You were Mr. Naofumi's test subject yourself, Ruft, so we don't need to hear from you," Raphtalia replied.

"Oh my!" Ruft exclaimed, channeling the killer whale sisters.

"Mamoru?" Cian said, noticing Mamoru silently watching our exchange unfold. There was no need to expand this conversation any further. We needed to get to Holn and Keel.

"Well, whatever. That's enough chatter. Let's just go inside! Keel might just be having a nice chat with Rat's favorite monster," I said hopefully. That's what I really wanted to be happening here, and I pushed the door open, clinging to that idea.

What we found was . . . no one at all.

"There's no one here," Raphtalia said.

"I see that," Wyndia replied.

"No Mikey either," Rat commented. The large tank in which he was normally located was empty.

"What about Keel?" I muttered, checking her location. It looked like she was diagonally downward from our current position. I didn't recall any way to get below this room. Now I was starting to get concerned.

"Mr. Naofumi, where's Keel?" Raphtalia asked. I didn't say anything, just indicated a downward direction with my eyes.

"Imiya, you guys have some residential space beneath the village, don't you?" I confirmed with her.

"Yes, that's right. But we haven't excavated anything around here. Causing a sinkhole under some of Rat's research might be bad for the entire village," she explained. The lumo slaves whom Imiya so ably represented were a pretty thoughtful bunch. I'd been aware of their digging, which was careful not to cause any collapses. When I'd checked their living space, it had been very well shored up with lots of pillars for support and had felt like a well-planned underground residence.

"Having the killer whale sisters around would make this spatial awareness stuff so much easier," I commented. They could use ultrasound to even tell what was behind walls, making them perfect for finding people quickly.

Rat headed over to the terminal placed in this room, a machine unique to this world that looked like a stone tablet. She started to operate it.

"Hmmm. Looking for anything out of place . . . huh? This is strange. I'm not sure what's going on here," she muttered. She operated some more, and I started to have a bad feeling too, so I opened up the camping plant controls. Then I said the password.

"Supervisor authorization. Critical item, lock release. Open." This was a backdoor that I'd added when we created the camping plant, allowing me to get inside even if the village kids tried something silly like locking themselves inside. It also had basic programming that meant it could not betray my orders, even if another hero tried to use nefarious means to control it. If these measures were destroyed, the camping plant would become completely unresponsive and then self-destruct. I'd given the camping plant to everyone, so I didn't want anyone to be able to use it for just their own selfish needs.

Of course, I could also initialize everything.

With a heavy grating sound, stairs leading downward appeared in the middle of the lab.

"Ah! What's this?" Rat seemed to have discovered something too. "Duke, look! There's a pipe here that I don't remember installing!" Rat was pointing at the tank. Beyond it there was a hole, just like with the stairs.

"This is smelling fishier and fishier," I said.

"Not to mention, after creating this underground facility, she concealed it perfectly by making the camping plant excrete more coagulant. Even you wouldn't have spotted this, Duke," Rat said. I looked over at the one responsible for the individual in question—Mamoru—and he looked away quickly, sweat on his brow.

"It seems pretty obvious that Holn is behind all this," I stated.

"I would say so," Natalia agreed, joining me in looking at Mamoru. "This is just the kind of setup that an evil alchemist loves." There was no defending her now, surely.

"It definitely looks that way, but I don't know a thing about this!" Mamoru replied. I saw Cian look down at the ground when he said that, as though maybe she had some idea about all this . . . but it was Holn, surely. That much seemed plain.

"I guess not. You wouldn't have walked in here with us so casually. That said, if she's trying to pull some kind of fast one over on us, we need to find out what she's planning," I said.

"She's an intelligent person. Why would she do something like this?" Raphtalia lamented. Ren and Fohl looked like they were asking the same question.

"Trying to pull something like this on you, Naofumi . . ." Ren said.

"She knows no fear," Fohl finished. I wondered about that as a response though. Just once I would like to know exactly what they all really thought of me.

"What this definitely means," Fohl said, "is that we need to continue the search for Keel as quickly as possible. When we were discussing the trauma treatment for Keel and the others, I heard Holn muttering something about not being asked to help out!" he suddenly recalled. It was a little late for that! We could have used that information at the point when we arrived here.

Something nasty was swelling inside me. It was a

combination of Holn, Keel, and Rat's favorite monster. I really didn't like what that was suggesting. She had some plan to cure Keel's trauma, and I didn't think I was going to like it!

"Let's get down there!" Rat headed first toward the stairs.

"Right with you!" I said.

"I'm not in a forgiving mood right now! Ancestor or not, if she's done anything to Mikey, I'm going to dice her up and turn her into an experiment herself!" Rat seethed, sounding like a pretty dangerous switch had been flipped in her head. She normally wouldn't say stuff quite as dangerous as that.

"Come on! Let's move!" I said.

"Ah, Shield Hero." Wyndia stopped me. "After we've gone in, can you be sure that that woman's ancestor isn't going to escape from here?" she asked.

"Good point," I said. Wyndia knew Rat well, which maybe gave her this insight. "Wyndia, Imiya, you stay here and keep watch. Ren, Fohl, go and order the entire village to watch the lab from the outside. I don't want a single ant to escape!" I wasn't sure they would get that expression, but they nodded anyway.

Then the earth started to shake.

"What's going on?!" We hurried back outside the lab, to see towers made from bioplants growing up around the village. "Towers?!" I exclaimed. The very top of each tower was glittering and shining. I was starting to have a really bad feeling about this. I narrowed my eyes to see the name of a monster: tower plant. Then a voice sounded from the lab.

"Oh dear. It seems you're on to my little game."

"Holn!" Mamoru shouted, his brow furrowed. "What are you planning?!" She ignored him—maybe she wasn't listening, or maybe this was all a preset recording—and carried on.

"If you want to get inside the research space I've created just for little old me, you'll need to put someone on standby at the top of each of the towers positioned outside it and then touch the devices placed there simultaneously. There's a total of seven towers, so good luck with that. I'll just hang out and see if you can meet my conditions, okay?" she announced, and then the voice vanished with a scratching sound. Mamoru's shoulders slumped and he put a hand to his forehead.

"Just the kind of twisted game she loves," he moaned. "You've been able to provide just the toys she needed for this." By "toys" I presumed he meant the bioplants. She really had gone crazy, from the look of it. She'd even set things up to completely negate my orders, and so there was nothing I could do to control it. It was like she had taken the idea of the bioplants and turned them into something else completely of her own making.

"Now she's really gone off the deep end, right? You'd better punish her for this!" I said to Natalia.

"I would like to, trust me, but when she's done things like this in the past, the subsequent wave has featured the same kind of tricks. I hate to admit it, but we only made it through thanks to her," Natalia said. This was the first I was hearing of stuff like that coming with a wave. I had always thought they were just about a bunch of monsters coming out to be defeated. I looked over at Ren, and he averted his gaze and nodded.

"I do remember seeing something for setting up events to coincide with waves. They only ran for a limited period. I also remember they required teamwork to complete, so they were a pain when playing solo," he recalled. Events like that were a real pain in the ass.

"I doubt she intends to take this far enough to kill anyone, but it's still a big problem," Mamoru said, shaking his head. "She's planning something we can't see yet, that's for sure."

"Okay. Can we just chop this stuff down?" I asked.

"I'll give it a try! Hundred Swords X!" Ren shouted, unleashing a skill that sent countless swords—okay, maybe it was a hundred of them—flying toward one of the towers. They smashed through the barrier protecting the tower and chopped it to the ground in short order . . . but immediately afterward, another tower grew in its place and started to shine.

"It looks like we'll have to disarm them, like she said," Mamoru commented. "They seem to just grow back, so destroying them is pointless." I cursed—more shit we didn't need!

"Dafu!" said Dafu-chan. She seemed eager to help tackle this.

"Naofumi, we'll deal with these towers. Can you take a party and try to find a way to get beneath the lab as quickly as possible?" Ren asked, sounding a little unhinged. He wanted to coordinate the pain-in-the-rear task of climbing seven towers, while we tried to circumvent the entire thing anyway. That sounded fine by me, if we could get away with it.

"Okay. It has to be worth a try. You handle things here," I told him.

"Mamoru, I want to go too," Cian said, taking Mamoru's hand.

"Cian has proven herself to be unexpectedly good in a scrap already," I said. "She might help us catch Holn by surprise."

"Sure, okay," Mamoru eventually said. "Cian, are you willing to help out?"

"Yeah!" she replied.

"Okay! Let's go!" I said. With that, we started down the lab's underground passage.

Chapter Six: Mikey

We were heading into the new underground facility discovered below Rat's lab. I did a quick head count, just to make sure I knew what was going on. I had Raphtalia, Ruft, Rat, Mamoru, Cian, Natalia, the Water Dragon, and the two Raph-chans with me. Everyone else was either climbing the towers outside or running recon for any possible escape routes Holn might have set up. There was no way she was going to try to pull this on us and then get away. We had the lumo here in the village, experts at underground excavation. Even if she had made an escape tunnel, it would be easy for us to fill it in. S'yne and R'yne weren't here yet, but they had to be watching and so would surely arrive soon.

We hurried through the underground facility and came quickly to a strange invisible barrier blocking the bleak-looking passage.

"Some kind of defense mechanism?" I wondered, tapping on the barrier.

"It looks like your own Shooting Star Shield, Mr. Nao-fumi," Raphtalia commented. I agreed. I signaled Raphtalia with my eyes to try and break it—she was the one with the highest attack power here. Just trying to smash our way through seemed like the best idea. Raphtalia gave a small sigh and raised her Katana to attack.

"Instant Blade! Mist!" she shouted. Sparks radiated out across the mysterious barrier as her blade slashed across it. It looked good for a moment, and I thought maybe it was going to work, but then the wall immediately recovered and returned to its original state.

"No matter how hard we attack, it's pointless if it's just going to recover," I said. "It was to be expected, but this is still a pain." It didn't look like we could just slip through as we were cutting into it. I placed a hand on the wall and tried to make a float shield appear inside it, but it was immediately bounced away.

"It seems to have a repulsion effect too," Raphtalia said. So these defenses were tight. I wondered how Holn had created something quite so hard. Our invasion had run right into a wall.

There were sounds coming from above. I imagined it was Ren, Fohl, and the others attempting to clear the bioplant towers.

"I was hoping it wouldn't go this way . . . I don't think we can muscle through," I said.

"Doesn't the Shield Hero have some idea about how to get through a barrier like this?" Ren muttered irritably. The barrier looked like an application of Shooting Star Shield, that was true. I just had to think of it as a Shooting Star Shield that was being controlled remotely. Maybe "Shooting Star Wall" was the correct term. So what was the weak point of Shooting Star Shield?

In my case, even if a life-force-infused attack was used to destroy it, only the Shooting Star Shield would be destroyed; I wouldn't take any damage.

"Anyone it recognizes as an ally should be able to slip right through," Mamoru said in the same moment I explained the same thing to myself.

"If you are in the same party, you should be able to just pass through. If we can get it to recognize us like that, those towers won't be needed," I said.

"Okay, and how do we do that?" Raphtalia asked.

"Good question. Knowing what we need to do and pulling it off are two different things," I said. I turned to look at the Water Dragon. "You created a mystery barrier in Q'ten Lo. Don't you know about this stuff? Also, think about where we are. There are sakura lumina growing here to protect the village," I reminded him.

"Yes, that could work," said Rat, seeming to also get an idea. "We could crash a barrier into a barrier and carve out an access passage for us." She climbed the stairs and started to operate machinery again. The camping plant proceeded to extend tendrils toward the barrier, and the tips of them started to glow.

"A barrier against a barrier," I said. Mamoru and I synced

up and deployed our own Shooting Star Shields, then pushed toward the impediment. But we simply bumped into it again and couldn't go any further. This was going to be even harder than I'd expected.

"Raph!" said Raph-chan.

"This is all such a pain . . . but we do need to resolve this quickly," the Water Dragon said, moving forward and touching the barrier. "We need to apply the structure of the Q'ten Lo barrier with the pulse of the sakura lumina . . . Hey, are you going to help?" the dragon said to Natalia.

"Very well," she eventually replied. Then she took a deep breath and drew out some kind of protective charm from inside her clothing.

"Five Practices Destiny Field Expansion," she said. I'd seen this before too, when Raphtalia had used it to create a field and activate the power of the sakura stone of destiny.

"I can help with that too," Ruft said, stepping into the field and starting to incant as well. I quickly looked at Raphtalia. If she didn't take part now, she'd have been branded a muscle brain forever!

"Mr. Naofumi, no need to look at me like that. I know what I must do," she replied, adding her voice to those of the others.

"Although this isn't normally allowed, having three of us really increases the output," Natalia said.

"We have the sakura lumina too. That should make it

easier," the Water Dragon said. "The issue is the timing. If those outside can capture at least one of those towers, that would make this easier." I wasn't sure if that was a possibility, this quickly, but we'd see how it went. "The Shield Heroes aren't very compatible with this though. Back up."

"Okay, okay," I said. The field Raphtalia and the others created extended forward and hit the barrier, causing more sparks to fly. Rat directed the vines to head in again, causing even more sparks, and then something magical started to flow into the barrier. This was a pretty impressive sight, but I didn't like the fact that Mamoru and I were just sitting on the sidelines.

With the three barriers clashing together, I could tell it was hard on Rat too. Everyone continued to work together, and before long we had carved out a hole large enough for one person to pass through.

"Okay, looks good!" I said.

"I'm not so sure," the Water Dragon said. I could hear the strain in his voice.

"I'm managing to nullify the repulsion effect while fudging the party recognition. I can maintain it thanks to the dragon and the Heavenly Emperors, who are supplying the power for our barrier, but if they stop, then this all goes back to normal," Rat explained, coming back down the stairs. I was impressed at how well she had followed the situation from above ground.

"Which means . . . Raphtalia and the others can't move?" I said.

"Not quite," Natalia replied. "The Water Dragon and I should be able to maintain what you need. In fact, it's becoming difficult to manage so much power flowing from other people. Please, carry on inside and take care of that alchemist."

"That should work," the Water Dragon said. "But both of you Shield Heroes need to keep a barrier up at all times. Do not underestimate the strength of the repulsion inside here."

"And is it asking too much to bring a load of reinforcements through this hole?" I asked. Both the Water Dragon and Natalia made painful faces at the suggestion.

"Okay. We'll either capture Holn or at least bring this rampage to an end as quickly as possible. Just hold on here," Mamoru said to Natalia and then headed through the hole with Cian, throwing up another Shooting Star Shield as he went. It looked like we didn't have much of a choice. I started sending up Shooting Star Shield too and stood in place to hold it over the hole, making it easier for everyone else to go through.

"Raphtalia, Ruft, and the Raph-chans," I said.

"Okay . . . Natalia, can you handle this?" Raphtalia confirmed with her ancestor.

"Underestimate me at your peril," Natalia replied. Raphtalia still had a look of concern on her face as she passed through the hole.

"I'm breaking off too," Ruft said, ending his contribution and starting forward.

"We need to prioritize accessing the device that is creating this barrier over capturing that woman. Keep that in mind," Rat said as she followed Ruft. That was a good point. If we could take the barrier down, it would be easy to capture Holn after that. Being underground had to be making it hard for S'yne and R'yne to get here, but we also didn't have the time to wait for them to show up.

Raph-chan and Dafu-chan were the next ones through the hole, leaving only me on the wrong side of it. There was sweat on Natalia's brow now. The departure of Raphtalia and Ruft clearly increased the burden placed on her.

"Please, hurry up. I can't hold this much longer," Natalia said.

"We'll be quick," I told her. A quest with a time limit. If we failed . . . Holn would end up experimenting on Keel. With that thought burning in my mind, we left Natalia doing her thing and started onward.

The passage appeared to lead into a sequence of small rooms. Holn wouldn't have been able to create a sprawling facility beneath our village, what with the lumos and other monsters that lived underground being so active here. If she bumped into one of them, then the whole thing would have been exposed, and it hadn't even been that long since Holn first came to the village. Maybe the camping plant could have been used to achieve all of this, of course . . .

I stopped thinking and opened the door.

"Check it out," I said. We entered a room with a large water tank. There was a large Raph species creature floating inside the tank—about four meters long—and it looked to be in the middle of some kind of treatment. Both Ruft and I immediately gave loud and unfiltered gasps at seeing this behemoth of a Raph presented before us. It was even bigger than Raph-chan in big-and-fluffy mode. I was already imagining what it would be like to take a ride on that mountain of fluff. Raph-chan would do that if I asked, but Raphtalia was always watching.

"Mr. Naofumi, that isn't Keel, is it?" Raphtalia asked with some trepidation.

"If it was, she'd definitely be getting more attention from me," Ruft said. I could only nod at that, but the signal from Keel was coming from further inside.

"Do you think she's making that massive monstrosity in order to placate Mr. Naofumi?" Raphtalia mused to Rat.

"I'm not sure," Rat admitted. "She did seem very interested in the Raph species, and I can't deny the possibility that she'd try to make something to win favor with the Duke." I had to admit, Holn was winning me over—*ahem*, I mean she was proving herself an excellent judge of character. If she could make these kinds of wonderful additions to the Raph species, I might even be able to forgive her for this misconduct.

When I looked more closely, however, the massive Raph

didn't seem especially structurally stable. Its lower body looked all malleable, like clay. I wondered if it was just not finished yet. I might have to order her to continue this research.

"Holn . . . what the hell are you playing at . . ." Someone had a very different take on the situation to me—and that someone was Mamoru. Ruft and I just had a thing for the Raph species, that was all. But I couldn't deny that it looked like Holn had gone completely off the rails on a crazy train. If one of my party pulled something like this, I'd have something to say about it myself.

"Mr. Naofumi?" Raphtalia said, her hand on her sword.

"Raph!" said Raph-chan.

"Dafu!" added Dafu-chan. I knew what was coming.

"No destroying this beauty, thank you," I cautioned Raphtalia carefully. "You'll flood the whole place, for one thing. We don't need to be wading through water down here."

"What makes you really say that?" Raphtalia asked, putting me on the spot.

"I want to see the finished thing. Very badly," I admitted.

"I'm destroying it now!" Raphtalia shouted.

"Wait, wait!" I replied.

"Her research has struck exactly at the Duke's weak spot. Impressive stuff," Rat breathed.

"Do you think she was chosen by the Whip seven star weapon because the Whip Spirit desired the creation of something like this?" Ruft mused. That only rocked me harder, right to my core. What fantastic research! I had to see this finished!

"Enough wasting time here. Come on! That massive Raph species isn't going anywhere," Raphtalia said. She was right, but I still had to tear myself away from the tank.

We opened the door to the next room. In this chamber, we found something that looked decidedly core-like, glittering and hovering in the center of the room. My first thought was that it was some kind of power source. It also reminded me of my battle with Kyo inside the Spirit Tortoise, which made me pretty uncomfortable.

"This might be the chamber from which that barrier is controlled," Rat suggested. She hurried over to what looked like a control terminal and started doing her thing again—which immediately triggered an alarm. Something that looked like a holographic projection of Holn appeared in the middle of the room.

"Interesting. You have reached this point faster than I expected. The future Shield Hero gets things done!" she cackled.

"This isn't our first time at this," I replied, "and we have Natalia and her dragon helping out. If you don't stop all of these games, you aren't going to like it once I actually get my hands on you."

"Oh my, so scary, I'm shaking in my little old boots. I'm not doing this out of malice. Your allies are suffering from severe trauma in their hearts, future Shield Hero. I'm only trying to resolve that issue for you. I expected gratitude, to be honest," she said.

"What are you doing to Keel? Stop it at once!" Raphtalia shouted.

"Your little puppy—" Holn started, but then the sound system crackled and Holn looked over to the side, rolling her eyes. "Your brave dog wanted this. I'm just trying to put her brain right. If everything goes well, this could be the solution for everyone suffering from the same malady." Seeing how she was calling her "dog" now instead of "puppy," it sounded like Keel was there and still in one piece, at least.

"Do you have Keel there? Let her go!" Raphtalia said, but Holn was not interested in Raphtalia. Instead she looked over at Rat. Rat ignored the attention, continuing to fiddle with the controls of the terminal.

"You shouldn't expect to break my little old security like that," Holn commented.

"Enough out of you!" Rat seethed. "If you've laid a finger on Mikey, you will pay dearly!"

"Still, I don't think I can afford to let you play with that any longer. It seems the situation calls for a little of the rough stuff with your little poochie!" I thought it was funny that she would call it a poochie. Then there was a bubbling and I heard a glugging sound from the room we had just come through. I turned around to see the fluid draining from the tank with the massive Raph specimen inside and the sides of the tank opening up. The massive Raph specimen stood up with a resounding thud . . . and then slowly opened its eyes and started walking.

It was already finished! I felt like giving a whoop of joy, even if it looked far too big to fit inside this room. I wondered if it had the Raph-chan ability to shrink down. I raised my shield in readiness, just like Mamoru, and watched the scene unfold.

The massive Raph specimen reached the doorway. I expected it to just smash its way inside, but its method of entry was very different. It extended an arm and placed it inside the room. Then the rest of its body turned into a kind of liquid-flesh state and changed shape to fit through the doorway. The specimen then reformed inside the room. I almost threw up. So it looked like a Raph species on the outside but was something completely different inside!

"You tricked us!" Ruft and I shouted in perfect unison. What kind of bullshit was this?! It looked slimy to the touch, not soft and fluffy, and was completely ruining the best parts of Raph-chan!

"Raph!" said Raph-chan as the massive fake Raph specimen swung its tail to take us out.

"I've got this!" Raphtalia shouted, swinging her Katana toward the massive fake Raph specimen. With a satisfying sound, the head of the massive Raph specimen was sent flying to the side . . . Still, I didn't like the image of her hacking into a Raph-chan.

"Raph!" said Raph-chan. The chopped-off part returned to a liquid state and then reconnected with the body. That ability seemed like a possibility from the way it had entered the room, but now I was sure. This was some kind of slime monster, which meant just chopping off its "head" wasn't going to be enough to stop it!

The massive fake Raph species pointed at Raphtalia.

"Fake!" it said. I took a moment to process that.

"Who are you calling fake?!" Raphtalia shouted.

"Ah, my apologies," Holn interjected. "As I know the pacifier, I am acquainted with who would be coming here soon, so I installed a function to identify the current pacifier and I forgot to remove it."

The fake Raph species pointed at Ruft.

"Raph!" it said, making a normal Raph species noise. It proceeded to do the same thing with Dafu-chan and Ruft.

"Why did it make that normal noise for Ruft with his Heavenly Emperor connections, but it called me a fake?!" Raphtalia raged.

"It might be fun to investigate that phenomenon," Holn said.

"Not fun for me!" Raphtalia retorted. The scene was almost becoming comical, but we still had to fight the thing.

"Mamoru!" I shouted.

"Okay! Shield Boomerang!" At my shout, he immediately unleashed his shield, throwing it into the body of the monster. It made a noise that sounded like something hitting a wet surface but failed to pass all the way through and then vanished before returning to Mamoru's hand. It wasn't the first time I'd seen it, but I was still conflicted about Mamoru having such natural, easy access to attack skills. Even I couldn't reach the level of Ren, Motoyasu, or Itsuki. I would have loved to have a bit more versatility—by which I meant any attack at all—when it came to fighting.

"How about this?" Rat said, dodging capably through the incoming attacks. She did know a lot about monsters. She threw some syringes at it. This was the attack that had knocked even Filo out in the past. Her syringes splashed into her target and unloaded their chemical contents. If that slowed the thing down enough, Raphtalia and the others could just pile on and finish it off. Mamoru and I could keep our shields out and make it easier to fight, at least.

The massive fake Raph species proceeded to rip the syringes out and continued toward us as though nothing had happened. So much for that idea then.

"I'm not finished with you yet!" Raphtalia shouted.

"Fake!" the creature replied. As Raphtalia was jumping toward it, it popped out three tendrils from its back that rapidly attacked her. They slipped through my Shooting Star Shield and thumped into Raphtalia's side. She grunted and flew backward.

"Raphtalia!" I shouted, moving to intercept her.

"I can't predict where attacks like that are coming from!" she said.

"It's like a super-powerful slime-type monster," I said. "It might look like a Raph species, but fighting it like one is only going to get us hurt."

"Naofumi . . ." Ruft said, concern in his voice as he touched my hand. I couldn't believe that massive fake Raph species had attacked Raphtalia by passing through my Shooting Star Shield.

"Pathetic. You won't defeat the body I have created like that!" Holn crowed.

"My drugs aren't working either," Rat said.

"Raph!" our assailant shouted, swinging one arm in a thundering smash attack.

"I've got this!" Mamoru said, taking the impact on his shield. But more tendrils proceeded to snake out and add additional whacks. This thing was hard enough to defend against already, and its attacks could also pass through my Shooting Star Shield! I needed a moment to work this out. Rat, standing behind Mamoru, was getting her fair share of whacks too, and they sounded painful.

"Do you understand where we are?" Holn asked. "Passing through any barrier that you might create is no problem for me here." It pushed Rat violently back, and then the massive fake

Raph specimen closed in to finish her off.

"Raph!" The massive fake Raph-chan locked eyes with Rat.

"Hold on. Mikey?" Rat asked.

"Raph?!" the creature replied. A moment later the massive fake Raph specimen grabbed its head and started moaning and wailing.

"What's the meaning of this?!" Rat shouted.

"You did well to work it out! That's right, this is what your precious monster wanted for himself," Holn explained.

"That doesn't give you the right!" Rat wailed back. I paused for a moment, taking in this new information. So this massive fake Raph species was actually Mikey, Rat's favorite monster.

"Rat, is that really your Mikey?" I asked her.

"Yes, I'm sure of it. I would know!" she replied. She sounded completely confident, but I really couldn't tell at all.

"Just like the way you and Ruft can pick out Raph-chan from among a horde of Raph species, Rat must instinctively know Mikey," Raphtalia said. That sounded reasonable to me, and I grinned. Rat had impressed me again.

"Impressive, Raphtalia!" Ruft said.

"Please, I wish you wouldn't accept such crazy theories so easily. It makes me sad," Raphtalia replied.

"It happened when I was here, conducting research in this village," Holn said, like she was giving some kind of lecture on the results of her research. "Little old me was taking a little old look around your lab, and I happened to knock on the tank he was inside. We talked for a while, and your favorite told me that he wanted to be able to fight and help everyone, but you couldn't understand that. I made sure to get his full consent for everything. He told me he was ready to face whatever experiments may come." As though complementing her presentation, images of Holn conducting the enhancements to Mikey were now displayed before us. "That's why I used all the modification methods I have at my disposal, including the powers contained in the Whip vassal weapon. Bio customization, alchemy, and even . . . genetic modification." She must have used some kind of crystal to record the images. It was a little much, if you asked me.

"Go ahead," said the Holn in the footage. "Imagine for me the strength that you want to obtain. I can make it come true." The fluffy ball still floating in the tank—Mikey—gave a nod and something started to appear on the tablet in front of Holn. "I see, I see. So this is the extent of the power that you crave. You want to withstand all pain and all curses!"

The footage continued, showing Holn making modifications to Mikey. It was a pretty strange process. She turned him into something very different from how he looked now—a round, red ball of crystal. Then, for camouflage, she dressed him in a costume that looked like the original fluffy ball. That was how she had been hiding him, making him look like nothing had changed.

In the next clip, a large Raph specimen was floating in the tank. The footage finished showing the large Raph specimen swimming in the tank.

"That's why little old me gave him power! What do you think? I do great work, don't I?" Holn said.

"No, you don't!" Rat replied flatly. "This was for me to do, not you! My goal was to enhance Mikey safely! I'll never forgive you for being as reckless as this!"

"Holn! Even if you had the consent of the monster, doing this to one of Naofumi's allies is just too much!" Mamoru said.

"Hah! Like you understand my pain, Mamoru. The pain in my brain at realizing something I simply have to do! You've never complained about the other things I do though, have you?" Holn retorted. I wasn't sure what that meant, but I wasn't sure about half the things she said. If it was some kind of thing between the two of them, I was going to need them to explain it later.

For now, though, we needed to focus on defeating the Mikey monster that was standing right in front of us. We'd consider destroying it if we had to . . . but accurate analysis was important first. The video had revealed that he had been turned into that red crystal first and then turned into this form by putting something over the top of that. That red crystal . . . like a stone or core . . . Just what was Holn involved with? When she was in Piensa, she had been involved with dragon research, if

I recalled correctly. She'd also made comments about enhancing balloons, if she had to, to take the throne of the mightiest monster away from dragons. Now we had Mikey, who looked like a slime based on the Raph species. I called on my own knowledge of RPGs to refer to what kind of a monster slimes were. Apart from all being gelatinous creatures, they tended to be single-celled organisms. Sometimes they had a core to be destroyed. This one had joined back together when cut apart and was wearing camouflage to look like its original form. That meant that fluffy stuff wasn't actually its fur.

"Raph!" said Raph-chan angrily.

"Dafu!" said Dafu-chan, just as enraged, the pair of them up on my shoulders.

"Raph!" the big one replied, electricity practically crackling in the air between them. They were ready to fight at the drop of a hat.

"Rat, first let me ask you, what do you want to do? If we decide we need to defeat Mikey, could you accept that?" I asked.

"Of course not!" Rat snapped back.

"Sure, I mean, I can see that . . ." I deflected. He looked so much like a Raph species now; it was hard for me to fight him too, but I would if I had to.

"Do you think you can reach the next room if we don't take Mikey out?" I asked her.

"That won't be easy. I'd need you and the others to buy me some time," Rat replied.

"No need to worry!" Holn said with a cackle. "Once I'm finished modifying my second subject, I'll have him stand down!" Dammit, we were on the clock with Keel too!

"I'll never allow you to harm Keel!" Raphtalia raged.

"We're out of choices. Rat, this is going to be rough on you, but just listen to the plan, okay?" I said.

"Hold on! What are you planning?" she asked.

"I'll cast attack support, doubling the damage we cause to him. Then, Raphtalia, immediately attack, but not with a slice. Use an impact attack, a skill that causes an impact over a wide area, to blow Mikey's body off," I explained.

"Huh? Mr. Naofumi, surely that's the same as defeating him," Raphtalia said.

"I'm betting he'll be okay. If I'm correct, his real body is just the red crystal. If we can take the flesh off from around it and expose that crystal, we might be able to capture him alive," I said. It looked like transforming flesh, probably based on the same principles as the Dragon Emperor core. The Spirit Tortoise had been similar too, now that I thought about it.

There was no guarantee that Holn hadn't made the Spirit Tortoise.

"Oh my, the future Shield Hero is pretty sharp. That's the correct answer! But it won't be as easy to do as you think. Not with how I made it."

"Raph!" Mikey said and proceeded to split into two, then

four, each individual one moving independently around the room.

"What now?!" Rat exclaimed.

"The body can be controlled remotely over short distances," Holn explained. "Can you guess which is the real one?" We watched the scattered Mikeys running around the room before they gathered together and formed back into one. He reminded me of a boss in an action game I played once. A big impact when joined together would knock it back and expose the core to attack, but when split up, there was no way to do damage. That boss had been a real pain in the ass.

I cursed Holn's name again. She'd made her modifications with the intent of keeping the monster alive for as long as possible, to buy herself more time. If Mamoru and I busted out our shields, it would just go all soft and stick to them.

"If it's okay to just take it out, I think Raphtalia and the others could pull it off," I said. Rat didn't say anything, but I could feel the pressure emanating from her. Keel's body or Rat's trust—it really looked like I was going to have to sacrifice one of these two things.

"Do you have time to think so hard?" Holn quipped. In that moment, I decided I'd had enough of all of this.

"Let's get real here. However Keel ends up, she asked for it, so she has no grounds to complain. I hope she can overcome her trauma and feel better doing it," I said.

"Mr. Naofumi?!" Raphtalia yelped.

"Naofumi?!" Mamoru joined her, both surprised by my offhand declaration.

"From everything we've heard so far, it seems Holn doesn't do anything her subjects haven't asked her to do. I'm not entirely sure about her methods, but however this turns out, I'm sure it means our fighting strength will be enhanced," I said. I was starting to understand why the Whip seven star weapon had taken such a liking to her. If you considered all of this as being required in order to overcome the waves, it was possible to give a certain degree of latitude to the methods used. In this case, her deeds had been exposed, but Keel still desired the modification. So Holn was trying to buy the time to finish.

"Dafu! Dafu, dafu!" said Dafu-chan, seemingly not pleased with my answer. She was hitting me repeatedly on the shoulder, but I didn't really care about that.

"Just too much hassle for you, huh, Naofumi?" Ruft said.

"Raph!" said Raph-chan, her paws raised in the air as she shook her head.

"Yeah, to be honest," I admitted. "I'm not sure I've got the energy for this crazy comedy routine over junk that doesn't really matter."

"Mr. Naofumi, do you understand what you're saying? If you give up now, then Keel is surely going to suffer!" Raphtalia countered.

"Suffer? At worst, she's going to end up like the Raph species . . . and she may even come out like Ruft," I said.

"No! I will not allow that, never!" Raphtalia said emphatically. I was losing the will to continue this charade, even as Raphtalia got more pumped up. She had grabbed my shoulders and was seething with murderous intent, her eyes practically boring into my head. "Mr. Naofumi, are you looking to really make me mad?"

"Raphtalia, I know what you're trying to say. But even if we make it through this room, capture Holn, and save Keel, can you promise that Keel just won't do something like this again?" I asked her.

"I'll talk her down," Raphtalia said. "That's what my treatments have been about!"

"And yet Keel chose Holn over those same treatments, Raphtalia. If we do capture Holn, what are you going to do? Kill her? Mamoru, could you accept that?" I turned to him and asked.

"Well, that wouldn't exactly be desirable . . ." Mamoru's eyes shifted around, sweat forming on his brow. He was breathing hard too—almost hyperventilating.

"Mamoru, it's okay!" Cian said, looking worried as she gripped Mamoru's hand. I might have put him on the spot a little, but he still seemed far too shaken by my question. In fact, it looked like he was suffering the same kind of trauma as Keel and the others.

For the moment, though, I needed to deal with Raphtalia. Mamoru's reaction had told me how things would play out.

"Do you see, Raphtalia? Even if we take Holn alive and free Keel, she's not going to give up until she gets modified. We can't kill Holn, which means Keel will probably go right back to her."

"But . . ." Raphtalia said futilely.

"And even if you talk Keel down, can you promise that someone else isn't going to get the same idea? Ask for the same thing? This is physical enhancement! Can you be sure that others in the village won't want the same thing to make us happier by growing stronger?" I asked her. Their trauma didn't matter anymore. Everyone in the village knew how hard our battle was going to become, had seen our struggles so far, and were trying to get stronger as a result. They wanted to cover the losses in the battle with the Phoenix—indeed, wanted to surpass that strength and help keep the village safe. It stood to reason that some of them would do whatever it took to obtain such power. No matter how we tried to stop them, if the means were there . . . some of them would take it. Just like we'd done whatever we could to get stronger ourselves, they would do it too.

Even after all that, Raphtalia was looking at me pleadingly. She still seemed to want to say this was wrong, and I could understand that. But that didn't mean Keel was going to choose the right way of doing things either.

"Hold on! What about Mikey?" Rat asked.

"It's too late for him. Just give up—or have Holn conduct some more modifications as soon as possible," I told her.

"You're just giving up completely, Duke?" she retorted. I'd had enough of all this, that was for sure. It would be so great if the problems I constantly had to deal with could be resolved with a little muscle. But no, I always had to deal with these complex, twisted, soul-sucking conundrums. I wondered if this was karma. Maybe that was it. I needed to fundamentally change my ways.

"The future Shield Hero has quite an enlightened perspective," Holn commented.

"I don't think Raphtalia is going to give up though, Holn. Can you give her a chance to talk Keel into changing her mind?" I asked.

"That sounds reasonable," she replied. "I've been pushing your hospitality a little, I know, and I want to continue my research into areas other than modification too." Holn seemed to have accepted my proposal. The doors at the back of the room opened, and then the pressure on my Shooting Star Shield faded away as well.

"Glad we could discuss this like rational adults," I told her.

"The same back at you," Holn replied. "You've got complete access to the entire facility now." Most of the people we ended up fighting had no intention of listening to anything we said. On that point Holn was quite refreshing. She totally sucked, for sure, but she was doing it for what she thought were good reasons.

"Raph!" Mikey beckoned us over, moving aside to let us pass. It sounded like we'd reached an agreement and might even resolve this one without fighting. The main problem was we needed to explain all of this to Natalia and the rest of the village.

"Mikey?" Rat peered intently at Mikey.

"Raph?!" Mikey didn't seem to like having her stare at him.

"Just how much trouble were you planning to cause?!" Rat shrilled. At her voice, Mikey's fur all stood on end. "I really was worried about you! And yet you helped out her crazy scheme and placed more trust in her than in me! Why didn't you say any of this to me?" she asked.

"Raph," Mikey said uncertainly, showing his tummy in an act of submission and begging for further forgiveness.

"You seem to understand that I'm angry! I'm not being kind to you today! Look at everything you've done!" Rat said. Mikey gave a weak "Raph." They seemed to have a clear hierarchy in their relationship—almost like trust between them. "Duke, I need to lecture Mikey a little, so you go on ahead. Once I'm done here, I'll go back and explain to the Heavenly Emperor what has been happening," Rat said.

"That would be a big help. Come on, Raphtalia," I said.

She didn't reply. "This is Keel we're talking about. First listen to what she has to say, and then think about what to do next."

"Okay," Raphtalia finally said. She didn't seem happy with it, but she gave me a nod. It was certainly going to be interesting to see what happened next.

"We're making pretty good progress," Ruft commented.

"Raph!" said Raph-chan.

"Dafu!" said Dafu-chan repeatedly. Ruft and Raph-chan seemed to have accepted it pretty easily, but Dafu-chan was still stamping her foot in dissatisfaction. I knew she didn't like it, but this still seemed to be the better solution. I told Dafu-chan to give it up and then continued with Raphtalia toward the next room.

Chapter Seven: The Raph Species Upgrade Plan

The next room looked like some kind of control chamber, with a gaggle of pipes coming from the previous room and leading into the next one. The place looked like it was still under construction. For the moment, I had to keep my promise to Holn, so I didn't order any destruction. Not yet.

Raphtalia still had a slightly troubled look on her face. If we were still here to just smash our way through, I probably would have given that order. Mamoru seemed to have recovered a little from his shock in the previous room and was following quietly behind as he held Cian's hand.

"I really am sorry about all this," he eventually said.

"Don't worry about it. We treated her too much like Rat, who was mostly harmless, and left her without supervision. That's on us too," I replied. There were issues with how Holn was doing things, but at the root of it all, she was trying to meet the request I'd made of her. She could create all of this in such a short space of time, after all; that was exactly the kind of person we wanted researching how to get us back to the future.

"She's giving us this chance to talk Keel down, so that's something. The issue now is what kind of decisions the other villagers might make after we tell them about this." It was scary to think that they might all choose the same path. I'd made all sorts of modifications to the village already, it was true, but it felt like this was definitely crossing a line. I kept coming back to the same thought: had I made the villagers too transfixed on becoming stronger? But we still had a long fight ahead of us, and they wanted to become stronger too. When playing a game, even ace players could end up losing a battle through sheer numbers, even if their allies weren't close to the same level. Just like Takt had and S'yne's had sworn enemies too. The more people I needed to protect, the easier it would be if those people were stronger. That just made sense.

It depended on how the current situation shook out, and also the actual content of Holn's research, but I definitely wanted to discuss the possibilities.

"Is everyone going to want to be a Raph species?" I mused, mainly to myself, but Raphtalia twitched as she overheard me.

"Mr. Naofumi! That made my spine tingle like never before!" she said.

"I phrased it as a question!" I replied defensively. We could achieve that by having the Raph-chans perform a fresh class-up on everyone though, so we didn't need to ask Holn for that. I considered just limiting this new development to Ruft.

In any case, this was only going to increase Raphtalia's concerns. It felt like I was the one increasing them too. Like it was my fault for all the monsters who became Raph species.

I wondered if she felt like she was getting more and more relatives. It might be time for me to confront my Raph-chan addiction head-on.

I opened the door to the next room and went inside to find Keel in a capsule with a pissed-off look on her face and Holn waiting in a chair. She was still on her guard, however, as there was a transparent wall dividing the room, keeping us from getting to her easily.

"Here we are then. Nice of you to come. Chat away," Holn said, pointing in Keel's general direction.

"Bubba! Raphtalia! What are you getting in the way for?!" Keel said.

"You need to rethink this. Holn is clearly bad news. You shouldn't be doing anything with her," I said.

"Mr. Naofumi is right!" Raphtalia said. "You're already more than strong enough. Your heart is what's important! If people could heal such trauma this easily, no one would ever have to suffer."

"You're lying! You overcame your trauma so easily because Bubba did something for you, that's all! He won't do it for me, so I asked Holn to!" Keel yipped.

"That's not the case at all," Raphtalia replied. "I didn't overcome it easily at all, I assure you. You've been making good progress too! You're almost there!"

"Your treatments have been helping me, I admit, but then

when I wake up and realize it was all a dream, the pain just comes flooding back!" Keel whined, showing no signs of calming down yet. That sounded like a problem we should have been prepared for. Showing them a dream of being powerful, of resolving the crisis that cracked them, was all very well, but ultimately that was still just a dream. Having the feeling of achievement at defeating a feared enemy from the past did not change what actually happened. Under such circumstances, they might be able to do more than before, but it was hard to say they had overcome their trauma completely. This was a world in which stats existed and strength could be turned into numbers; facing something like this trauma required the last bastion of unknowable strength. I could understand why someone might be lured by an easier choice.

"Keel . . . the past is . . ." Raphtalia started but seemed to lose her way and looked over at me. I realized where she was coming from—we were in the past right now. If we could turn things to our advantage a little, we might even be able to prevent the terrible things that had happened to Raphtalia and the others. We were in a place where anything could happen. Raphtalia was looking confused now herself, having realized this possibility.

"Trauma is an issue you have to face for yourself. No one would struggle with it if a little physical upgrading could change that. If you're letting her mess around inside your head, that's just brainwashing," I stated. We didn't know what the rules for this time travel stuff were. When we went to find Natalia, for example, we'd seen a fox monster defeated. If that was the fox who had been part of Takt's crew, then the future had just been changed. Yet here we were, with our memories of that same fox creature. Even if we could return right to the point that the first wave happened . . . we might not be able to change anything.

I looked over at Holn, and she didn't even seem to be listening to us. Instead, she was looking at Mamoru. He didn't seem to like that much. He had a frown on his face.

"Bubba, you're the one who told me to decide my future for myself! That's why I asked Holn to make me so strong. I'd never be afraid of a monster like a cerberus ever again!" Keel replied. I had expected this argument and didn't really have a counter for it.

"Holn," I said after a pause.

"What now?" she replied.

"If you were to go ahead with modifying Keel, can you assure me that it isn't going to fail?" I asked her.

"All experiments can fail, one way or another. But if this particular one fails, I'd probably have to commit suicide from shame," she replied. So she sounded pretty confident. "To be quite honest about it, this one isn't half as much fun as my first attempt."

"Why not?" I asked, not sure I really wanted to know.

"I find nothing so boring as having to investigate how future demi-humans and therianthropes have changed and then track back those changes," she said. I didn't really understand that statement either.

"Holn!" Mamoru chided her sternly, a glare in his eye. But she just gave him a devil-may-care look back. I needed to rethink this.

"Next question: if you modify Keel, will that actually allow her to overcome her trauma? What kind of modifications do you even intend to make?" I asked.

"Ah. That's the little old question I've been waiting for," Holn replied. She started operating the terminal again, and it displayed something for us. It looked like her plans to modify Keel. "First I activate the weapon technique 'bioethics,' then work in parallel with bio-customization to expand the subject's body with the desired strength and enhancements. Of course, this will all require a considerable volume in materials, magic, and SP."

"Bioethics? What materials does that come from?" I asked.

"Oh, even I don't know much about that. It was already there on a weapon when I obtained it," Holn replied coyly. She sure knew how to hold her cards close to her chest. But then there were also unique shields like the Shield of Rage that appeared after you used emotions as materials. Holn was an alchemist, meaning something supplementary to that might have automatically popped up for her. If I kept on playing around the bioplants and evolving them, and obtained new shields too, eventually it might have popped up for me as well. I already had similar techniques in my arsenal.

"And what will happen to Keel once you're done?" I asked.

"It depends on exactly what we modify. There are certain options there, like giving up the demi-human form completely and just going with the therianthrope one," she replied. I pondered that too. It sounded like she could make Keel into a real monster if she wanted to. "If we take it too far, she could lose control completely, so I'm recommending we keep things in check a little."

"And this will allow her to overcome her trauma?" I asked.

"If she's satisfied with the changes, it will lead to further confidence for her. There are risks, of course, but yes, I think it will allow her to leave the past behind," Holn asserted.

"What about drugs? You use any powerful chemicals to do this?" I asked.

"Please. I'm not some street-level hawker of quick fixes," Holn scoffed. I pondered on this too. Just from Holn's description, I really couldn't make a determination as to whether Keel would be able to overcome her trauma or not. Holn seemed pretty confident about it, that was true though.

"What method are you using then?" I asked.

"There's an experimental element to this, but it should be

possible to revert her to a more ancestral state, like a shifted therianthrope," Holn postulated.

"What? Keel can already turn into a therianthrope," I said. She's been in her dog form most of the time recently.

"And I'm talking about ancestral power. Don't you have those in the future? Shifted therianthropes? Shifters? They turn into something that looks almost like a monster at a glance. They need a lot of training to reach that point, of course," Holn explained.

"Are you talking about beast transformation?" I asked. That was a powerful form that only a few I knew could use, such as Fohl and Sadeena. They could only achieve it when I used beast transformation support on them, the conditions for which were still a mystery. I honestly hadn't even thought about all this for a while. It sounded like Holn could let me perform that transformation at will. That Aotatsu with Takt had pulled a trick like that, now that I thought about it. Takt had been master of the Whip vassal weapon, so maybe he had activated some kind of technique of his own to make that happen. In any case, if Keel could pull off that complex and difficult-to-maintain maneuver on her own, that would be quite something.

"It's the realization of a powerful latent ability that only a very small number of demi-humans and therianthropes have access to," Holn said.

"When you say 'very few,' how few do you mean?" I asked.

"Just based on my own little old research, I think only a handful of types from all the demi-humans in the world," she said. So there were only a handful of demi-humans who could use beast transformation like Fohl and Sadeena. It was a pretty crazy thing—more like simply turning into a full-on monster. "I compared Fohl with sample data here in the lab from subjects called Sadeena and Shildina and discovered one striking difference between them," Holn continued.

"Something different between Fohl and Sadeena?" I asked. They had both used beast transformation in the past. Holn really could learn a lot from a small volume of material.

"This Sadeena, at least, is able to achieve true ancestral recall. I would very much like to get my hands on her," Holn said. I didn't want to break it to her, but taking Sadeena and Shildina alive would be impossible for her. The two of them would be more likely to manipulate Holn into doing whatever it was they wanted.

"Fohl's mother was human," I told her. His demi-human side showed through strongly, but his mother was Trash's younger sister. That might be the reason Holn had spotted some kind of difference.

"Nope, that doesn't matter," Holn said flatly. "I'm talking about ancestral power here. To put it another way, this Sadeena shows no signs at all of having been modified or magically enhanced—she has a completely pristine body." I wasn't really following this, but it sounded like Holn thought I was making some kind of mistake.

"Stop beating around the bush. If you've got something to say, spill it," I said.

"I thought I was being pretty clear. Having one human parent isn't going to make a difference to this," Holn replied. It sounded like she was saying that the hakuko and orcinus species were fundamentally different in some way. Traces of modification or magical enhancement . . . it almost sounded like the Whip power-up method was having a genetic effect. There was an item called "descendants prosperity" under the Whip power-up method. It could also be used to enhance your basic nature at the cost of levels, increasing your stats in the long-term. All of these benefits weren't restricted to just heroes either; they could be applied to any trusted companions. These enhancements were quite intensive on resources and could only be used a limited number of times, so one common use was to apply them to children in order to give the next generation a boost. Here it looked like they were being applied to monsters, who had a much harsher lifecycle than humans, to enhance them across the generations. The Japan back in my world had done similar things. It was like domesticating wild dogs.

This seemed to be a way to do that more easily . . . but it would be pointless for humans or demi-humans. Managing species with such long lifespans over the period of time it would take would be almost impossible. Which meant these were enhancements that didn't mean much, even if we had access to them.

I presumed that some of the races in this world were the offspring of ones who had received such enhancements. That meant Sadeena was from a pure bloodline that hadn't undergone any such modifications. That just made her incredible strength even more . . . incredible.

"We are getting off track," Holn said.

"You're right. So this will allow Keel to use a more powerful beast transformation?" I confirmed with her.

"That's right. I can give her that power, like I'm giving her ancestral recall," Holn replied.

"What? Naofumi! If that's a possibility, then I want to do it too!" For some reason, eyes sparkling, Ruft chose that moment to throw his hat into the ring. In his case—and based on his current appearance—that was likely to push him even harder into becoming one of the Raph species. In light of what Sadeena and Fohl had turned into, he might be able to become a massive Raph. But Raphtalia wasn't able to do that, and so maybe they were a race that simply didn't have the aptitude.

"Ruft, we can come back to this later. Raphtalia is right there," I said.

"Sure, okay," Ruft said, not wanting to get killed. Raphtalia was looking over intently already—there wasn't a glare in her eyes, not really, but the intent to destroy us was nevertheless hanging heavy in the air. It was even scarier than it had been earlier. If we didn't cut it out, Raphtalia might bring out her Curse Series Katana vassal weapon.

"If you make it so Keel can use beast transformation, what will she look like?" I inquired. "Will she turn out like a Raph species?"

"Bubba! You're still planning on turning me into a Raph?!" Keel growled threateningly.

"If we get to choose, that might be a fitting punishment," I replied.

"Are you serious?! Holn! Please, don't do that!" Keel pleaded with Holn desperately. If I pressed this line of thinking, we might be able to get Keel to give up.

"I'm not sure . . . No, it's nothing," Raphtalia said, giving up. She was unlikely to be pleased with the outcome, no matter what happened next.

"This is a suggestion from the future Shield Hero, so I can't easily discount it. Little old me thinks it sounds more fun," Holn said. Her "little old" bit was getting a little old.

"No! Bubba! Seriously, don't do it!" Keel squawked.

"Are you ready to give up then?" I asked her.

"No! I'm going to become strong enough to keep everyone safe!" she replied defiantly. Bah. She was stubborn, that was for sure.

"How about I use a simple method, with no aftereffects, to let you experience beast transformation and we can take it from there?" Holn suggested. She pressed a button and the liquid inside Keel's tank started to bubble like crazy.

"Keel?!" Raphtalia shouted.

"Don't worry. I'm using factors extracted from the Raph species to provide a magic effect for a limited period. It's a one-time-only deal. A little old 'try before you buy' kind of thing," Holn quipped.

"Is it a bit like Raphtalia using illusion magic to let Keel see herself transformed for a while?" I asked.

"Pretty much," Holn affirmed. "She'll see what she would be like if I complete all her requests." I heard the sound of the liquid draining away and looked over to see, well, a three-headed . . . cerberus where Keel had been. However, it wasn't the slobbering hellhound that Raph-chan had turned into, but a cute, heavily stylized, mascot-like cerberus. It was like if there was a basketball team called the Hell Dogs.

"Huh? Wow! See, Bubba? I've overcome my trauma!" Keel said excitedly.

"I'm sorry to say I'm just doing this to give the future Shield Hero a taste of what you might look like. You can't actually turn into that yet," Holn revealed.

"What? So what is this?!" Keel asked.

"Like a costume, nothing more," Holn said.

"You're joking! And why can't I look down on Bubba and the others? I thought I was going to get big!" she asked. I promptly turned my shield into the Otherworld Kingdom Mirror Shield and let Keel take a look at herself. "What's going on? I can't get any bigger than this?!"

"I'm not sure that's the point you should be getting hung up on," I told her. She looked like a baby cerberus that had gone through a cute machine. If this was the finished thing, then it seemed pointless to go ahead.

"That's how Keel is going to overcome her trauma?" Raphtalia asked. I didn't know. Raphtalia knew more about Keel than I did—she should be telling me what was going on. Still, turning into the thing she was afraid of could possibly have beneficial effects. It was like that primitive, shaman-like thinking: defeating a powerful enemy and eating them could bring you that strength. A bit of a crude analogy, but it was something like that. Keel believed that she could overcome her trauma by becoming the object of that trauma.

"Raph!" said Raph-chan.

"One thing though, Keel," I said.

"What is it, Bubba? Why are you looking at me with those eyes? Not angry, almost pitying me?!" Keel asked.

"Your position as a therianthrope is already something more like an animal . . . You're the cute village dog, a mascot character like Raph-chan here," I said. Keel's doggy form was loved by all, and she had such a friendly personality, which made her really popular around the village. "The reason your trading always goes so well is because of that cute appearance and how friendly you are. That's different from being cool," I explained to her.

"Whatever are you talking about?!" she exclaimed. That seemed like a bit of an overreaction. She had to have had some idea about this herself. Some of this was definitely coming from a desire to avoid reality.

"Keel is very cute, that's true," Ruft said. "If I hadn't met the Raph-chans, then I would have been totally hung up on her."

"You think the same thing too, Ruft?!" Keel exclaimed. "Holn, can't you make me cooler?" she pleaded.

"I'm sorry, but that's the only possible outcome. It's the core part that comprises you. It's something I can never change or take away," she replied.

"Dammit!" said Keel, about as blue as I'd ever seen her.

"In terms of combat capabilities, this is what we're looking at." Holn brought up the predicted stats for Keel. The cutie cerberus would give her basically a fifty-percent boost across the board. Not bad. "The cost of this is that she'll lose control for confectionary and will gain a weakness to sleep attacks." So it was a power-up with some built-in disadvantages. All sounded pretty standard so far.

"Okay. What if you push Keel closer to the Raph species?"
I asked.

"She'll retain the cute features but give us some leeway on
the stats front," Holn said.

"Hey! No! I said not to do that! I don't want to become another Raph-chan! Raphtalia, help me!" Keel yipped loudly as I
chuckled with Holn. No wonder she was asking for Raphtalia's
help. Then, with a puff of smoke, Keel's temporary transformation came to an end.

"Raph . . ." said Raph-chan.

"Dafu, dafu. Dafu, dafu!" said Dafu-chan. Raphtalia was
shaking her head in sheer amazement.

"Keel, give up this insanity. You can overcome this on your
own. If you want to look like that, get S'yne to make you a
costume," Raphtalia suggested.

"No way! I want to become stronger, even stronger! I want
to be able to do a super power-up like Fohl and Sadeena can!"
she replied. She was starting to sound like L'Arc when he had
been insisting on apprenticing with the accessory dealer. I had
to give them this though—both of them were taking action
based on serious considerations on their part.

"She should be able to get stronger if we remove some of
the unnecessary optional stuff," Holn said.

"Let's try that then," I replied.

"Mr. Naofumi!" Raphtalia said, incredulous.

"Straight to the point. I like it," Holn said. "If we just expand the basics as much as possible, this is the kind of ancestral recall she'll be able to pull off." She pressed a different button, and Keel was submerged in liquid again . . . to become a different-colored Keel. The pattern on her coat seemed to have changed a little, and she looked bulkier as well. But otherwise, she looked exactly the same. Still a cute dog, just a little bigger. Not much difference.

"What's going on here? I've not changed at all!" she exclaimed.

"This one is based on affinity variation," Holn explained. "Using beast transformation like a combination skill will allow her to take on all sorts of different abilities depending on the affinity of the other skill."

"Okay, that sounds useful," I said.

"This is a magical form that a lot of therianthropes in our time use to enhance themselves," Holn said. Indeed, this seemed to match with the magic that Keel could unconsciously use to protect herself.

"In our time it's said to be hard to separate affinities out. Looks like this is beast affinity," I said. She had access to howling magic, stuff like that. She was able to give herself a boost by howling. It sounded suited to Keel.

"Do you not have moon affinity in the future?" Holn asked.

"Moon?" I asked in return.

"It's also called 'night,' or 'twilight,' depending on the region. An affinity expressed by the darkness of the night, and beasts, things like that," Holn explained.

"All sounds pretty similar," I said.

"The pattern I just showed you is based on Dragon Emperor transformations," Holn said.

"Wow, okay. Our Dragon Emperor keeps a pretty fixed form most of the time ... but the Demon Dragon transformed herself, that's true," I recalled. That had to be a similar thing. If it would allow her to casually change her transformation patterns, that could be useful too. "Keel moves around a lot, so it would be great to boost her speed."

"In which case I can add some wind or lighting affinity magic," Hold suggested.

"Hey! Stop trying to decide what I turn into, Bubba!" Keel interjected. "I thought I was going to get to choose for myself!"

"This is surely going to be better than a cutie cerberus, okay! I want to see what you turn into," I said.

"Me too. I think I might be able to shoot for something big here," Holn mused.

"Might be able to!? Did you hear that? And what do you mean 'cutie' cerberus? That's not the kind of cerberus I'm aiming for!" Keel continued, as energetic as ever.

"Mr. Naofumi, can you please stop proceeding along the line of thinking that we're actually going to modify Keel?" Raphtalia asked.

"What do you want then, Raphtalia?" I turned to her. "Do you want Keel to become a Raph species?"

"There's no need to default back to that position either!" Raphtalia replied. With that, we put a pin in the whole "modify Keel" thing. The issue was that after she transformed once, she would never be able to come back, and so we put a stop to it. Holn had apparently been proceeding with the entire thing under the presupposition that we would have to approve it anyway.

"That was fun, wasn't it?" Holn said brightly. "This is for you, future Shield Hero. It should be perfect for the Raph species." Holn pressed another button, and something popped out from the wall in front of my eyes. They looked like green leaves.

"What's this? Leaves?" I asked.

"Raph?" said Raph-chan quizzically. Raph-chan took one of the leaves and showed it to me. It looked like a tree leaf a tanuki used to transform in Japanese folklore. It really suited Raph-chan, that was for sure. It might look good on Raphtalia too.

"It's an accessory that can draw out the power of the Raph species. It was made using the concentrated power of the sakura lumina," Holn explained.

"Impressive . . ." I said. She'd clearly made this to try and curry favor with me—and it was working.

"Of course, the Heavenly Emperor can use it too," Holn added. Raphtalia looked pretty conflicted by that.

THE RISING OF THE SHIELD HERO 21

"What about this brown leaf on the bottom?" I asked.

"That's something else. I mixed different factors into that, for you to use, future Shield Hero. Try putting it into your shield," she suggested.

"Okay," I replied. From its appearance, it didn't seem to have any strange magic on it. I didn't want to end up getting cursed again by putting strange stuff into my shield. As I had that thought, though, the gemstone on the shield gave off a soft glow. It seemed to be saying it was okay to put the leaf inside. I proceeded to do so.

Conditions for Shield of the Beast King II unlocked!
Conditions for Shield of the Beast King III unlocked!
Conditions for Sakura Stone of Destiny + Shield of the Beast King unlocked!
Conditions for Dragon King Shield 0 unlocked!

Shield of the Beast King II 0/C
<abilities locked> equip bonus: boost abilities of beast transformation users (medium), skill "Beast Transformation Support Expansion" "Beast Transformation Additional Access"
  special effect: power of loyalty, power of trust
  mastery level: 0

Shield of the Beast King III 0/C
<abilities locked> equip bonus: boost abilities of beast transformation users (large), skill "Beast Transformation Support Expansion" "Beast Transformation Additional Access" "Voluntary Beast Transformation Support" "Cost Reduction (Large)"
special effect: power of loyalty, power of trust, army roar
mastery level: 0

Sakura Stone of Destiny + Shield of the Beast King 0/C
<abilities locked> equip bonus: skill "Pacifier Support"
special effect: pacifier beast
mastery level: 0

Dragon King Shield 0 0/0 C
<abilities locked> equip bonus: reincarnation recognition, beginning of 0, skill "Transformation Support"
special effect: primal dragon
mastery level: 0

That was a lot to take in. An expansion had popped up from the shield that I copied in the special room for the Shield

Hero in Siltvelt. It was mainly focused on expanding use of beast transformation support—making that annoyingly obtuse skill easier to use.

I also had to wonder about this series with 0 on it. This one had developed from Shield 0, but apart from the special effects and abilities, the stats were the same as the Shield 0.

"Has it unlocked something?" Holn asked.

"Yeah, the Shield of the Beast King series. Other stuff too," I replied absently.

"What about me?" Mamoru asked. He'd kinda been on the sidelines until now, that was true.

"Nothing for you, Mamoru," Holn replied brightly.

"Why not?!" he retorted.

"Because this is something that I created for use by the future Shield Hero. It isn't something you need, Mamoru," she explained. I took a moment to appreciate that. It was all pretty weird-looking, but I might be able to make use of it. "I think you would get completely different weapons—probably ones that support ancestral recall."

"Impressive that you know all this," I said.

"I made it to complement those kinds of weapons. Future Shield Hero, this should help you to further aid your allies," Holn said. She was right on that score. All the new shields had some kind of support features, but the 0 one was the outlier on that score.

"Reincarnation recognition" definitely caught my eye. Maybe it would let me spot the resurrected. If so, that would be super convenient. I'd have to unlock that later.

Moving on . . . The 0 series, the Shield of Wrath, and the Shield of Compassion trees were connected by unlocked shields. I didn't know how to unlock them . . . but the conditions were gradually being filled in.

"In any case, after all the loyalty I've shown you here, I hope you'll overlook certain other things," Holn said.

"I get it. Now start by getting rid of those towers placed around the village and turning off your other security measures," I said.

"Of course," she agreed. With that, Holn returned the village to normal. In regard to the towers that grew in the village, even in that short time, the others had gotten close to clearing them all. Holn said we had displayed far greater collaboration and strategy than she had expected. Ren and Fohl had been up there, after all. This was proof that they could act quickly when it was required.

"Raphtalia, I'm sorry. We're going to have to ask the others in the village if they want the same treatment as Keel," I said to her.

"I understand . . . but I hope they won't go for it," she replied.

"We'll have to discuss this later," I said.

"Raphtalia!" said Keel, tears in her voice. "It was totally not what I was expecting!"

"That's what we call karma, Keel," Raphtalia said. "This is why you don't go off with strange scientists."

"Raph!" Raph-chan agreed.

"Dafu, dafu!" said Dafu-chan.

"So great! I wish I could become exactly like Raph-chan!" Ruft said enviously. I ignored his casual comment and turned to Mamoru instead.

"It looks like we avoided all-out war," I said. "But you need to have words with her."

"I really am sorry about all this!" Mamoru replied. He'd been doing little but apologizing for a while now. Cian was acting like a cat, licking her hands like paws to clean her face, looking unperturbed. That was a true cat reaction, ears, whiskers, and tail. "You need to think hard on this too, Holn!" Mamoru said pointedly.

"This isn't going to be enough to curb my little old curiosity," she replied. She was incorrigible.

"If you get too carried away, my Heavenly Emperor might throw caution about future generations to the wind and try to off you," I warned her.

"That does seem like a possibility," Holn admitted with a nod, perhaps having sensed the same terrible intent to destroy emanating from Raphtalia. "I'll pay attention to that."

Hopefully that would keep her in check a little. In any case, that brought the fun and games Holn had triggered to an end. It went without saying that we had Rat and Wyndia constantly watching Holn from that moment onward.

After we resolved things with Holn, we came out of the lab with her to find Natalia and the others looking down.

"You need to stop this nonsense or I really will punish you," Natalia warned.

"I was just doing what I was asked to do. Or is the little old Whip telling you that I've stepped off the path of a hero?" Holn goaded. She showed the Whip seven star weapon to Natalia, with a cheeky but completely unbothered expression on her face. The gemstone on the Whip did glow for a moment, but that only made Natalia bite her lip in frustration.

"Personally, I think you could clock her one. I'm not taking responsibility, of course," I chimed in.

"Naofumi, I don't think that's especially appropriate . . ." Mamoru warned, and Ren arrived just in time to nod his agreement.

"Hey, I don't discriminate because she's a woman. Ren, you understand, right?" I asked, but Ren just looked away.

"I wouldn't stop you if it was Bitch, that's true," he said finally. I couldn't think of anyone who would seek to stop the punishment of Bitch. It was strange how attitudes changed when we were talking about someone different.

"We shouldn't be getting too emotional about this," Natalia finally said. "Very well. I will back down." I hadn't expected Natalia to give up and I wondered what had brought on this change of heart. She seemed to be looking at me pretty intently. "That said. I think the Whip Spirit should take the punishment this time." With that, Natalia swung her hammer toward the Whip that Holn was holding.

"Huh? I guess we have to accept that," Holn replied. She didn't avoid the attack but took Natalia's hammer right on the whip. An actually quite pleasing clang rang out, and the Whip gemstone flashed.

"Whip Spirit. Vassal weapon spirit or not, you need to learn your place," Natalia said. It sounded like responsibility had been shifted from Holn to the weapon.

"I'm not going to be able to use the Whip for any fun stuff for a while, am I?" Holn muttered. Maybe the punishment had been some kind of restriction of functions. It sounded like fair measures, anyway. It was better than just letting them have their way. She was still surely quite capable even without the power of the weapon.

"You can even punish spirits," I noted. She could render a vassal weapon completely inoperable. I'd kind of done the same thing when I stripped the seven star weapons from Takt. Maybe this wasn't a form of punishment that was only available to a pacifier. I had to wonder if it had any effect on the temperament of the spirit inside the weapon.

"Even the spirits can sometimes step off the path," Natalia said. "Under the current circumstances, though, taking it further than this would be too heavy of a punishment. We have the waves to consider too, and there's no time to search for someone to use it instead. I also don't want to trigger any rebellious backlash." I was pleased to see that the pacifier had her eye on the waves too. During such a dangerous time, it would be difficult to kill a holy weapon hero even if they did step off the path. Natalia was just going to have to suffer a bit longer.

"So this is the work of a pacifier. Pretty different from things back in our time," I commented.

"Oh? What happens in the future?" Natalia asked.

"They hole themselves up in Q'ten Lo and never come out," I replied.

"Before you came, Naofumi," Ruft said, "there was a period when the Q'ten Lo dragon hourglass kept on shining really brightly. But Makina said it was nothing." That had been the call to action, for sure. That twisted hag had completely ignored it.

"The world is in constant flux," the Water Dragon said, "even with my supervision. That is just a mark of how much things will change."

"I'd say you guys got left behind, pretty much," I commented. Not to mention the wistfully laconic Water Dragon was the one who would end up bringing us in to help out. I shook my head, not knowing what to say.

"I don't really want to hear any more of this," Natalia said. "You'll get me thinking about how to change the future."

"Good luck with that. Make a better future for us all!" I chirped.

"We might have our own problems if things change too much," Raphtalia said.

"We could do with working out how that is all operating," I said. One possibility was that our coming to this time was already something that had happened to shape the future that we knew. That said, the waves were a phenomenon that involved the fusing of worlds, as caused by the one who assumed the name of god, and yet now—with the involvement of enemies from another world, admittedly—we had been kicked back into the past, and so that really confused the issue. A single line of the past, present, and future was now being mixed with other lines. If there was a future beyond our own time, figuring out the waves might explain it. If the waves defeated us, the world was wiped out, after all. S'yne had already experienced that. It was a fact that the time we had come from was either the leading edge of this world or at least a key point in its history. It proved that worlds fusing together was the route this timeline should take . . . but the only way to know that was to jump further into the future.

I wondered how I would feel if heroes from further in the future came back to our time, like we had shown up in Mamoru's time. I decided I wouldn't like it. I didn't even know what kind of structure this world had anyway. The little information I had gathered so far was all I knew. Working all of this out would be hard without another chat with Atla and Ost. Maybe I could ask the Demon Dragon personality that appeared when I cast magic. I tested my connection with it, and it seemed to be there.

Of course, it was just a simulated personality, so it might not be able to think about unexpected things. Maybe waves were happening in all times, at the same time, in the past, present, and future, all at once . . . That might be possible too, but I also wasn't going to get an easy answer.

Natalia began speaking again. "In any case, this was quite a stimulating welcome. I've got a lot of notes I'd like to share with you, but I think I understand the situation. As a pacifier I don't want to get too involved, but very well. I'll be praying for your return to the future as quickly as possible," she said, making a clear statement to all of us. She likely thought a little less of us after all of this, but at least she wasn't choosing to take us out with the trash. "I can't promise I will stand by this if you start to use the holy weapons or vassal weapons viciously—that is to say, using the spirit implements for evil," she warned.

"I've got you," I replied. "So what next?" I actually didn't have any idea what Natalia did.

"I've already warned the Bow Hero. The nation he is affiliated with seems to have cooled down . . . for now. That's all the big stuff I've handled. Now I can just clean up any outliers in readiness for the coming battle," she said. Of course, she also had her eye on things like Piensa and their desire for global warfare. "There have been rumors about the Shield Hero bringing in heroes from other worlds, but now I know the truth. No one would ever guess that you're actually from the future."

"About that. When I asked you about ways to get us home, you said you didn't have any idea. Is that true? You really don't know?" I asked.

"Why not ask that evil alchemist?" Natalia suggested.

"I'm working on it," the evil one replied. "I just haven't found any clues yet."

"Very well. I'll send an envoy home and see if the previous Heavenly Emperor has any ideas," Natalia said. She was going to ask someone smart back in Q'ten Lo. I just had to pray that would provide some answers. "I haven't seen that talkative winged girl yet today, now that I think about it," Natalia added.

"You mean me?" R'yne put her hand up, accompanied by S'yne. I wasn't even sure how long she had been there—it was so hard to keep track of who was around at any given moment, and for once she had been keeping her mouth shut.

"There you are . . . but I don't need you. How long are you planning on spending here? Why don't you go off and defend your own world?" Natalia asked.

"Don't have to," R'yne replied cheekily. "My friends there know what I'm doing, and they are fine with it." She was so easygoing! I presumed it was the same principle as Raphtalia's Katana. Anyway, if things at home got bad, her weapon would take her back. "How are things going here? It looks like we've missed all the fun."

"There was no fun here at all, I promise you. What a joke," Natalia said. She seemed to get along with R'yne about as well as Raphtalia did. Such was the lot of the pacifier, having to observe the heroes—whomever they might be. At least the Q'ten Lo guys didn't seem to be coming after Raphtalia's life this time. In my time, they would have done anything to try and take out someone they considered this dangerous. That thought made me think of Kizuna—and realize why sometimes heroes ended up fighting. In her world, they had already lost their Heavenly Emperor.

In any case, if the Bow Hero from this time or other vassal weapon holders made a play for us, we could shut them down using the power of the sakura stone of destiny. They could fight amongst themselves as much as they liked once we were safely back in our own time.

"And you're the future Sewing Kit Hero," Natalia said, looking at S'yne.

"That's right. She's called S'yne," R'yne interjected. "She's probably, like, related to me or something. She's super cute, huh?" R'yne stroked S'yne in a very familiar manner.

"You really don't change, do you? That's exactly how you treated your own sister," Natalia said.

"Oh yes! I can't tell heads or tails of things these days!" R'yne replied. S'yne looked pretty disgruntled by the whole thing. Maybe it was because R'yne treated her in the same way her own sister did.

As the banter continued, I noticed Keel a little distance away, talking to the rest of the villagers.

"Keel, how was it?" Fohl asked.

"How was it? It sucked! Bubba almost turned me into a Raph species!" Keel replied.

"That sounds truly awful," Fohl sympathized.

"But if we ask Holn, she'll give us stronger enhancements than the Shield Hero, right?" another villager said.

"Didn't she just say she couldn't do anything for a while?" Keel asked.

"That's a shame . . ." the villager replied.

"Ah, hold on. She's grinning! I think maybe she can still do that much!" Keel yapped. I'd thought maybe they were chastising Keel, but it sounded more like they were just interested in what was going on. These guys were a hardy bunch.

"Oh, what should I do?" Imiya pondered.

"What kind of modification would you like?" Keel asked.

"Yes, well, about that . . ." Imiya said. They were already having exactly the conversation I had expected. They needed to think about the methods a little more. Raphtalia was already glaring over at them.

"Are you going to ask to become a little more human? For the Shield Hero?" Keel asked. I wondered why they might think I'd want that. Imiya was already a therianthrope, so what would it mean to make her more human? Close to a demi-human, maybe.

"Why would you want that? Any fun reasons?" Holn asked.

"Well, you see . . ." Imiya replied. Holn was chatting with the slaves like she was one of the gang.

"Huh, that's no fun at all," Holn said after Imiya finished explaining. "It would be more fun for me if we sent you back to ancestral recall." I shook my head at that too. She'd just finished being punished! "There's something else. My investigations have revealed that each Shield Hero possesses certain characteristics—a common trait: they don't treat anyone differently based on their race." I wondered what she was talking about now. At this line from Holn, even others removed from the conversation looked over at Mamoru, Ren, Fohl, and me too.

"Atla did take an instant liking to him," Fohl said.

"I don't think I've ever seen Naofumi concerned about race. He always interacts with everyone earnestly, honestly, and with such care," Ren mused. I just wanted them to shut up. This wasn't helping things! People were only going to start believing this crap! I wasn't so noble!

"Do you know the story 'The Hero and the Beast?' There's a version in which true love's kiss from a Shield Hero is the only thing that can turn a maiden back from being a monster. Very famous," Holn said. "The commonality is that the Shield Hero is someone who falls for what's inside, not the external appearance." I didn't know a thing about that! She was making the Shield Hero sound like the prince who suddenly showed up at the end of a fairy tale! "This is a marked difference from the Bow Hero. There's no need to be concerned about race when dealing with the Shield Hero," Holn summarized.

"Holn, I'm not entirely sure that's what Imiya wanted to know," Keel said.

"Why not? Still, the future Shield Hero does seem to have a thing for the Raph species. She might be better to modify herself in that direction," Holn mused.

"That might be . . . a little too much for me," Imiya admitted apologetically. That was fine. That was what I wanted her to say. Whatever my daily attitude, I liked Imiya a lot.

"You make a good point." Just when I thought it was over, Natalia stepped in with a follow-up attack. "I've seen records concerning the Shield Heroes from the past regarding the closest friend of the very first Shield Hero. The other heroes who were summoned immediately after him called that friend 'lizard man,' or so the records say," Natalia stated. "I've also heard that the bloodline of the Shield Hero's partner shows up strongly in their children."

"I've heard the same kind of thing in Siltvelt," Fohl mused. I didn't need to hear any more of this—especially if Fohl seemed to have heard it before too.

"I have to ask, why does all the talk about me recently seem to come back to sex?" I muttered. I had stroked Raphtalia to avoid all this. I wished they could just take the hint. It was starting to look like I'd need to stroke Raphtalia like she was Raph-chan in order to make this topic go away.

"Everyone, please. This isn't very fair on Mr. Naofumi and Mamoru, so maybe we should leave this topic alone. I think I would appreciate that too," Raphtalia said, stepping in and calling for an end to this line of discussion. I decided to back her up—I wanted to disperse it completely.

"Okay, enough time-wasting. Clean this mess up. I think this served to show how quickly we can act in an emergency situation. If something like this happens again, I want you all to work even harder to resolve it," I told them. They all offered various levels of agreement and then went their separate ways. "Natalia, this is pretty much how things work around here. We're going to be stuck here a while longer, from the look of it, so I hope you'll help us out."

"I think I understand the general situation," Natalia replied. "There's definitely an energy to the place. If you can offer powerful aid against the wave, I can overlook the smaller stuff."

"Really?" I replied. "I thought you would want us to keep out of things, considering we might change the future."

"A risk I'm willing to take. We need all hands on deck right now. If that's going to change the future, I say go ahead and let it change, if it means we can keep this world safe," Natalia responded.

"If we can use them to prevent the waves from going the way our enemies expect, we've no choice but to do so," the Water Dragon said, winding around Natalia and placing his head on her shoulder. He seemed to like the position. "We just have to hold on until help arrives." It sounded like Mamoru and his allies were also waiting for someone to show up who would fight the one who assumed the name of god. I wondered if this mystery helper actually did (from our future perspective) come to this time. Information on that had been pretty vague in the future. Fitoria had seemed to recall fragments of something though. Maybe they were going to show up.

"I will continue to observe you closely," Natalia finished. She was going to be in the village for a while. I quickly convinced her to teach Raphtalia and Ruft some new tricks. Melty also had an incredulous look on her face when she heard about everything that had happened, since she was completely removed from it all this time. Eclair, for her part, had a look on her face like she would rather have taken part than have been off guarding Melty—but who cared about that?

Chapter Eight: The Troubles of the Shield Hero

A semblance of everyday life returned to the village for a while.

Raphtalia's healing and Raph-chan's illusion magic helped treat Keel's trauma, and the simulated fights with the cerberus seemed to be having a positive effect too. We were putting together a comprehensive plan that included letting those who were still suffering consider Holn's modification. Piensa was desperate to simply quell their own internal unrest, and it didn't seem likely they would make a big move anytime soon. Melty and the others were giving them the runaround, in the best possible way. With Natalia resident in Siltran now, it made it even harder for Piensa to send heroes into battle. We just had to pray they didn't make a stupid mistake.

One evening when we had finished our trading for the day and I was suggesting to Raphtalia that we return to the village, I noticed Cian—who was also along for the ride—looking at me like she wanted to say something. I gave Raphtalia a puzzled look for a moment.

"What's up?" I asked Cian. There was no reply, and she just looked down. Maybe I needed to take this to Mamoru.

"What's going on?" Keel said, coming over. She had helped bring in a lot of customers again today.

"You're the Shield Hero from the future, right?" Cian finally asked.

"Yeah," I replied.

"The same as Mamoru, right?" Cian said, seeking further confirmation.

"I mean, sure—I'm the Shield Hero. That's the same, at least," I told her.

"And you've managed to fix Keel's trauma?" Cian continued. I looked over at Keel. It seemed we were making progress in that direction. I wasn't sure exactly how much, but it seemed wise to give a definite answer here. Something was up with Cian.

"Yeah," I confirmed.

"Does that mean . . . you can save Mamoru too?" Cian asked.

"Save him?" I replied. Mamoru was the one saving Siltran, surely. Then I remembered something from the whole Holn security breach fiasco. When I asked him if he could deal with Holn, he had almost started to hyperventilate like Keel. I had suspected that there was something going on there, and now it seemed that Cian knew the truth and was looking to do something about it. Mamoru took good care of these kids, and they were an energetic and helpful bunch. They had helped out a lot with the trading too. He had made a good relationship with them. "Why are you bringing this to me?" I asked. "Surely you'd be better off asking Holn or R'yne?"

"I don't think they can help. Looking at Fohl made me think that only another Shield Hero could do something about this," she replied. There did seem to be something there with Fohl, but he seemed to struggle a little with her, without even really knowing why himself. "I'm going back to the castle now. Once night falls, will you bring the charm that Holn gave you and come in secret to meet me?" Cian asked. It sounded like she wanted to show me something. She didn't normally talk this much and was very shy—still, she seemed to quite like me.

"Sure, I guess I can do that," I replied, still a little unsure where this was going.

"Thank you. But don't bring too many people. Especially not that person who looks like Raphtalia," Cian said.

"You mean Natalia?" I asked. She nodded. I wondered why Natalia in particular would be undesirable. She did seem to have an Eclair-level streak of inflexibility, so maybe that was it.

"You can bring Fohl and Raphtalia too," Cian continued. Raphtalia, Fohl, and me. I wasn't sure how she was making her picks, but combat-wise, that wasn't a bad party.

"Raph?" asked Raph-chan.

"Sure. If you're good at hiding, you can come," Cian replied, stroking Raph-chan as she moved over to her.

"Dafu," said Dafu-chan. It sounded like she had gotten permission to join us too.

"What about me?" Keel asked hopefully.

THE RISING OF THE SHIELD HERO 21

"You always make a big noise, so definitely not. Don't bring any filolials either," Cian said, crossing her arms in front of her to shut Keel down completely. The two of them still couldn't understand everything the other said, but they were reaching a mutual understanding.

She was being pretty strict on who to bring though! This wasn't a game-type thing where party members were restricted, but there had to be some reason for this.

"Hmmm," I pondered.

"Bubba, what do you think?" Keel asked.

"I don't know exactly what Cian wants to tell us, so this isn't an easy choice. Considering our relationship with Mamoru and Siltran, though, we can't really afford to turn her down," I reasoned. The way Cian was acting, this seemed like a pretty serious issue. It felt like we would be letting something big slip past if we just ignored it. If it was going to be a problem, we needed to get the jump on it now. "Okay," I finally agreed. "We'll see you later."

"Good. Watch out for sentries and security devices. You need to make sure you aren't seen, no matter what," Cian asserted.

"Sure, we'll be fine," I said, a little offhandedly. We returned to the village, and then took Mamoru's allies back to the castle in order to swap them with Melty and the others. Melty was in a great mood, the restoration of Siltran going very well.

Then it was back to the village. We finished eating our evening meal, and then I put together the party as Cian had requested—Raphtalia, Fohl, the Raph-chans, and me—and sneaked in past the Siltran castle gate. Raphtalia and the two cuties had concealment magic, and with our levels and physical training, it was no problem to just climb the walls. We dropped down on the other side and reached our intended destination, the castle garden, to find Cian waiting for us.

"Here we are," I said, keeping my voice low. Cian's ears pricked up and she looked over in our direction.

"Hold on. Don't reveal yourselves," she said, pointing toward the castle wall just as Raphtalia was about to end her concealment magic. There were a number of birds circling around in a fixed loop above the castle walls. Birds at night were definitely out of place.

"Those must be familiars," Raphtalia said. Castle security was using familiars too then.

"If they spot anyone, they make a loud noise. That's how they are set up," Cian said.

"Okay. What do you want us to do then?" I asked.

"Keep noise down to the absolute minimum. I have a pretty good idea where you are," Cian replied. If she could sense us even through Raphtalia's brand of concealment, that meant she had to be super sensitive. "You're there, right, Fohl?" Cian said.

"That's right," he replied haltingly. Cian couldn't see him

THE RISING OF THE SHIELD HERO 21

but still reached out and took his hand, then started off. Fohl didn't seem that happy with the arrangement, but we followed along behind her. Fohl really did seem to have a problem with Cian. He had looked after Atla for so long that he shouldn't have any issues with taking care of kids. I wondered what his deal was.

We proceeded through the Siltran castle as I mulled over these thoughts. It was pretty quiet, all things considered. Back in the village, the nightly ruckus would only just be getting started. Some people would be getting training in after dinner, or taking a bath, or chatting with friends about the day. I'd thought Mamoru would be doing the same with his friends at this time of day. I looked around again. This place was just too quiet.

Thinking about our arrival, I realized the same could be said of the Siltran castle town. There had been some activity, but it hadn't looked like the people had been enjoying themselves . . . just resting, waiting for something. An odd feeling. Even for a small nation, which easily got swept up in conflicts, there seemed to be too much tension in the air. It was almost like they were putting on a show just for us, lively when we were around but quiet when they thought no one was looking.

We continued through the castle.

"Wait a moment here. You absolutely must not make a noise beyond this point," Cian warned us. She released Fohl's hand and then pressed a part of the wall that until a moment ago had just looked like a dead end. With a rumbling, stairs appeared, leading downward. This was becoming a bit of a pattern recently, especially if this was also the work of Holn. She'd made modifications to the castle too.

Then what looked like a monster—it could have been Chick in a slightly more developed form—poked its head out the stairway and looked at Cian with a chirp.

"Fijia, great work on the lookout," Cian said. The monster called Fijia raised one wing in reply. I had all sorts of questions but had been told not to make a noise. The chick thing was chirping enough, that was for sure.

"I know. We're coming," Cian said. Hurried along by this Fijia creature, Cian started down the stairway, beckoning for us to follow her. We proceeded cautiously behind her. Fijia pressed the wall again and the entrance closed up behind us, and then she returned to her post and started preening her wings. Cian said goodbye to Fijia and we started down the passageway. I was still intrigued by the bird. I hadn't seen anything like that here before. Raphtalia seemed to be having similar thoughts and was also having to hold her questions in. Cian, however, was pressing forward, seemingly intent on not letting us waste time with chatter.

A moment later, it felt like we had passed through a membrane of some kind. I looked around the vicinity to see Cian turn back and make a leaf shape with her fingers. She was indicating the accessory that Holn gave us. Maybe it was some kind of key to get through all this security. The passageway itself was much like the hidden base Holn had created for herself in our village, with a sequence of corridors and rooms. She seemed to have spent a lot of time on this one, because we passed numerous doors along the way, but Cian just ignored them and carried on. One of them looked like a prison cell, with a grate to look through. I peered inside and saw someone who looked like a therianthrope sleeping, snoring loudly. That only made this all the more confusing. I couldn't even tell what kind of therianthrope it was. It looked like a sheep but then had fangs and muscles that were more like a wolf. Some kind of human chimera, perhaps. It was a strange thing to see here though—we were still in Siltran, after all.

We continued quietly forward, and then Cian stopped.

"Walk exactly where I do," she told us, as though muttering to herself, and then she started out. I put the Raph-chans on a float shield and followed after Cian, putting each foot carefully after the other. Raphtalia and Fohl then had to follow behind, but this was all going to be too much hassle. I decided to cover the ground with an Air Strike Shield and make it easier for them to proceed. I triggered one for them, and they continued along behind me. There was another door with a gate, so I checked that one too. This time there was a monster that looked a bit like an eagle suspended in one of those cultivation tanks. It was red, a burning, fiery red.

"Next you need to crouch down . . ." Cian said, pointing ahead. I didn't see anything of notice at first but then spotted delicate wires suspended in the air. They might have had cutting effects, but that was meaningless against me. I could just push through them, if I wanted to. If they were connected to some kind of alarm, however, we were finished. The security in here was no laughing matter.

We made it through the traps arrayed against us and continued onward. Eventually, a kid appeared, who looked to be on watch. She looked kind of familiar too. She had a bit of a spaced-out vibe about her, a pale blue color . . . and a rucksack on her back.

"Good evening, Fitoria," Cian said, raising her hand in greeting. Hearing that name made me do a double take. She did look a bit like a younger version of the Fitoria that we knew. It was almost enough to make me make a noise, but I held it in. Fitoria might have sensed something coming from us, because she tilted her head in puzzlement and reached out toward me. I managed to avoid her hand.

"What are you doing?" Cian asked, watching as Fitoria chopped at the air and looked around intently.

"It's like . . . there's something here," Fitoria replied.

"Like what? An invisible man? Just get back to your post," Cian said lightly.

"Okay," Fitoria agreed, still looking a little suspicious as she turned away. That was a close one—and I was still spinning out over having found Fitoria here! This was more than someone else who looked a bit like her. She had feathers on her back and everything. I was sure—pretty sure—that I wasn't wrong.

Cian was clumping along, perhaps trying to make some extra noise to cover us being there. Still unable to talk about anything, we followed where Cian led. Eventually, she brought us to a certain room.

"Hey, Cian. Where have you been?" The speaker was Mamoru. He was in the room, looking at Cian with gentle eyes.

"I wanted to get some night air, so I went for a walk in the gardens," Cian replied.

"I see. It's a modeling day today though, so you need to be on time," Mamoru chided gently. The scene in the room provided the rest of us with a bigger surprise than just having encountered Fitoria. To the right of Mamoru, there were countless cultivation tanks, and inside them were the children who Mamoru looked after. They had their eyes closed, as though they were sleeping. On his left, there was a bird monster like the one from the stairs, but this one looked a bit more human in form. Right in the back, there was one tank larger than all the others, with a single girl floating inside it. She had a face a bit like Fitoria, maybe with some R'yne mixed in. She was also like S'yne and Filo. I wondered who she was.

I also wondered what the hell this entire place was.

"Hey, Mamoru," Cian started.

"What is it?" Mamoru asked. He was attempting to show her to one of the tanks, and Cian had clearly plucked up her courage to speak to him.

"I want you to change back to the old Mamoru," Cian continued. "I can tell how sad you are. That's why we want to get stronger and why we asked for you to give us this strength. If the experiments aren't going well, then we can ask someone other than Holn to help . . ." But Mamoru shook his head, an intensely sad expression on his face.

"I know what you're trying to say," Mamoru replied to her. "But we can't. That isn't an option." What he was saying, combined with his gentle tone, created a strangely prickly atmosphere. "This is the most important time. If we can just make it through, no one will have to suffer anymore. We can make it through the conflict . . . without having to make any sacrifices." I was sure a sound like a puzzle piece clicking into place rang out from inside my head. "Today we're going to be practicing therianthrope transformation. Get inside here . . . I'll lead you into it. Everyone is waiting." But Cian shook her head.

"Mamoru, I'm not going to say I don't want to be strong. I don't think it's a bad thing. But will this really make you smile like before? You only seem to be suffering more and more, recently . . ." Cian said.

"It's fine, Cian. Just do as I say," Mamoru replied.

"I'm sorry, Mamoru. I need you to think ahead!" Cian exclaimed. Then she looked in our direction. Mamoru looked over too, wondering what was going on. That seemed to be our signal. I gave Raphtalia the nod and she dropped the concealment.

"You seem to be conducting some pretty shady experiments down here," I noted sardonically. Mamoru looked like he'd been hit in the stomach.

"Cian!" he roared at her. But Cian was just scratching at her face, as nonchalantly as a real cat might be. "What have you done? You've ruined everything! We're finished!"

"Finished why, exactly? Because of your human experiments on children? Or because Natalia is going to find out about all of this now?" I asked. I was starting to see why Natalia had been sent here from Q'ten Lo—and it wasn't about Holn stepping off the path of a hero or the Bow Hero planning to pull something nasty. It was because Mamoru was dipping his toes into waters best left undisturbed by the Shield Hero. Maybe he had even been corrupted by the Curse Series. Cian had said something about him returning to the "old Mamoru." Based on what I'd seen with the other heroes, I could tell something was going on here. Ren had started out with a strong sense of responsibility, for example, but in many ways, it had been too strong. That had conversely kept him from wanting to get too involved in the affairs of others, along with a fear of making things worse by getting involved. That was why he had started out alone . . . or just with a small group of elite fighters, people he was confident he could protect. Ultimately, although he had overcome the arrogance derived from his gaming history, when I left him in charge of the village, the responsibility had crushed him, leaving him bedridden.

For Itsuki, his overbearing sense of justice had worked against him, sending him on a rampage in which he gave no thought to the situation of others and just followed what he believed was his own justice. He had ultimately lost his individuality as a result of a cursed weapon. While being treated for that, he had been given time to think and mature, and now he had calmed down a lot.

Motoyasu . . . wasn't even worth considering. He was the worst of the bunch by a mile. Now, though, I had to admit, he was also the one among us who wanted to save other people, wanted to believe in other people, the strongest. There were issues with his approach there too, of course, and he didn't think too highly of people. In fact, he only really cared about Filo and the filolials and was becoming a bit of a troublemaker for everyone.

Even I had a totally different personality now from when I first came here. And Cian wanted Mamoru to return to how he had been before.

"This place has just been one surprise after another," I quipped.

"You said it," Raphtalia agreed. "In all sorts of ways. Can you please explain all this?" she asked Mamoru.

"I'm sorry, but that's not on the table," he replied. "Even if you are heroes from the future!" Alarms started to ring out inside the facility, and the doors behind us opened up at once. R'yne came in and then shook her head as she seemingly quickly picked up on what was going on.

"Check it out. The cat's out of the bag, huh?" R'yne said.

"You were in on this too?" I asked her.

"In a roundabout way," R'yne replied. She didn't seem all that happy about it, but she also didn't seem ready to back down, turning her sewing tool into a pair of scissors and popping out her wings. It didn't look like we were going to be able to avoid a fight. "You definitely helped out by keeping Natalia's attention on Holn."

"The alliance between us ends here!" Mamoru exclaimed.

"Cool it. We just want to talk. Can we start with that? We were friends a moment ago," I said. Mamoru had been very cooperative, almost since we first met. There was some shady stuff going on here, but we could work through it.

"I can't stop now! Everyone needs this!" Mamoru ranted.

"Listen to me!" I shouted back. But Mamoru called out a shield with a suspicious-looking aura around it and was fiddling with something in his field of vision. It looked like maybe he had dug up some hidden weapons after all—like something from the Curse Series.

Then the liquid in the cultivation tanks containing the children started to bubble. In the same moment, Cian sank down to the ground, clutching her chest. Then the kids all started to transform . . . following the exact same process that Sadeena and Fohl did when they became therianthropes. I could tell right away that this was something being done to them, however, rather than something they did voluntarily.

Cian had always had some slightly odd things about her. There was that time she moved at super speed onto the back of the ultros and slashed its throat, for example. That kind of behavior, almost instinctual, didn't really match with her level and combat experience. Meaning she was able to rely on some kind of special instincts in battle. That had been a sign of her human modifications—she'd been set up to unconsciously use such abilities.

As I watched Cian turn not into a cat, but a white tiger— the exact same form as a therianthrope hakuko—my guesswork changed to conviction. The other kids were also changing, into shusaku, genmu, and aotatsu therianthropes.

The Shield Hero prior to me had done great work. One of the things he did was act as a go-between for the demi-humans and the humans. I didn't know exactly when that had been, but it was likely around the time that Faubrey was established. The name "Faubrey" suggested to me that the four heroes had worked together to establish the nation. In any case, this was definitely something that happened after the period we were currently visiting.

Then there was also his establishment of the nation of Siltvelt and the affection the four primary races showed him. In this time, though, those four races didn't even exist. There was something about the characteristics of the four primary races of Siltvelt that nagged at me a little—the question of exactly what kind of demi-human they were. I had met a variety of demi-humans and therianthropes in my time here. Every race had characteristics that pointed to a single animal. Raphtalia was a tanuki, Sadeena a killer whale, Keel a dog, and Imiya a mole. There were plenty of others too, and all of them had been animals I recognized.

Apart from the four primary races of Siltvelt, it was easy to say "white tiger" for the hakuko, but something seemed off there too. There had already been enemies like the Phoenix and Spirit Tortoise that seemed rooted in Chinese mythology, and the hakuko seemed more along those lines—like the mythical byakko white tiger. For shusaku, genmu, and aotatsu, there was also the legendary suzaku, genbu, and seiryu. But if seiryu was the dragon, what did that make the other dragons? Exceptions to the rules, perhaps. They could increase their numbers without intervention, after all. This was another world, meaning creatures of their bloodline could exist here too. There had been kappa in Q'ten Lo and I hadn't batted an eyelid—I was well past the point of such things bothering me.

It looked like my original thinking on the matter—that races living in the world of the Sword and Spear had come to settle in Siltvelt after the fusing of the worlds—had been incorrect, anyway.

"Fohl," I said.

"What?" he asked.

"I've worked out why you feel odd around Cian," I told him. It made sense if she was his ancestor—on his father's side, of course.

"Brother . . . this is hardly the time," Fohl replied.

"I'd expect no less from Mr. Naofumi," Raphtalia chipped in. Cian finished her transformation with a growl and looked around. The situation was not especially rosy.

"Cian, can you hear me?" I asked, but she only growled at me angrily in reply. It looked like an incomplete and out-of-control therianthrope transformation. Cian was clearly trying to hold in her aggression, gripping her right arm with her left hand hard enough to draw blood.

"Confusion Target!" Mamoru said, pointing a finger toward us. All the kids immediately turned their aggression toward us and started to measure up the space between us. It looked like even if they lost control once transformed into therianthropes, Mamoru had a skill that he could use to make them attack a specific target. "C'mon Fimonoa!" With that shout, the three-winged birds we had seen on the way here appeared around him. Then I realized what they were—familiars. So he had a skill to summon them, the same as I did for Raph-chan.

I looked around myself, seeing that we were surrounded by Mamoru's allies.

"Shooting Star Shield, Air Strike Float Shield, Second Float Shield!" I set up some barriers and deployed some shields, just in case they attacked. The question now was, how the hell did we get out of this situation?

"Mr. Naofumi," Raphtalia asked, wanting to know what to do.

"Brother," said Fohl, wanting the same thing, even as both of them also prepared for the worst.

"Mamoru, are you serious about fighting us?" I asked him. I couldn't see any reason to go ahead with it. The circumstances seemed different than with the resurrected, and it felt more like he was losing control just because his secrets had been exposed.

"Dafu!" said Dafu-chan, up on my shoulder and making aggressive gestures toward Mamoru. Raph-chan was also up on Raphtalia's shoulder, warning off would-be attackers as well.

"Of course," Mamoru replied. "You've seen all of this now."

"Hah. Mamoru, you're forgetting one important thing," I said. "You've been so worried about Natalia . . . but do you really think Raphtalia is any less strong?" Certain things might have been lost along the way, but Raphtalia was still the Heavenly Emperor in the future. Not to mention, he had to know we had a sakura stone of destiny. Picking up perfectly on what I was doing, Raphtalia and Fohl both changed their weapons to the sakura stone of destiny Katana and Gauntlets, respectively. These anti-hero weapons hadn't been available in Kizuna's world, but it seemed going back in time wasn't enough to stop them.

With this, we could win even if it came down to just shooting skills at each other, meaning experience would be the deciding factor. We could stop their weapon modifiers from working, but the issue was pure stat increases, like those offered by the Whip power-up method that couldn't be nullified until we had the sakura stone of destiny barrier in place. Mamoru was obviously worried about us getting to that point.

"You won't make your pacifier barrier," Mamoru said, lifting his shield and deploying something strangely colored from it. It seemed he had countermeasures in place. "We can still fight you, with the proper preparation." They already had some measures to combat the sakura stone of destiny—of course they did, or things wouldn't have gotten to this point. We'd only come along because Cian had asked, but we ended up being exposed to some pretty crazy secrets.

"Ma, mo . . . no . . . no more . . ." Cian managed to force down her violent urges and force out a few words to Mamoru.

"It's fine, Cian. I'm not going to punish you for something like this. You were only thinking of me. It's fine," Mamoru said, but there was something like pity in his eyes when he looked at her. She wasn't reaching him at all.

Or maybe she was. Maybe that was why he felt so full of betrayal.

We were facing the therianthrope kids, who looked ready to pounce at any moment, Mamoru's familiars, and the girl who looked like Fitoria. Behind us, blocking our escape, was R'yne. It didn't look like we could use portals down here, so even escape would mean smashing our way out.

"Brother," Fohl said again.

"Fohl, I know you don't want to do this. I don't want to either. But I can't see a way out without a bit of fighting," I told him.

"But . . ." he started, and then Mamoru raised his hand and gave the order.

"Go!"

We were going to have to fight.

Chapter Nine: Confusion Target

"Raphtalia!" I said, signaling her with my eyes.

"I know!" she replied amid the growls of the children. We needed to knock them out without getting too . . . fatal. Raphtalia swung her Katana at the first of the incoming therianthropes. "I'm sorry about this. It might hurt a little!" She slashed out with her blade at incredible speed, heading directly for the lead attackers. But the shusaku-like kid skillfully dodged her attempts to hit them. Then they descended upon Raphtalia in a flurry of violence.

"Air Strike Shield!" I shouted, blocking the attacks coming for Raphtalia.

"No way!" Raphtalia was still processing them dodging her attack. Speed-wise, Raphtalia definitely looked like she had moved faster, and yet they had managed to dodge her attack. I wondered if this was due to enhanced physical abilities over reliance on status. Something built into the enhanced therianthropes, perhaps.

"They moved liked Sadeena and Atla do," Raphtalia said.

"Yeah, they do that exact same thing," I replied. Sadeena spent a lot of time honing her skills, but it was still impressive when she dodged attacks in her bulky killer whale therianthrope form.

"But it didn't look as beautiful as when Sadeena does it or Atla did it," Raphtalia added.

"The shusaku can sense wind and fire instinctually, sister!" Fohl shouted. That actually made sense—they were sensitive to the movements of the air and so detected the changes in air pressure caused by Raphtalia's sword and dodged accordingly. That was superhuman for sure. They really shouldn't be pulling stuff like that.

"Over here! Don't forget about me! Scissor Shock!" R'yne shouted, coming at my Shooting Star Shield with one of Mamoru's chirping familiars. A loud noise rang out. R'yne then dropped back, the epitome of hit-and-run tactics. She unleashed a flurry of feathers from her spread wings that also hammered into my barriers. Those wings seemed pretty useful. I'd been hoping S'yne would pick them up before something like this happened.

Fohl was having a hard time of it too, a look of pain on his face as he fought the incoming kids. He didn't seem to be putting his back into it though, as the kids he did send flying quickly recovered and came back at him.

"Air Strike Shield! Second Shield! Dritte Shield!" Mamoru launched his own succession of skills at Fohl, who had stepped out of the protective range of Shooting Star Shield. Shields appeared at Fohl's arms, back, and legs, trying to box him in.

"Hey, are you forgetting I'm the Shield Hero too? Second

Shield, Dritte Shield!" I said. I moved in my float shields to give Fohl some protection, watching out for interference from something like Change Shield. With a grunt, Fohl leapt to the side, trying to get away from the enemy shields. In the same moment, Mamoru started to cast some magic.

"Spirits! World! The Shield Hero makes his plea. Entwine together my opposing magic and the power of the hero. As the source of your power, the Shield Hero implores you. Lend these others unbreakable strength!" Mamoru commanded. I'd never heard this incantation before. Mamoru incanted so quickly, and it included phrases I was unfamiliar with, meaning I couldn't block it with Way of the Dragon Vein. It still felt similar to the magic I'd used in the past, but the way he incanted it was totally different.

Something I'd read once in a magic book passed through my mind. Long ago in this world, there had been a category of magic called "ancient magic." It was one of those tropes in which a powerful technique had been lost to history rather than passed down.

"My turn!" said the Demon Dragon's voice in my head, and in the same moment a breakdown of the magic Mamoru had used was displayed in my field of vision. The Demon Dragon was super annoying, like an unwanted parasite dwelling in my shield, but I had to admit, she could also really help out at times. The Demon Dragon's analysis was that Mamoru had used a direction aura magic that boosted all stats, Liberation-class hero magic. I couldn't let that stand without some kind of reply.

"I, the Shield Hero, order heaven and earth. Cut free the bonds of truth, reconnect them, and spout forth pus. Power of the Dragon Vein, I form power by fusing magic and the power of the hero. The source of your power, the Shield Hero, now orders you. Reconsider the state of all things once more and provide my intended targets with everything. All Liberation Aura! All Emancipation Power Aura!" Now we had both cast auras across all of our allies.

"Oh, look at that. You cast your magic after Mamoru, but it triggered at the same time, meaning you must be the better magician," R'yne quipped lightly, snipping away with her scissors. Powerful shock waves started to batter my Shooting Star Shield.

"I might have a few magic tricks," I said deprecatingly. Magic tricks like a strange onboard personality that popped up and helped out. But I wasn't going to reveal that. I didn't want to keep relying on it, but when it came to reducing magic casting speed, there seemed no reason not to.

"Shield Boomerang!" Mamoru unleashed his fallback physical attack. Raphtalia slashed down with a sword, attempting to send the shield flying away. Then I noticed Mamoru smiling.

"Raphtalia! Don't!" I shouted. She made a puzzled noise. At the same time I shouted "Shooting Star Wall," Mamoru shouted "Change Shield!" I put up a Shooting Star Wall and caught the incoming boomerang. It immediately turned into something like my rope shield and bounced off. The flying shield was also fixed with a sphere containing a mysterious liquid, which splashed over the barrier and hardened. Mamoru made an annoyed noise.

"We're both Shield Heroes, right? Did you think I wouldn't see through that?" I asked him. I had some Change Shield tricks up my own sleeve as well, but I'd only performed them using Air Strike Shield, and I didn't even have Shield Boomerang. So I couldn't do the exact same thing.

I could do something similar using my Frisbee Shield, but that was a little demeaning. I mainly used that to play with Gaelion and others from the village—now that was some extreme Frisbee action. But it couldn't be used with Change Shield anyway.

"You wanted to shut Raphtalia down, but you'll have to do better than that," I quipped. Mamoru scoffed. Even if the sakura stone of destiny erased any incoming skills, he had clearly been hoping to pin Raphtalia down using that hardening liquid. It wasn't going to be that easy.

"Then we'll just pile on!" Mamoru exclaimed. His familiars all moved up into a protective formation and he started to incant some magic.

"Spirits! World! The Shield Hero makes his plea to break

these chains. Oh, hear our plea! Entwine together my opposing magic and the power of the hero. As the source of your power, the Shield Hero implores you. Tear these others apart with blades of pure air!" Mamoru shouted. His familiars were chirping.

"Raph, raph, raph!" said Raph-chan.

"Dafu, dafu!" added Dafu-chan. The two of them started up with their own magic. A request for cooperative magic promptly came over to me. Since I started using Liberation, I'd had cases of not being able to use cooperative magic all the time.

"I see. That's an issue with the output of those you are collaborating with, surely. This is where I come in!" the Demon Dragon said inside my head, offering an explanation I didn't ask for and then supporting my incanting. It felt like something that hadn't been working for some unknown reason had suddenly clicked into place.

"Take two powers and imbue them with illusions to confuse all foes, turning a destiny of defeat into a future of victory . . . Dragon Vein! Hear our petition and grant it! As the source of your power, we implore you! Let the true way be revealed once more! Show our enemies illusions to confound them!" I shouted.

"Raph, raph, raph!" joined in Raph-chan. In the instant we finished the incantation, a wind whipped up around us.

The Demon Dragon's parasitic personality was letting us know that it thought Mamoru's familiars were trying to use some wind attack magic.

"Mamoru! Please, stop it!" Cian grabbed onto Mamoru from behind in an attempt to stop him, but it did not sway him and he unleashed the combination magic.

"Tornado Corridor!" Mamoru shouted. His familiars instantly unleashed countless small tornados.

"Sister! Watch out! Air Strike Tornado Blow X!" Fohl shouted in response.

"Hah! Swallow Fall!" Raphtalia responded with a skill of her own, the two of them smashing the tornados down, avoiding them. They were capably handling both the highly mobile tornados and the wild attacks from the children.

The magic was actually weaker than I expected. It seemed that Mamoru's main magic was more about impeding the movements of his enemies than causing damage. We were both Shield Heroes, after all—there was no getting away from certain things. The next issue he was going to face, however, was a fundamental flaw in his selection of magic.

"Emptiness Is Form: Hollow!" I shouted.

"Raph!" added Raph-chan. We completed our own combination magic and unleashed it. I could tell this was a powered-up version of the Emptiness Is Form we had used before. We directed it at Mamoru's allies, the children, and R'yne.

"Ah, uwah . . . Naofumi, you're playing dirty . . ." R'yne put her hand to her forehead and moaned.

"Unfortunately for you guys, I can't use attack magic thanks to this shield. Even my combination magic tends to turn out like this," I replied. It might not be all that effective against other heroes, but it was still combination magic imbued with the power of the Raph-chans and myself. It was going to have a certain degree of effect.

"Mamoru can attack, can't he?" R'yne managed. She was still harping on that. We were both the Shield Hero, so I had no idea why I couldn't fight too—at least a little.

The kids seemed to have lost their target and were now growling and rampaging around on their own. What had actually happened was that they were still seeing their targets—us—but just a massive number of us. This was the illusory power of the Raph-chans.

"I'm not finished yet! Cian! Get off!" Mamoru barked. Cian cried out and then weakly called Mamoru's name as he tossed her aside. "You all only know a Shield Hero specialized entirely for defense! So now I'll show you a fighting style you've never seen before!" Mamoru changed the shield on his arm to a jet-black one. I'd never seen one like it. It was cross-shaped, like a black version of the Spirit Tortoise Heart Shield. I could feel something nasty from it though—something similar to rage. I had a really bad feeling about this. It definitely wasn't your ordinary shield!

"Mamoru! You really are getting serious," R'yne said, bracing herself. "Naofumi, you might want to make a run for it." She didn't seem able to move herself, perhaps still caught up in the illusions. She didn't know which ones were the real us and was basing her actions on what Mamoru was doing, seeing as he was unaffected.

"Guardian Shield! Hate Reaction!" Mamoru activated another skill. Raphtalia and Fohl were affected by the Hate Reaction and started to shake their heads over and over to try and escape it.

"It really is unpleasant to have your skills used against us, Mr. Naofumi," Raphtalia said.

"Hate Reaction is a skill that draws enemy attention, right? What happens when it affects you?" I asked.

"It actually increases attack a little while lowering defense. It also makes it harder for you to look away from someone," Raphtalia said. I hadn't known any of that, but I could tell that any difference it was making was only minor.

"It can also interrupt magic casting," the Demon Dragon offered inside my head. I could use fewer interruptions like that!

"We need to get Mamoru under control first. Raphtalia, Fohl!" I shouted. They responded affirmatively and leapt forward, beginning to attack Mamoru with each of their weapons. They were using life force and wielding weapons made from the sakura stone of destiny, so it was likely to do more than just sting a little. They'd keep it to just knocking him out, I was sure.

"Spirit Blade! Soul Slice!" That was Raphtalia's offering.

"Air Strike Stun Blow V!" added Fohl. Mamoru took Raphtalia's Katana on an unbreakable shield and then grabbed Fohl's arm and tossed him away. I blinked, unsure what had just happened. "I'm not done yet! Sorry, but I'm not giving up this chance! Afterimage Palm VI!" Fohl shouted as he recovered at once, going into his own therianthrope form and charging forward. He had formed semitransparent clones who fought alongside him. They seemed to offer physical attacks. The two additional ghost-Fohls matched Fohl's movements and struck with follow-ups at Mamoru. That was a pretty convenient-looking attack. I hadn't expected much from him recently, but maybe I had to rethink that. Mamoru defended against all the attacks, but with heavy impact noises. He was letting his life force flow out from his feet. Those techniques were the same as the ones we used.

"My turn! Eight Trigrams Blade of Destiny Combination! Formation One! Formation Two! Formation Three!" Raphtalia was right there, following up seamlessly behind Fohl. Her selection was a three-strike, vastly powered-up edition of her Eight Trigrams Blade of Destiny. A very surprising attack. The combination almost looked like too much, but Mamoru took Raphtalia's attacks on his shield while letting Fohl's hit him in the body.

He did grunt at that though, and some blood spilled from

his mouth. Perhaps hesitating a little at that reaction, Raphtalia and Fohl leapt back. I watched things unfold, kind of hoping— somewhat naively—that this would take Mamoru down. But apart from the blood, nothing else changed.

"That's it? That's the best you've got? If you want to stop me, you'd better try and kill me!" he raged, taunting us further. I took a mental step back and looked at Mamoru's shield. It had a large gemstone in the middle, like the Spirit Tortoise Heart Shield. But I noticed it had a suspicious purple light flickering there. I didn't like that much either. The damage we had caused to Mamoru was gradually being healed. I didn't know if it was an effect of the shield or some physical modification he had performed on himself in this strange facility, but it was definitely going to be a pain to fight it.

We'd started fighting, but I'd also made a promise to Cian; we couldn't afford to kill Mamoru. I'd been hoping to just knock him out, but when I thought about the enemies we had fought in the past . . . it was going to be hard to hold back. He wasn't someone we could incapacitate by taking his weapon away, like we had with Takt. And while the sakura stone of destiny weapons could nullify his attacks to a certain extent, they couldn't actually cut through his shield. We might be able to nullify his power boost, but Mamoru didn't seem that picky about magic in that regard, so it would create an opening for him to exploit.

"If you can't do better than this, we're finished here!

Confusion Target!" Mamoru shouted, unleashing his skill to command the rampaging children again—perhaps finally losing patience with us completely. But rather than attack us, the growling kids started attacking him! The confused kids were still suffering from the illusions we had unleashed on them, seeing copies of us all around them. And so he'd ordered them to attack himself—their ally! They crowded all over him, but he withstood all of their attacks.

They might have lost all reason, or they might have understood what they were doing, because the kids had tears streaming down their faces as they attacked Mamoru. I looked on with my allies, each of us aghast at what was unfolding here.

"What's he even thinking?" Raphtalia asked. I was analyzing his actions too, and it was starting to dawn on me. This was something that perhaps only the Shield Hero could understand.

"Even if you are the Shield Hero from the future, there's no way . . . you know about this shield! With all your sarcasm, you underestimate the weight of being Shield Hero. You will never reach these heights! Now face its power!" Mamoru ranted. The light around the crystal in Mamoru's shield was sparkling brightly now, even as the kids continued to beat on him. That was the moment when my patience finally shattered.

"You've got a bigger mouth than I thought!" I shouted. He made it sound like I was some casual lightweight who made fun of everything. I might have started to think maybe I didn't have it so bad compared to what Raphtalia, Keel, and Imiya had been through. But I'd still been through my fair share. My irritation started to peak, and I lost the desire to hold back against Mamoru. Thinking about it, I realized Cian had shown us here and we'd witnessed the negative side of Mamoru. That was all that had happened. Yet it had now blown up into a whole big thing.

We need to prioritize working out what Mamoru was planning on doing. I'd been something of a gamer myself back in Japan, and so multiple options came to mind. I was also the Shield Hero myself. So that provided me with more possible attack patterns he might be using—if certain shields that I personally didn't have access to existed.

"Raphtalia, Fohl. Get back!" I shouted. Raphtalia sounded surprised.

"Brother, we should press the attack," Fohl said.

"Piling onto him won't work now. Just drop back!" I told them. When I gave that order, Mamoru unleashed an evil aura with a raging shout. The aura sent the kids tumbling away from him and also cancelled their targeting commands. As the kids started to chase around all the illusions we had created for them again, Mamoru dashed forward to defend R'yne. Then he pointed his eerily glittering shield in our direction.

It looked like one of my hunches had been right.

"Fimonoa!" Mamoru shouted. His bird-like familiars all chirped again, including the girl called Fitoria. She turned into her bird form. They all moved over to Mamoru and spread their wings. Then the birds' wings started to sparkle too, scattering a sparkling barrier around themselves—almost like they were acting to discharge the heat coming from Mamoru. It looked like he was using the discharged energy to reduce the damage to his allies. That could be convenient.

"Mr. Naofumi, is this . . . what I think it is?!" Raphtalia asked.

"Yeah, Mamoru is going to use some kind of special attack. Get back!" I said again. We didn't know what kind of powerful strike he was going to unleash, so trying to avoid it would be risky. There wasn't much room to move around inside the narrow chamber anyway, so Mamoru could simply redirect the attack even if we tried to get out of the way.

I was presuming the skill or attack that Mamoru was attempting to unleash involved accumulating power through the attacks he had taken on the shield and then unleashing it after building up a certain amount of energy—a powerful special attack. I was feeling jealous again. In terms of attacks I could use, among those without severe repercussions, Iron Maiden was pretty much my only choice, and that was hardly worth it. I could never sustain combat while using something like Blood Sacrifice.

In regard to the Shield of Wrath, the curse on it was too powerful; I could use it as float shield, perhaps, but if I brought the actual shield up, I knew I'd get swallowed by the anger. My only option there would be to change to the Shield of Compassion before I sank into a complete rampage. That was how dangerous the Shield of Wrath was after being enhanced by the Demon Dragon, even if I used enhancements to purposefully lower its stats.

I took a look to see that an item sealed by the Shield of Compassion was active again thanks to the Demon Dragon—or maybe the Shield of Compassion itself. I'd failed to overcome my wrath completely, meaning I'd been unable to completely unlock the power of compassion. That might make sense. The Shield of Wrath had the powerful counter-effect called Dark Curse Burning, but that could only be triggered by being attacked.

My jealousy surged again. We were both the same Shield Hero, and yet he had access to all sorts of attack shields.

"Sorry, but I'm not joining your pity party!" I shouted. "Change Shield!" I sent my two float shields toward Mamoru and his minions, turning them into the Shield of Wrath and the Shield of Compassion. I'd pulled this off before because the Demon Dragon was around, so I couldn't be sure it would work again, but it had to be worth a try.

"Raph!" said Raph-chan.

"Dafu!" added Dafu-chan. They were up on my shoulders again, and I felt something similar to when I'd done this with the Demon Dragon. Raph-chans really could pull out all sorts of tricks!

"This will finish you off! Karmic Overload!" Mamoru retorted. Black flames blazed up from his shield, forming a single flickering black line that came right for us. I lifted my Sakura Stone of Destiny Shield and brought together my Shield of Wrath and Shield of Compassion float shields in order to try and block the attack. I immediately grunted as the brunt of it hit me—it was powerful! I'd been hoping to redirect it off to the side, but it was too powerful to do that easily. I'd caught the attack on the shields of compassion, wrath, and sakura stone of destiny, and yet light was still flickering around the edges to burn my skin. This was while I was using the Sakura Stone of Destiny Shield, with its boosted effects against heroes. The raw power of this attack was not to be underestimated.

"Mr. Naofumi!" Raphtalia shouted.

"Brother!" Fohl cried out.

"Stay behind me!" I told them. An attack of this power, the heat radiating from it, it reminded me of a moment from the past—the moment when the Phoenix self-destructed. The moment I stepped forward, to protect everyone, and then when Atla had stepped in just when I realized I wasn't going to be enough.

I let out a roar through clenched teeth, begging the Shield of Wrath and Shield of Compassion to be enough. I couldn't suffer such a defeat, such a trampling again. I would defend those behind me, no matter what. I was stronger than I was back then . . . and I'd sworn to protect everyone. I'd overcome whatever trials I had to face in order to achieve that. If what the Demon Dragon had said was true, that failing to overcome my wrath was holding back my strength, then I'd overcome that too.

The two emotions seemed at complete odds with each other—to forgive someone, while being anger with them, and to bring wrath upon an enemy who had to be defeated, with no room for compassion. Yet if they would let me protect everyone, that was what I would use!

I continued my roar, and the Shield of Wrath and Shield of Compassion started to spin around together. Black and white . . . as they spun, they drew closer to the design of the Sakura Stone of Destiny Shield and its yin-yang stylings. I used the resulting shield to take the full brunt of the attack. Still shouting, I saw my Shield of Wrath and Shield of Compassion float shields were finally able to shred Mamoru's attack to pieces.

"What? Impossible! How were you able to block that?!" Mamoru seethed. The black light he emitted finally dissipated away.

"Hey, predecessor . . ." I growled, breathing hard as the smoke cleared. "You'd better not underestimate me! What do you mean, the weight of the Shield Hero? Pathetic! If you think you've got it hard, then you've no idea how hard things can get!" He was worse than Ren! If he was going to go on about how hard it was to be a hero, he wasn't going to make it very far into the future. He had no idea of the volume of shit I'd been forced to wade through. I'd lost track of it myself. There were more stars in the sky than moments of pain I had suffered. But I carried the pain of the Shield Hero, for Raphtalia, for Atla, for everyone. I didn't need to take out my own cursed weapon and take part in some pity party!

"Mamoru, when you say it's the end, what do you mean? What's the problem here? You need to stop judging other people so quickly. Just take a look around. Come on!" I raged. Right behind him there was Cian, desperately trying to control her therianthrope transformation, and then around him there were the rampaging kids and R'yne. There were loads of other people in this underground facility too.

Mamoru still looked stunned that I'd withstood his special attack. If he didn't start to show some decorum, I'd order Raphtalia to attack the precious-looking tank stored in the back.

"What kind of hero are you?" I asked. "Bow? Sword? Spear? Is this the best way for you to fight?" Mamoru gave a moan. We were both shield heroes, and there was a difference in the way we fought, but I still couldn't believe this situation was the best for Mamoru. If it was, then I'd overestimated him considerably. If that did turn out to be the case, I'd have to report him to Natalia.

"Okay . . . we're all played out," R'yne said. She seemed to have recovered from the illusion's effects and sat down on the spot with her hands up.

"R'yne, don't give up!" Mamoru said.

"Mamoru, can't you see? Naofumi is taking care not to destroy those things precious to you," R'yne replied. She pointed down at the cultivation tank at the back.

"Please, Mamoru . . . please. No more fighting . . ." Cian managed, still collapsed on the ground but reaching toward him nonetheless.

"But . . . but . . ." Mamoru stammered, but he also dropped his fighting stance and changed his shield. It looked like the fighting was over, at least for now.

"Brother believed in you . . . and he still wants to," Fohl said. Mamoru didn't reply. "Please, tell us what's going on. We'll do whatever we can to help." Fohl looked over at the floating Shield of Compassion as he spoke. If Atla's brother was willing to go so far, I guess I could negotiate a little, in the name of the Shield of Compassion.

"Let's get some details then," I said. "How have you changed? What's been eating you so badly? Don't waste what Cian tried to do here," I told him.

"Mr. Naofumi, don't be like that," Raphtalia chided me.

"Brother . . . can't you be a little gentler?" Fohl added. I was going to have to take that under advisement; this seemed about the right level for me. I was still under the effects of the Shield of Wrath too.

"Hah!" I scoffed. "I'm just a sardonic semi-hero who takes my responsibilities too lightly, right? So what do you expect?"

"If I had to choose one, right now you are the Mirror Hero, Mr. Naofumi," Raphtalia said gently.

"So you do get it?" I replied. Raphtalia knew how to handle me, I'd give her that. I knew I was acting like a moody child. But that was just my personality. I couldn't sit still unless I got to put the boot in, at least a little. I needed to say my piece.

"Okay . . . R'yne, Cian, everyone . . . I'm sorry," Mamoru said. Then he started to treat each of the children in turn. Whatever he was doing reversed the therianthrope transformation, turning them back to normal, but they were still unconscious. Then he returned each child to their own empty cultivation tank. "Please, can you help?" Mamoru asked. "If we don't put them back into the tanks, it will take longer for them to recover."

"Okay," I finally said. Tending to wounds and recovering physical strength were two different things. Liberation Heal could treat wounds, not stamina. Other magic could be more useful in that regard, but it would also increase the burden on me. The kids had been in the middle of being modified too, which meant giving them the wrong treatment could simply mess them up. It would be for the best if Mamoru could heal them with whatever technology he had here. So we helped to carry each of the collapsed kids back to their cultivation tanks.

"Keel's . . . Shield Hero . . ." Cian moaned as I lifted her up.

"I'm here," I replied.

"Mamoru . . . isn't a bad person . . . Forgive him . . ." Cian managed to say. "I'm sorry for attacking you . . . Please, forgive him . . ."

"We're the ones . . . at fault . . ." said another kid. Each one of them, barely conscious, was saying the same kind of thing. It hit me hard. The kids were clearly the victims here, but all of them were still trying to protect Mamoru. That not only told me how likable Mamoru was—or had been at one point—but also how the kids still trusted him, even after this outburst. It almost reminded me of the women Kyo and Takt had kept around, but there was a fundamental difference.

Those bitches had given orders. These kids pleaded and begged.

Takt's women had ordered us to stop beating him. These kids were asking us, begging us, not to punish Mamoru. We had to approach this from a place of discussion. That was what Cian had wanted too.

"Mr. Naofumi. . ." said Raphtalia.

"Brother . . ." said Fohl. The two of them were also helping take care of the kids while looking at me with concern on their faces.

"Raph!" said Raph-chan.

"Dafu!" said Dafu-chan. The two cuties seemed to understand the gravity of the situation as well, with troubled looks.

"Mamoru . . ." Cian turned back from her therianthrope form and looked over at Mamoru.

"Cian, we need to treat you too," Mamoru said, but Cian shook her head.

"I'm fine . . . no need." Cian had used her powerful mental capacity to prevent herself from going on a rampage. All the other kids had lost it completely, but not her. That was proof enough of her incredible mental fortitude.

"One last thing, then . . ." Mamoru operated a terminal and the tanks containing the kids filled up with liquid. The kids' suffering quickly seemed to be eased, and they floated in each of their tanks as though simply sleeping. All the pain from moments before was gone.

"Now that that's handled," I said pointedly, turning back to the two people who hadn't been put into that goop. "Let's hear it. Mamoru. R'yne."

"You finally finished asking questions?" I turned around at the voice to see Holn coming in, like it was the most natural thing ever. "Oh, don't worry about little old me. I've no intention of fighting you." She raised both hands to prove her point.

"Why aren't I surprised to see you here? You knew about all this?" I asked. She'd given me that leaf accessory because she'd expected this to happen.

"You bet. That's why I caused the ruckus in your village, of course. That was all about the trauma Mamoru carries around with him too. That's also why I gave you that leaf accessory." Considering how similar this had all been to that time, I had thought they were related. "I expected this confrontation, so I wanted to train you for it. Now, future Shield Hero, listen to what Mamoru has to say." I shook my head. She was a master manipulator. Mamoru furrowed his brow at Holn's attitude but took a deep breath and started to speak.

"Why have we strayed so far from the path . . ." he muttered before starting to share what were clearly painful memories. "The beginning was . . . when Filolia died, I guess."

"Filolia?" I asked.

"Yeah," he replied. That name gave me pause too—it was only one letter off "filolial." Maybe it was the name of the one floating in the tank at the back of the room. Maybe they'd taken a page from Rat's playbook. Mamoru's familiars, now turned into small birds, gathered on his shoulders, chirping. Mamoru stroked them gently with obvious tender care.

"I didn't make the introductions yet, did I? These are my familiars, Fimonoa, Fijia, and Fitoria. Filolia is the one who named them. They are familiars derived from her," Mamoru explained.

"Raph!" said Raph-chan.

"Dafu!" said Dafu-chan.

"Although they don't have the same level of awareness, they might be like those familiars you love so much, Naofumi," Mamoru said. Raph-chan climbed down from my shoulder and went over to greet Fimonoa and the others. That made sense. Just like I'd made Raph-chan as a familiar from Raphtalia's hair, Mamoru had created these familiars from one of his allies. Mamoru was still stroking his familiars, smiling . . . but with a sad look on his face.

"I see," Raphtalia said, accepting that situation.

"Filolia was quite something," Mamoru continued. "She was summoned here as the Claw Hero from the same world that R'yne comes from."

It was the story of the dead user of the Claw vassal weapon and how Mamoru had lost someone impossible to replace. After Mamoru was summoned here as the Shield Hero, he started his activities in Siltran and then met with Filolia, who had also been summoned here to be the Claw Hero. Filolia had at first been bewildered at being summoned to another world, but she adapted quickly and had soon become Mamoru's right hand in fighting. Fighting for such a small and weak nation as Siltran, Mamoru had lacked other allies. He had made it through those trying times by combining his strength with that of the girl called Filolia.

"I met up with Mamoru when I came looking for my missing sister," R'yne said. "It was pretty crazy for me too.

My precious little sis suddenly vanished, and when I worked out where she'd been taken to . . . she was the Claw Hero in a completely different world." Filolia was also the connection that brought R'yne and Mamoru together. Filolia had been summoned here from another world to be the Claw Hero. The world she had come from was R'yne's world, and Filolia's sister was R'yne . . . Kind of a complex relationship. It was similar to the situation Shildina was in, perhaps. It seemed likely that she hadn't originally been summoned because she'd been in Q'ten Lo, and once she left, she had been summoned to Kizuna's world as the Ofuda Hero.

"We fought for Filolia's attention for a while, didn't we, R'yne?" Mamoru reminisced.

"That takes me back," R'yne replied. "We didn't really get off on the right foot." Both of them seemed to be enjoying this trip down memory lane. It was an interesting development for sure. They hadn't looked like a happy couple, exactly. Now I knew why R'yne was hanging around in this world—to take her sister home. Maybe she was even going back and forth, popping in to see her sister sometimes.

"Back then . . . things were hard, but we all truly believed that by working together we could overcome anything," Mamoru continued. The change had come when they fought Suzaku, one of the guardian beasts. "The battle took place close to the Siltran castle town itself. We were desperate to hold our enemy back, but it wasn't going well for us . . . and Suzaku was about to attack some of our allies who couldn't get away in time." Mamoru had stepped up to defend the people of Siltran but had been unable to stop the raging attack from Suzaku, and those people were about to be killed.

"That was when Filolia stepped forward and defended everyone . . ." R'yne said.

"It was our fault," Cian said. "We wanted to support Mamoru, so we'd sneaked out and hid to watch the battle." It sounded like this girl called Filolia had used her body to shield Cian and the other kids from the rage of Suzaku. "Filolia knocked us aside as hard as she could toward Mamoru . . . and then, right in front of our eyes . . ." Cian could barely finish, eventually managing to say that Filolia had been hit by the blazing fire from Suzaku and simply turned to ash.

"After that," Mamoru said, his voice shaking with memories he didn't want to relive, "somehow, we managed to defeat Suzaku . . ." He paused. "I was in love with her. She and I managed to win R'yne over, and after the battle with Suzaku, we were planning to hold a wedding."

"Just a little longer and I would have got to see my sister on her wedding day," R'yne said. Happiness found on the battlefield had then turned to despair. It reminded me so much of Atla it made my head ache for a moment.

"Sadness wasn't going to end the battle though. It wasn't

going to end the waves," Mamoru continued. "I couldn't allow
there to be another Filolia. I couldn't afford to remain so weak!
That's why . . . I started seeking further strength." It sounded
like he was pretty aware that he'd stepped off the path, but also
that he never wanted to lose anyone again—no matter what it
took. I'd had similar feelings after losing Atla and the others.
"No matter what it took, no matter what would rain down on
me, I didn't care. In order to not lose anyone again, to defend
everyone, to stop anyone else from dying . . . I needed strength.
Holn started teaching me all sorts of things . . . and I started
using alchemy to modify everyone."

"That's right," Holn stepped in. "I've been teaching him
various things." All of this would have been hard for Mamoru
to do alone. But I wondered if that meant he was doing it all
himself, just within the range Holn taught to him, or if Holn
was just helping to cover Mamoru's mistakes.

"So you've been modifying the Siltran people so that they
can survive any possible battle?" I asked.

"That's right," Mamoru eventually admitted. "I didn't want
to lose anyone else. I wanted them to be able to face any possible danger." His voice was trembling.

"We feel responsible too . . . so we asked Mamoru to do
this. We wanted to do whatever we could to help him . . . wanted
to cheer him up, however we could," Cian added.

"That explains why you've been modifying Cian," I said.
"But you didn't hold back, did you?"

"We discovered that the materials from the guardian beasts—Byakko, Suzaku, Genbu, and Seiryu—including some we received from R'yne and other worlds—would provide incredible modifications. So we started embedding them into the kids. It took a little time for them to get used to the changes, but they were reborn as new races. Bringing in the beast transformation process, which only a few races have access to, should make them even stronger."

"Future Shield Hero," Holn said, offering additional explanation. "When I saw Keel's factors, I understood what was going on. You have all sorts of races in the future with access to therianthrope transformations, correct? I think most of them are probably the result of the work Mamoru and little old me did back here."

"Which means . . . everyone in this world who can turn into a therianthrope have the factors that you and Mamoru introduced, and those factors will then be passed down to their children, creating all the therianthropes in the future?" I asked.

"That's likely the case. That's why I said it wasn't any fun," Holn replied. So this was what she meant when she talked about a pain in her brain at realizing something she simply had to do. It was like the results of her own research coming from the future to meet her. Some people might be further motivated by knowing the results, but for Holn . . . she wanted to take on the unknown, something with no idea of success or failure, and so that was why she didn't like it.

It was like gambling for her. A game you were definitely going to win might be fun for a while, but just winning all the time would eventually become boring. For someone who lived for the pleasure of winning or losing, that would be very dull.

"There are other things too, but we can't afford to pack too much in. Let's keep the discussion moving," Holn suggested.

"What about that, then?" I pointed down to the back of the room, to the tank that was separate from the ones with the kids inside.

"That . . . is my attempt, by whatever means . . . to get back my lost Filolia . . ." Mamoru said. Another trope reared its head, but I could understand this one too.

"So while researching your experiments on the kids and people of Siltran, you were also looking for ways to bring someone back," I said.

"That's right. But it's not easy. Filolia was killed by one of the guardian beasts, Suzaku . . . which means normally Suzaku would absorb her soul and use it in the barrier that protects the world," Mamoru explained. I remembered Ost saying that the Spirit Tortoise had similar properties—that those killed by the guardian beasts went on to protect the world. "But I couldn't give up. I was able to obtain a part of Suzaku . . . a part with Filolia's soul inside it, before it melted back into the world." It sounded like he'd obtained the power of the barrier. That was something sure to make the Shield Spirit mad—maybe that was even why Natalia had been called in. If we had access to that technique S'yne's sworn enemies used—being able to bring someone back so long as you had their soul—we might have been able to resolve Mamoru's problem. Still, even that might be tricky if part of the soul had been absorbed. "So I've been analyzing the factors of the Suzaku and gradually working on how to bring Filolia back before her absorbed soul is blended into the world completely. Luckily, we have some of Filolia's genetic material here . . . in the form of Fimonoa and the others," Mamoru continued. I couldn't help but click my tongue in annoyance and frustration.

"Brother . . ." Fohl said. This was all making me feel awful. It was like this was some shared fate of the Shield Hero, some horrible rite of passage we all had to go through. Losing a precious companion to a guardian beast! It was like the world was mocking us.

"It's so similar. It seems like some sick joke," I said. "A horrible coincidence." History repeating. None of us needed that. "Cian," I said, managing to push down my irritation.

"What is it?" she asked.

"This really is such a strange fate," I mused. Cian was probably Atla and Fohl's ancestor. Cian had seen the pain in my own heart and had asked me to help convince Mamoru to stop.

Things might still have been better for me. Atla had been hit by the Phoenix's attack, but she hadn't died right away. I'd been able to put her inside my shield, preventing the Phoenix from taking her and providing me with a chance to see her again. But I couldn't be sure I wouldn't have taken the same route as Mamoru if my circumstances had been different, if someone else, someone like Raphtalia, had simply been erased from existence by a guardian beast in an act of self-sacrifice like Filolia. It reminded me of when Takt first got the jump on us. If Raphtalia really had been killed then . . . It made my spine shudder. Even though we were here from the future, we had no way of knowing if Mamoru would finally succeed in reviving his lost love. Taking that a step further, we had no idea if Cian's wish could come true and Mamoru could return to his old self. But that wasn't going to stop me from trying. Cian had come to me because Mamoru was so lost.

"Mamoru. You're forgetting something important," I told him. "What's the power-up method for the shield holy weapon? Trust, right? The people of Siltran believe in you. That's why they're offering up their bodies and seeking further strength. What's going to happen if you repay that by showing hesitation and concern?" The Shield Hero got stronger by believing in people and having them believe in him. By taking on the expectations of others and fighting alongside them. I thought it was kind of corny myself, but I wasn't going to hide behind that now.

I'd decided to defeat everyone who wanted to harm me or

my friends and to protect the world. I might not be the Demon Dragon, but I was still willing to aim powerful rage at my enemies.

Cian began to speak. "Filolia said it was strange that Mamoru was always on the front lines. That her own world was suffering under the waves, and so we couldn't leave it just to the heroes. But we were weak . . . so all we could do was run from the fighting," Cian said. That was why she had sought this new strength. Siltran was a small nation that had always been picked on. It raised up Mamoru as their hero and decided to fight alongside him. "But even after we raised our levels and abilities . . . we still couldn't hope to hold our own against the fighters the Bow Hero and Piensa raised."

"Really?" I asked. Back in our time, it wasn't just limited to the villagers—pretty much anyone could become strong with some training.

"No matter how much you raise someone's level, ultimately their innate nature is going to come shining through. Do you know what I'm talking about, future Shield Hero?" Holn asked. I thought for a moment. I decided it was best to refer to Sadeena as an example here, as she had the most honed combat instincts of my allies. In terms of performance in battle, she was at least five times stronger than anyone at the same level. If she fought with Raphtalia at the same level . . . I was sure Sadeena would win. No question. Raphtalia and Sadeena had trained together before we came to this world, and Sadeena had hardly broken a sweat fending off a powerful flurry of attacks from Raphtalia. The old Hengen Muso lady had said that apart from using Hengen Muso Style to control life force, she had nothing to teach Sadeena.

And this was against Raphtalia, one chosen as the Katana vassal weapon holder and excellent in battle. Keel and Imiya simply wouldn't stand a chance against her under any circumstances I could imagine. No matter how hard they worked to reach that same level, there would always be a gap between them.

In the case of Siltran, we were looking at herbivore-type citizens with almost no combat sensibilities. My villagers were making gains because I was raising them from the ground up, but I couldn't vouch for what would happen if they fought people enhanced in the same way Mamoru was doing.

"Even if we use my Whip power-up method, it's difficult to catch up with those who have already been enhanced over a long period of time. Even worse, such enhancements are hardly passed down at all and will completely vanish after maybe three generations," Holn added. So the first generation was enhanced by the hero and obtained powerful strength. The second generation was trained and raised by the first, reaching a reasonable level of strength. But by the third generation, we reached a point where they didn't even know the struggles of the first. "Wealth only lasts three generations," they say. But who wouldn't want an age of peace to last longer? I could see why Mamoru had been modifying everyone to make them stronger, including his desire for peace in his actions.

"Mamoru, I've been keeping this quiet, but let me fill you in. Getting my answers from the future is really, really boring. But I can tell you that they are going to stabilize very soon. They won't need permanent supervision anymore," Holn said.

"I see," Mamoru finally replied. It sounded like it wasn't going to be long before the four primary races of Siltvelt showed their faces to the world.

"Mamoru. What would your precious Filolia say if she could see you now? Shouldn't you be trying to be the kind of person who would make her proud?" I asked him.

"That's rich, coming from you, Mr. Naofumi. Look what you've done to poor Ruft!" Raphtalia said.

"Sister, please, read the room," Fohl interjected. It was true though; I probably wasn't making Raphtalia especially proud of me.

"That said . . . I do think Mr. Naofumi has what it takes to lead us all as the Shield Hero. Look at the way he searched for Keel," Raphtalia continued.

"He can be a little too forward-focused," Fohl said. "Cautioning him is hard work." I looked over at the cultivation tanks and the kids floating inside them. They all looked like they were peacefully sleeping.

"Ethically speaking, I think you don't really have a leg to stand on," I said, "but in light of the future, this is the only possible choice. If you have to eat poison, why not eat the whole plate?" The people of Siltran had asked this of Mamoru, seeking to create the foundations for a lasting era of peace. They had already made the choice to be more than collateral to be protected.

I was impressed. The hangers-on around the resurrected tended to not do much for themselves, from what I'd seen of them. A bunch of irresponsible losers. They also used the power and authority given to them by the resurrected to try and make things always go their way, which was why there was no reasoning with them. Kizuna had struggled with them in her world too. At least in Mamoru's situation the people of his nation were willing to sacrifice something of themselves.

"Hey, Mamoru. We're going to keep doing our best. You're not going to suffer like that again, I promise. So even if you can't smile like you used to . . . you can lean on us, a little more than you do now . . ." Cian said. Mamoru looked down. She made a good point. Mamoru might have thought he was trusting them, believing in them, but really, he wasn't. "Maybe I can't be as strong as Filolia was, but . . . until she comes back to us, I'll do everything I can to help you. I want to be . . . your fangs, Mamoru." I wasn't sure what that would mean to Mamoru. Raphtalia had said she wanted to be my sword, and Atla had said she wanted to be my shield. Cian, meanwhile, wanted to be Mamoru's fangs—at least until this Filolia girl was resurrected.

"Everyone . . . I don't know what to say . . ." Mamoru fell to his knees, sobbing, and then Cian hugged him and started to cry herself.

Chapter Ten: Filolia

Mamoru cried for a brief while and then composed himself and looked at me. His face looked more confident than before.

"Mamoru, your choice could be considered arrogant and selfish. Even if the person you love is restored, you may find you can't accept them as the same person," I warned him.

"I know," he said with a nod, looking at the girl floating in the tank in the back. From my perspective, she felt like an artificial lifeform that had just been created to mimic the original. Maybe it was because of the Suzaku mixed in with her, but she had wings on her back. At a glance, she looked like nothing more than a sleeping filolial in human form. "Even so . . . from the Suzaku fragment we obtained . . . there's a part that is Filolia's soul inside that being that is returning to the world . . ." Mamoru explained. There was the slightest hope, then.

I was happy for him. It also made me think, however, that I might have been wrong to listen to Atla's last wish—that it might have been better to take Mamoru's route and try to bring her back, even if it meant creating artificial life.

"One of my allies, an uhnte jimna, is helping us to salvage Filolia's soul. You might not be able to accept it, but I want to bring her back, no matter what," Mamoru said.

"What did you just say? 'Aunty' what now? Do they have some kind of special power?" I asked.

"You don't know about the uhnte jimna, Naofumi? They look like . . . a weasel demi-human, I guess you'd say," Mamoru replied.

"Raph!" said Raph-chan. I recalled them now. When we first came to Siltran castle, Raphtalia had seen a demi-human with weasel-like ears.

"They're a little old race with powerful souls. With enough training they can do therianthrope transformation and ancestral recall. They have a special power to observe souls and keep them in this world for a while even after the host body dies. They are a race said to have been allied with the Shield Hero since ancient times," Holn explained.

"So with one of them helping out, you can salvage her soul?" I asked.

"The soul is likely heavily merged already, due to the Suzaku, but there's still a chance if we can cut it out before the merging is complete. That's about all I can say on the matter, however," Holn said. It sounded like there was still a chance then, but I was still pretty sure he wasn't going to be thrilled with the results. "Okay, maybe I can say some more," Holn continued. "The uhnte jimna are said to really be able to bring their power to bear after they have died, when they are still lingering in this world. If we can separate Filolia's soul from the Suzaku, you never know . . . but it's just a chance, not a sure thing." It sounded like Mamoru was going to have to call his aunty friend in order to salvage Filolia's soul from the Suzaku—and even then, it might not work.

"Filolia wouldn't want to come back at the cost of someone else's life," Mamoru said. "That's why . . ." If he didn't sacrifice the life of his ally, he couldn't even conduct the experiment to see if his dead girlfriend could come back. But if he did that, and it worked, his returned girlfriend would never forgive him. He was already doing some pretty shady stuff to his allies, but this would cross the line, even for him.

"Raph!" said Raph-chan, giving an exasperated sigh. She toddled over to the cultivation tank in the back, placed her tail on the terminal . . . and suddenly her tail fluffed up. That looked like magic, but I wasn't sure why she would be using it here.

An LCD screen turned on from the terminal, displaying . . . what looked like paint spreading slowly through water.

"Let me take a look at that," Holn said. Her face transformed from being completely unbothered to serious and intent. She stared at the screen that Raph-chan was operating. "Mamoru, future Shield Hero, come take a look," Holn said, beckoning us over. I stood behind Raph-chan and looked into the screen for myself.

"Raph, raph, raph!" said Raph-chan. She continued to delicately use her tail, causing more and more geometric polka dot images to be created. At a glance, it looked like Raph-chan was just messing around, but Holn's eyes were wide in surprise.

"Do you know what this is?" she asked.

"Based on what you were just talking about, Filolia's soul blended into the energy of the Suzaku," I guessed.

"I think that's probably right," Holn replied. The extraction of the soul hadn't started yet, but from what Raph-chan was showing us, it would be incredibly difficult to achieve. The shape of the soul was constantly changing in real time. Raph-chan was working overtime to keep it displayed. "Future Shield Hero, just what is this creature? All this time I've been thinking of it as nothing more than a familiar created from the elements of the future Heavenly Emperor," Holn said.

"Yeah, good question. She started out as a shikigami that was created in order to search for Raphtalia in a world different to this one. I guess she can see souls . . . I bet Glass could do this too," I replied.

"Another friend of yours, future Shield Hero?" Holn asked.

"Yeah, she's the companion to one of the four holy heroes in a different world from this one, and the user of the Fan vassal weapon. She's a spectral, also known as a spirit, a race created from a soul," I explained.

"Wow! That sounds like something I'd like to see," Holn exclaimed.

"Have you ever met one of her kind, R'yne?" I asked.

As the holder of the Sewing Kit vassal weapon, I guessed she had probably traveled through a number of other worlds before finally reuniting with her sister.

"Sorry, I can't say I've ever had the pleasure," R'yne replied.

"It sounds like S'yne did stop by . . . but very well," I said. She was moving around by crossing the waves, after all. It wasn't like she had much control.

As for Glass, just because we knew her didn't mean we could ask her to do this for us. It would be a massive responsibility, and a hero from a completely different world like her had no obligation to cooperate. But considering the personalities of Mamoru and the others here, I thought they could probably become friends.

"So Raph-chan is something created from technology coming from a completely different world. In which case, this might all make sense." Holn looked over at Mamoru. "If this creature can accurately divine the location of the soul, this might be worth a try." We had Holn for backup too. Things were sounding more hopeful. "There's still an issue though. We'll only have one chance. If we fail and the soul gets more merged, the salvage will be even harder."

"I bet it will. Also—and I hate to suggest this is what Raph-chan is doing—but there's a chance she's just doodling away there," I said.

"Raph," said Raph-chan, a little defensively, looking at me with a frown.

"I know, Raph-chan," I assured her. "You're doing your very best, but you have to consider what Mamoru might think this looks like." After all, we didn't even know why Dafu-chan had turned out like a Raph species. After the invasion of Q'ten Lo, I did see Raph-chan playing with what looked like a ball of fluff, and that vanished around the time Dafu-chan appeared. Maybe that ball had been the residual memories of the past Heavenly Emperor. If so, that meant Raph-chan had been able to bring them back to life. That really increased the mysteries surrounding her.

"Mamoru, what do you think?" Holn asked.

"No pressure at all," I told him. "We're not going to ask this much from your trust."

"No, I trust you, Naofumi, and your friends too. After all, what does the Shield Hero need?"

"Trust in others," I said, even though each word had to be dragged out of me. I wondered why the shield had to be the corniest hero. If you didn't believe, if your allies didn't trust you, then you couldn't fight at all. "Raph-chan, this is a big responsibility," I told her, putting my hand on her head and stroking her as she continued to operate the terminal.

"Raph!" Raph-chan replied, seemingly ready for anything.

"Dafu!" said Dafu-chan.

"I'm sorry to be . . . the voice of reason right now," Raphtalia said, "but I'm having trouble following why Raph-chan is suddenly our trump card."

"Sister, just breathe," Fohl told her.

"I'm breathing, okay? I'm breathing . . . and I see that Raph-chan can bring Mamoru closer to something he's wanted for a long time, but . . ." Raphtalia was starting to have a harder and harder time with all this stuff, and I was starting to feel responsible. I needed to back her up. "But if Raph-chan keeps on being able to do more stuff, and become more important, where does that leave me? You'll all be fine as long as you have Raph-chan . . . I won't be needed. My nightmares might be coming closer to reality . . ." Raphtalia continued, muttering mainly to herself. I hoped she was okay—she was starting to freak me out a bit, and I didn't like the talk about nightmares either.

"Looks like little old me is going into surgery. This is going to be a long night," Holn said.

"Oh wow! Looks like Naofumi and the gang are going to really help us out!" R'yne exclaimed, with her hands to her face.

"Your surprise is so fake I don't know where to start," I told her. I still couldn't really get a handle on R'yne. She had this jokey personality, different from Sadeena's, but I still didn't much care for it.

"Is Filolia coming back?" Cian asked, concern and expectation mixing on her face.

"It's going to be a bit of a gamble, but yes, if everything works out," Mamoru told her. It was like we were praying for the success of someone important who was undergoing surgery—and our doctors were Raph-chan and Holn. Hopefully they were good at their jobs.

I looked at the body for Filolia that had been created in the cultivation tank.

"There's one thing I've been wondering about. What's with the wings?" I asked. I pointed at her "body" as she floated in the tank. R'yne didn't have wings like that—at least not all the time—and even then, they weren't feathery ones.

"We needed to mix in a little Suzaku or the soul wouldn't take," Holn explained.

"I see," I replied. So they were a part required in order to make the resurrection work. "I'm just going to say it, okay . . . She looks exactly like a filolial in human form." Like a red filolial as a human. I could hardly tell the difference.

"Brother . . . there's a reason none of us said that," Fohl chided—which only meant they had been thinking it too. When we first met, I recalled Mamoru looking at the filolials with a sadness in his eyes.

"Future Shield Hero, allow me to explain. I think the name filolial is a contraction of the name Filolia Type L that I came up with," Holn explained.

"Mamoru made that though, right? You were only supervising, right?" I asked.

"That's true for Filolia's body, but I've been working for

many years on creating other forms of artificial life. This was another deal of mine with Mamoru," Holn replied.

"That has also led to me getting my cells harvested without my consent. She's also been messing around with Mamoru's familiars, in the name of powering them up," R'yne added with a sigh. It sounded like Holn had nabbed Mamoru's idea and was running with it. That reminded me: Holn had been complaining about the hierarchy in which dragons were the strongest creatures in this world, while filolials had a clear rivalry with dragons. They also hated griffons too. So we had filolials, unable to get along with other monsters . . . Did that mean . . .

Filolia Type L . . . Filolia-L . . . filolial?

"But why is your sister called Filolia, R'yne? Taking S'yne into account too, I was expecting a name with an *-yne* on the end," I said. Maybe S'yne's sister had a name like that too. Lyno had really looked like she hated that name and said we didn't need to know it. Then another name came to mind: Myn—but no, her name was Whore now. I didn't want to remember her either.

"She didn't like her birth name very much," R'yne replied. "So she changed it herself and used her new name once she was summoned here." So it was Filolia by choice, then. That kind of individual personality trait certainly sounded like a filolial to me—but there was no knowing the extent to which the original person would influence such things.

"What was her real name?" I asked.

"L'yne. She didn't like it because so many other people have similar names, making it hard to remember them all," R'yne explained. My head started to throb. If this Filolia did come back, it sounded like we might just be adding one more filolial to the fold.

"It sounds like . . . the filolials were created by Mamoru and Holn. Is that right?" Raphtalia asked, trying to change the subject. Holn's eyes lit up and she nodded.

"It certainly seems that way. That's why I was upset at seeing the finished thing. A creature I'm yet to make came to meet me from the future!" Holn cackled.

"Why do they develop differently when raised by a hero?" I asked.

"In consideration of the future, I made it so that hidden elements would not be activated unless a hero is the one raising them," Holn explained. "If I made monsters too powerful, it would simply replace the dragons and nothing else would change. I'm trying to do more than that." There was incredible confidence in her answer. "You know something of little old me by now. I've put the same kind of thing into all sorts of monsters, so I'm sure you've seen it before. Take the balloons, for example." That was right. When I raised a balloon, it had evolved into an adballoon. It had almost been ready to evolve again, and then it had turned into a Raph species.

"Why are you so obsessed with balloons?" I asked her. I didn't like them because they reminded me of when I first became a hero.

"I'm going to make a king balloon one day, you'll see," Holn replied.

"Hey, don't we have the option to shut her down and stop her making the filolial completely?" I asked.

"Mr. Naofumi, that would be going too far . . . Filo would vanish too," Raphtalia said.

"So how about we take back some of Raph-chan's genes with us and turn Filo . . . turn all the filolials into Raph species," I suggested.

"That might be fun," Holn said. "We can call them the 'Raphield' species due to their connection with the Shield Hero."

"Raph species have to be better than filolials," I stated.

"No!" Raphtalia said firmly, shutting us down.

"I have to say . . ." Mamoru chimed in timidly, "and I might not be in a position to say this, you helping you with Filolia, but . . . that would probably be going too far."

"How about setting things up so that we can return to the future and press a single button and all the filolial genes will change to Raph genes?" I suggested.

"That sounds fun too!" Holn said.

"No!" Raphtalia repeated.

"Sister is really suffering over here," Fohl reported.

"Mr. Naofumi, do you even understand what you're suggesting?" Raphtalia asked. "You're the one who said that it would be dangerous to change the future!"

"True, but let's be honest here . . . We've no idea what's going to change the future," I replied. The reason we didn't seem to have had much effect so far might be because we were so far in the past. There was a certain degree of latitude for history to autocorrect in the intervening years.

"You certainly do things at your own pace, future Shield Hero," Holn said. "Not a bad thing."

"Hold on though. It sounds like a monster created from Filolia and me is going to take over this world! I'd recommend making something that originated here, to be honest," R'yne said.

"R'yne! That I will not allow! I'm sure Natalia would have something to say about that too!" Raphtalia said, looking ready to fight R'yne tooth and nail.

"Come on then. Let's fight for it!" R'yne said.

"I'll stop you by whatever means possible!" Raphtalia replied. She was having a tough time—still, I'd started all this.

"What about Mamoru's familiars?" I asked.

"I've made all sorts of adjustments and enhancements to them to show me the kinds of things I can offer. Fimonoa is adept at flight, while Fijia has powerful magic," Holn explained. I looked over at the three of them—and especially at the one called Fitoria. "Fitoria has a fundamentally different composition from the other two, with a focus placed on carrying loads. She can carry the heaviest stuff around, no problem." So number one had flight strength, number two had magic, and number three had grit. I'd heard Melty and Fitoria talking about filolials that could fly and how they had been wiped out in a war with the griffons. It was starting to sound like there might have originally been three breeds of filolial. "We had a serious transportation problem here. These were modified to help resolve that and get things moving around."

"I know a Fitoria in the future," I eventually said. "But the one I know might be a different person with the same name." The familiar called Fitoria turned into her human form and looked over at me. She looked a lot younger than the Fitoria and Filo that I knew—maybe around seven years old.

"Wow, she's still alive that far into the future?" Holn said with excitement.

"We don't know for sure why she's lived for so long, but I can guess based on certain evidence that she took some kind of potion of eternal youth," I replied.

"Eternal youth? Life that doesn't age and break down is no fun. Something major must have happened for her to achieve that state while I was involved," Holn said. So she wasn't interested in eternal life. Strange, because that totally sounded like where her research was leading.

"Think how many things you could invent if you never died," I said, trying to tempt her.

"Don't you think our work shines because we have to make them within the limited time we have? You need a deadline or you'll never finish anything," Holn replied. She sounded like a manga artist, talking about "deadlines." It reminded me of something I'd heard back in Japan: it was the deadline that made the work complete. If you worked without a deadline, you would never finish. An issue millions of students faced each year with their homework for the summer holidays.

"Of course, there are lots more things I want to research, but I'm pretty sure they would lead me to somewhere truly terrible. That would make me no different from the arrogant ones who claim to be gods," Holn said. I didn't really understand what she meant, but it seemed clear she wasn't interested in eternal life. "Anyway. It's time to start the operation. Please keep out of our way."

"No problem. Mamoru, let's watch Raph-chan and Holn without getting in the way, okay?" I suggested.

"Sure, Naofumi. Thanks for all this," Mamoru replied. After offering his gratitude to me, he stood watching Holn work, holding Cian's hand the entire time.

The operation Raph-chan and Holn performed took the entire night. We returned to the village while they were working and let the others know that the incident hadn't been anything major. S'yne had realized she couldn't observe us anymore and started to track us manually, but she had been caught and detained by castle security. She didn't look all that happy about it, but I managed to summarize exactly what was going on. If I'd told her everything, she'd probably be first in line to get modified herself. If she was given the chance to become one of the primary races of Siltvelt, like Fohl, she'd surely jump at the chance. It might not be a bad thing, but if everyone ended up wanting to do it . . . Raphtalia was giving me a look, telling me not to let that happen.

We hadn't explained things to Natalia yet, either. She was starting to look suspicious about everything, so we'd have to tell her sooner rather than later—whether it came from me or from Mamoru. Melty also seemed to have an idea that something had gone down. She had a look on her face asking me to explain everything as soon as possible.

After that, Raphtalia and I returned to Raph-chan in the castle and did what we could to help out. We left Fohl back in the village.

We had fallen asleep, exhausted, in a corner of Mamoru's lab. I remembered Mamoru heading out to put the kids to bed. Their healing and modifications were finished for the night. Holn had asked him to get something for her, and he wasn't back yet.

Holn wasn't here either. I looked over at where Raph-chan was working at the terminal to extract Filolia's soul and saw what looked like a translucent human being. The figure—a girl's figure as seen from behind—had a longer tail than Raphtalia, small round animal ears, and brown medium-length hair. I blinked a few times and looked at Raph-chan.

"Raph? Raph," said Raph-chan, yawning. Then she turned, as though realizing the same thing that I had—but then there was no sign of the transparent girl behind her. I shook my head, wondering if I was seeing things.

Holn, Mamoru, Cian, and R'yne came back into the room.

"We're close, are we not?" Holn asked.

"Raph!" said Raph-chan, lifting both paws in victory.

"Oh, future Shield Hero, you're awake," Holn said. I nodded. Raphtalia, who had been sleeping at my side, was also awoken by the voices and looked around to see what was going on. "Nice timing, you two. You wouldn't want to sleep through this," Holn said. We stood up and looked at the screen where Raph-chan was working. It was displaying the percentage of the extract that had been completed, like some loading screen from a game, along with two quivering fires that were slowly being moved apart. It said eighty percent.

"Reaching this point, we can use Suzaku's power to take this home," Holn said. "Let's finish this thing off."

"Raph!" said Raph-chan. Holn proceeded to use the

terminal to transfer the soul that Raph-chan had spent the night separating into the homunculus body created for Filolia.

"Good . . . soul suitability is clear. No chemical or magic abnormalities, and no signs of rejection. All within acceptable numbers . . . Loading the memories from the soul . . . All green," Holn said. The soul eventually overlapped completely with the body and vanished inside it. In that same moment, a red light passed over the homunculus body, and the wings flashed a little. A moment later a light appeared, from nowhere in particular, and started to swirl around the girl floating in the cultivation tank.

"Hey, that looks like—" I started.

"Yeah, the spirit of the Claw vassal weapon. It looks like it recognized the soul of its owner," Holn said. That was a clear suggestion that this had worked. "Now we need to keep her stable until the soul settles completely. The Claw Spirit is lending us its strength, so we are close now."

"Finally . . ." Mamoru breathed.

"Raph!" said Raph-chan, coming back toward us and looking totally exhausted.

"Great work, Raph-chan!" I congratulated her.

"I have to say . . . thank you," Raphtalia managed.

"Raph!" said Raph-chan in reply. I picked her up and started to stroke her. She really was something else.

"When will we know for sure?" Mamoru asked.

"She should be out and about in maybe three days. That's my estimation," Holn said.

"That would be amazing," Mamoru replied.

"Wow. You really did just show up and solve this one, huh, Naofumi?! You guys are amazing," R'yne enthused.

"This was all thanks to Raph-chan, really," I replied.

"Naofumi, Raph-chan, and Raphtalia . . . thank you all so much." Mamoru bowed his head deeply as he thanked us.

"We don't know the results yet. Thank us once this is finished," I told him.

"No, please. I have to say this. I can't hold it in," Mamoru said. Even after stepping off the path, he was still a stickler for good manners. I could see where he was coming from though. This had been a bit of a gamble, all things considered, but it looked like they had extracted the soul at a far higher rate than they were expecting.

"Mamoru, if this sounds harsh, it's only because I'm the Shield Hero too. You aren't the only one who has suffered. Having allies who support you, and fearing for their lives, that's just normal. If you can't overcome that fear . . . you'll lose more allies in the future. You need to crush that trauma completely," I told him. Atla's death still burned brightly in my own mind. I wanted to see her, but I couldn't—and yet she was with me, inside the shield, at all times. I knew I had her support, and I had to protect everyone.

"Yes! I won't . . . won't lose anyone again!" Mamoru said. Maybe he hadn't overcome that trauma yet, not completely, but I still nodded at his words. "I'll do whatever it takes to protect Siltran. That's never going to change," Mamoru swore, with more conviction in his voice than before. He was like a combination of Ren and me. I was starting to get an understanding of him. It sounded like the trauma Cian had asked us to save Mamoru from was on its way toward improvement. I looked over at Cian to see her timidly bowing her head to us too.

"Thank you," she said simply. It was a little awkward, but for Cian, it was the very best she could do.

"Yeah. Good luck with all that," I said. The worlds were going to fuse—we already knew that—meaning they were ultimately going to be defeated. But word of the Shield Hero Mamoru Shirono would still be passed down by future generations. As a god in Siltvelt, and as a demon king in Melromarc.

It didn't quite resolve my worries about changing the future, but it seemed best for the world if that was where things finally settled once more.

"Thanks. Please, let us help you work even harder to find a way to get you back to the future. It's our turn to help you now," Mamoru said.

"That would be most welcome," I replied.

"First things first, then—" Mamoru started and then shifted his gaze to the side. It looked like something was up.

"Dammit . . . why now?" Mamoru cursed.

"Showing up as we just pulled an all-nighter. Nasty," Holn said.

"I was just in a good mood too," R'yne added. They all sounded pissed off about something, sighing and clicking their tongues.

"What's up?" I asked.

"It almost sounds like . . . you don't see this?" Mamoru asked.

"What? See what?" I replied. I checked everything over, but I couldn't see anything out of place.

"The forecast for the next wave was updated. There's a wave incoming in just one hour," Mamoru explained.

"What? That's quick. Was the seal on a guardian beast broken?" I asked. The time before a wave was normally stated far in advance, and yet here Mamoru was saying we were getting one almost with no warning. From my past experience, this felt like when the seal on the Spirit Tortoise was broken.

"No. This isn't a case of a guardian beast being released," Holn said.

"What do you want to do, Naofumi? You're not obliged to take part, if you don't want to," Mamoru said.

"You bet we're helping out. Anything threatening this world, we're there," I said. That's what we'd done even in Kizuna's world. It might even help us put off some of the problems we were facing. Not to mention, we now had access to the ability to attack the wave cracks with 0 weapons, like Kizuna had done in her world. There were more benefits to taking part than not. "Mamoru, we don't have long. Let me edit the party too," I said.

"Sure, okay," he replied. I received a request to accept authority for party editing from Mamoru, approved it, and was ready to get started.

"Good, thanks. Honestly, I'm still really tired, but we'll head back to the village and get ready for the wave. You do the same. Get ready, I mean," I told Mamoru.

"You bet. Please, prepare the best you possibly can. These waves aren't something that's easy to resolve," Mamoru said.

"I know . . . but I haven't felt all that threatened by a single wave for a while now," I admitted. Bitch and the forces behind her were proving more of a threat recently. They were the reason we were here in the past, for one thing.

"Big words! Mamoru, we have to show them what we can do!" R'yne said.

"Yeah. We don't have a way to defeat them yet," Holn said. "I hate having to sit around and wait for someone, something, to turn up and help out." We know the one who assumed the name of god was causing the waves, after all. The same pain Holn was feeling also ached inside me.

"Mr. Naofumi, let's go," Raphtalia said.

"Okay," I replied. "We'll see you at the wave," I told the others. Cian poked her head out from behind Mamoru, looking worried.

"I'll do my best too," she told me.

"Good for you. Support Mamoru however you can. You almost have Filolia back now, so don't give up!" I told her. Cian looked down in embarrassment at my words. This looked like a great opportunity to shift the target of everyone messing with me over to Mamoru! "We'll go get ready. Mamoru, don't count on us too much, okay? You're the Shield Hero in this time," I told him. Mamoru seemed to understand my intent and tried to call out to stop me, but we ran from the scene.

We needed to let everyone in the village, including Ren and Fohl, know what was going on.

"You bet I am! Don't you forget it! I'm your shield grand-daddy, you hear me? I'm not going to be outdone by you!" Mamoru shouted after us, seemingly a lot more comfortable with everything now. He had seemed tense and stiff before, but now he seemed looser and more relaxed.

"See you later!" Raphtalia said.

"Raph!" said Raph-chan. They both bowed and started after me. We took a portal back to the village as quickly as possible, and then we started to prepare for our next battle against a wave.

Chapter Eleven: The Imitations (Improved)

Our preparations were swift, however. Everyone in the village, including the heroes Ren and Fohl, had plenty of experience fighting the waves by now and were always ready for another battle. We had boosted our strength in numerous ways since the last one of these. That meant we should be able to end it pretty quickly.

"Bubba! We're going to show you how much stronger we've become too!" Keel said with an excited howl.

"Good. Do your best," I told her. At her side, Ren was gripping his sword and concentrating hard. Then he looked up and spoke.

"Naofumi," he started.

"Hey, don't get all stiff on me. You've collapsed once already under the stress," I reminded him.

"I know," he replied, glancing over to where Eclair was standing with Melty. Eclair gave a sigh and came over to put a hand on Ren's shoulder.

"We have Hero Iwatani with us. We just have to do our part," Eclair told him.

"I know that too. Just do our part. We don't have Itsuki or Motoyasu here, but having you with us, Naofumi . . . that is reassuring," Ren admitted. Honestly, I was more worried about what was going on in the future with those two that were left in charge. We could return to a real rampage. Itsuki was making good progress, so the issue was more likely with Motoyasu. We just had to pray that Trash was making good use of Filo. In fact, Filo might be the one we had to worry about the most with Motoyasu after her all the time.

"Oh, hold on! Holn said she made some 'little old cool weapons,' which she showed me back in the lab!" Keel said. With that, Keel rushed off to the lab and returned with Rat, Mikey, and . . . the ancient weapons we had found in the filolial ruins, which had appeared to be imitations of the four holy weapons.

"She really doesn't miss a trick, does she?" Rat said with a sigh. In her hands she was holding the ancient weapon (in the shape of a spear) that the high priest had used.

"Raph," said Mikey, who was carrying three more of them. He passed them to those who were good in battle, including Eclair and Dafu-chan.

"Those are out of magic, right? They can't even be used," I said. "What's she hoping to achieve with them?"

"Don't look at me," Rat said. "She started playing around with these all on her own. There's even a manual here on how to use them." Rat swung the spear she was holding and it turned into a sword. "This sucks down a little too much magic for me to use. She seems to have modified them so anyone can use them, anyway." Rat proceeded to read to us the instruction manual that Holn had left behind. She had modified the replicas of the four holy weapons, allowing for imitations of skills to be unleashed while only consuming a small amount of magic. The output was a ratio based on the volume of magic the user had access to. So those with more magic could get a bigger bang for their buck. If there was an issue, it was that they couldn't reach the same level of attack power as the actual holy or vassal weapons. They couldn't match weapons made from the best materials, like the guardian beast weapons or legendary weapons, but considering them as somewhat inferior holy weapons, we could probably still find a spot for them. They were able to re-create skills to a certain extent but couldn't match the real thing.

"Oh!" Keel exclaimed. "I've never seen a display like this before! Is this what you see all the time, Bubba?"

"Holn says here that it's slightly different," Rat replied, checking the manual again. "A simplified version."

"Honestly, I'm more impressed by this than I am by her work modifying Mikey and Keel," I replied. I had to wonder at how she handled herself, modifying these weapons like this but then leaving them lying around in the lab.

"She probably doesn't enjoy messing around with something other people have already created," Rat said.

"You're the same way, aren't you?" I quipped, causing her brow to furrow and her tongue to click.

"I guess I am. That's why I understand her urge to play around with things in her free time," Rat replied. In this case, it sounded like we had some versatile new weapons that were a little vanilla when it came to their output.

"Hey, Naofumi. Are you planning on deploying these during the wave?" Melty asked, looking a little concerned.

"I don't think we should be holding anything back," I replied. "If they start to seem too dangerous to use, toss them away. That should cover it." The others shouted their general agreement. Eclair turned hers into a sword and swung it around.

"I think I can handle this too," Eclair said. "I'll be doing my part too, Ren, so please don't feel the pressure too badly."

"Okay," he replied. "But please be careful. I don't have an especially good impression of these weapons." I understood where he was coming from. The high priest had been swinging that thing around like a lunatic, and now we were going to use it ourselves.

"They do seem to want to resolve the waves . . ." Natalia said as she watched this exchange, still a little unsure about us.

"I think they are proactively trying to discharge their duties as heroes," the Water Dragon said supportively.

"It sounds like something happened with Mamoru," Natalia said, a little pointedly. "Do you have anything to report to me?"

"Nope," I replied casually. "I was just letting him bend my ear a little. You know how it is. Being a hero is tough work." I wasn't lying. We'd listened to Mamoru's issues and helped him find a solution, that was all. "You're a pacifier, Natalia, so maybe providing a little mental care for the holy weapon heroes would make your job easier in the long run," I offered.

"A bold suggestion, future Shield Hero, but you are not wrong," the Water Dragon said, choosing to side with me in this. "Being a pacifier is about more than just killing miscreant heroes. You need to help lead the heroes along the correct path for the sake of the world." I almost felt sorry for Natalia.

"Very well. I will learn whatever I can from him," she replied, with an annoyed look on her face and a sigh in her tone that matched closely with Raphtalia.

"Dafu, dafu!" said Dafu-chan, seemingly fighting back. Maybe she had a problem with the Water Dragon.

"What was that? You think I'm looking down on her, making these proclamations without doing anything myself?" the Water Dragon replied. "I am watching over her. That's what I'm doing."

"Dafu, dafu, dafu!" Dafu-chan continued aggressively. She always seemed to be looking for a fight recently. I understood that she probably didn't like Holn or the Water Dragon very much, but I had to wonder again about her life. She was residual thoughts being held here in this world—we knew that much—but I wondered why she hadn't turned into her Heavenly Emperor form yet. Insufficient energy, perhaps.

"Oh boy . . ." Raphtalia had a troubled expression on her face. I hoped she wasn't about to spill the beans on Mamoru. It might still turn out to be a mistake, but if we reported on him now, then it really would be over. Dafu-chan had to understand that too, so hopefully everyone just kept their mouths shut. Raphtalia seemed to realize what I was thinking, because she came out and whispered to me, "I know what you want to say, Mr. Naofumi, and I'm not going to say anything, but this isn't ideal." She was worried about Natalia getting upset about being left out of the loop. She was serious about her mission, but also super intense. She might be a good pacifier, capable of keeping heroes in check, but with the waves going on, it was also tough for her to do that job.

"How are you going to handle this wave, pacifier?" I asked her.

"I'll help out, for the sake of this world, so long as none of the heroes go off on a rampage. My weapon should be able to help too," Natalia said. She was using a sakura stone of destiny weapon, along with techniques derived from those stones, which would provide excellent effects against heroes from other worlds.

"Okay then. Let's all get over this wave together," I said. Looking at the time until the wave in my field of view, I saw that there were only a few minutes left. I formed up our party, like normal, and performed the final checks to prepare for the wave's arrival.

"Brother," Fohl said, coming over.

"What's up?" I replied, hoping he would keep it short.

"A lot happened last night. I was there to see the beginnings of the hakuko," he stated.

"Yeah, I get it," I replied. Now we knew where the four races of Siltvelt, including Fohl, had come from. The filolials too. It seemed likely that Mamoru and the others would bring them out amid the confusion after the worlds were fused. Those from the Sword and Spear world would think they had come from the Bow and Shield one, and those from the Bow and Shield would think the opposite. That was one benefit of going to a real chaotic time. Pretty impressive too. This was what it meant to get a glimpse behind the veil of history. We would need to let Melty in on all this sooner rather than later.

"Fohl, try to get along with Cian," I told him. She was his distant ancestor, after all.

"I understand what you mean . . . but I'm not good at interacting with others. We hakuko are pretty hot-blooded," he replied. That was true; they could be quite a wild bunch. But Fohl wasn't a pure-blooded hakuko. He was also continuing the bloodline of his human mother.

"I think Atla would have got on with her better," I commented.

"Brother . . . I'll admit that Atla was pretty hot-blooded herself . . . but still, on second thought I don't want to admit it. She was a hakuko too . . . but in Siltvelt, Atla was . . ." Fohl rambled to himself. It sounded like maybe he had started to admit that Atla had been pretty hot-blooded herself. Right now he sounded like he was about to have a panic attack.

"Is it rude to compare Cian to Atla?" I pondered.

"Brother, what do you mean by that?" Fohl asked.

"Do I have to spell it out?" I replied. Fohl looked away at my question. He had to understand—Cian was far more docile than Atla had ever been. She was a cat. Not some raging tiger. She might become a tiger in the future, but for now she was a cat.

"I'll try talking to her . . . regardless of the hakuko connection," Fohl eventually replied awkwardly. That sounded fine to me. Fohl was good at taking care of other people. Cian seemed to sense something from him too, because she wasn't on her guard around him. He was an easy person to find a comfortable distance with.

Melty and Ruft came over.

"We don't know what's going to happen during this wave, but you can leave the rear to us," Melty said.

"Sure thing. You handle business," I said. Ruft was also a pretty good fighter, but we were better off having him support Melty rather than putting him on the front lines.

"Analysis of the monsters we will face, efficient securing of combat formations, there's all sorts of work to be done. We don't have my mother or father here with us, but I'll work to keep any damages down to a minimum," Melty assured me.

"Nothing to worry about!" Ruft chimed in. "We drove off Piensa, so we can handle this! There's nothing we can't overcome so long as we have you with us, Naofumi!"

"You said it. Past, future, I don't care. The waves aren't stopping us," Melty asserted. That was when the wave arrived. Since I was a hero, there was a problem for this world that I had to help with, and that was to minimize the damages of the waves.

My field of vision switched over as we were instantly transported to where the wave was happening.

Chapter Twelve: The Origin of the Waves

"Here we go! Here they come! The games are getting underway for today, guys and gals!" A high-pitched, already incredibly annoying voice rang out immediately after our arrival. I looked around, trying to work out which moron was treating this like a game. It didn't sound like anyone I'd encountered so far. I wondered if it could be the Bow Hero from this time. Mamoru and his crew were already here, standing there looking in what I presumed was the direction of the crack.

"What's going on here?" I asked, looking in the same direction . . . and then I gasped. There was definitely a crack, that much was for sure, but rather than like the cracks we'd seen before, this time it looked more like a mess of 3D polygons. There were countless rings floating around it, and we were seeing a vista that suggested a connection to somewhere else, different than to where the crack was coming from altogether. Within that cut-out space, there was a barrier floating. Above the crack, there was a figure in the air. It was . . . a person, from the look of it, with a microphone in hand and what looked like the head of some kind of cat-mascot costume. They looked super suspicious and appeared to be using some kind of voice-changing device. I thought that they could have been a hero from another world, or another one of the resurrected.

"Roll up, roll up! The game for today is—" A massive roulette wheel suddenly appeared next to the suspicious cat-headed person, and then a drumroll started to thunder out. A dart appeared, also from thin air, and stuck into the wheel with a thud. "Look at this! A thrilling battle between the Bow Holy Hero and the Brush Holy Hero! Let's give them a big hand! The other heroes will fight to the death against a horde of monsters kindly prepared by our sponsors for today, an eclectic mix of violent beasts and monsters from the heart of the wave!" Countless shapes suddenly appeared from the rings and started to run toward us. "The rules are simple!" the cat-headed figure continued. "You will explore a maze of unbreakable walls! The first side to escape is the winner! You can also use the traps and special tools we've prepared to kill the opposing heroes! That's also a win! I want to see people conniving and people stabbing people in the back! Stab, stab, stab! Do I need to even say that killing opposing heroes will bring you bigger rewards than escaping? Of course I don't! That's always the way this works! Good luck, losers!" With that, a gong rang out. "Hold on!" Cathead exclaimed. "Looks like we already have some forces from another world fighting here! Good, good, good stuff! Cameraman, don't forget the live broadcast!" My allies and I just watched this unfold in front of us, stunned. But Mamoru had his hand on his chest, actually looking relieved.

"Phew. Looks like this is a pretty safe wave this time," Mamoru said. "It doesn't look like we've got anyone crossing directly over either."

"What the hell is all this?" I exclaimed when I finally found my words. "What the hell are you talking about?" I looked at Mamoru with a dumbfounded expression on my face—we all did—and pointed at the crazy, complex-looking space that was apparently the wave crack. That was apparently . . . a wave.

"Your reaction tells me that maybe waves aren't like this in the future," Holn said, hazarding a guess.

"Just a little different!" I snarked back at her. "The waves we've fought in the future are like some kind of natural disaster, with a horde of monsters flowing out of a big crack. That's it." Raphtalia and S'yne nodded at my reply to Holn's question.

"The waves in the future and the waves we know about . . . are different?" Mamoru pondered.

"That's a little old mystery, to be sure," Holn said. "If we line up our knowledge on the subject, in both instances the monsters coming out of the cracks are controlled by the ones who assume the name of gods, seeking to overrun the world of men . . ." I paused there for a moment. She said "the ones," not "the one." I had Phoenix flashbacks, remembering that horrible moment when that mural on the temple wall had revealed we actually had *two* fire birds to fight. "The waves were called waves by the original heroes, far in the past, who defended against the first waves." That was interesting. I recalled hearing something like that in our time. The waves hadn't been named after a natural disaster, like tidal waves or anything like that, but rather the idea was to defeat wave after wave of oncoming enemies and enhance your own forces. "In the beginning, the word 'wave' was referring to something like tower defense against waves of attacks, if I remember correctly," Holn said. So that was where the word "wave" came from?

I was aware of the genre of games called "tower defense." They gave you a base to defend—not necessarily a tower, of course—and then you faced hordes of enemies coming along a fixed route, having to drive them off for a fixed period of time. The player placed all sorts of units to protect their base and prevent the enemy from reaching it and then took on wave after wave of enemies.

So we weren't talking about a tidal wave after all.

"They get harder with each successful completion, and recently we've been forced to fight to the death against heroes from other worlds more and more often. They are more like death matches between worlds at this point," Mamoru explained. I pointed at Cathead, who stood over the crack and gave a running commentary.

"That's one of those who assumes the name of gods. You've never met any of them before?" R'yne asked. I could only nod, still reeling from the information that there were more than one of these guys. We'd never seen anyone who could be said to be behind the waves.

"From my research into the topic," Holn explained in more detail, "we are talking about beings who belong to a completely different world from those from which the heroes come. It's a world that has achieved such technological advancement that its denizens have reached the level we would normally attribute to gods. They are immortal and all-powerful, and so they entertain themselves by making toys of other worlds." I shook my head, stunned. All sorts of records might have been destroyed in the future, but even then, we'd had no idea at all that something like this was going down!

"The level we would normally attribute to gods?" Melty repeated, with a mixture of disgust and anger in her voice.

"You know that a goal of alchemy is to achieve extended or eternal life, correct? We're talking about beings whose curiosity led them to those answers and beyond and created a civilization powerful enough to be known as gods," Holn explained. I shook my head, hardly ready for all these answers after all this time. So it was like someone from my time with modern inventions like a TV or lighter going back to a settlement of primitives and showing them off. How would those primitives—which was us, in this situation—react? Just thinking they were a magician wouldn't even be the half of it. Nope, they would be far more likely to think they were seeing a god.

It made sense. If a world did exist with technology far more advanced than this one—far more advanced than the Japan I came from—maybe they would develop the ability to look into other worlds. If they could do that, they might consider some kind of exchange or invasion. But if this god world had developed beyond even the need to do that, then maybe they would consider just using other worlds as their playthings.

When the worlds crashed together, a wave occurred, and monsters appeared. Those monster hordes had "Dimensional" associated with their names, so maybe they were some kind of defensive mechanism for the world. Considering the Spirit Tortoise and the Phoenix, I realized something else. Maybe they had been using souls as material to try and heal the damage caused to the human world by the waves. This led me to wonder what would happen if the heroes' weapons could heal that damage without having to use souls at all.

And the ones who assumed the name of gods were taking advantage of this natural defense mechanism and using it as a form of entertainment. Cathead had just said something about a cameraman and a live broadcast. They seemed to be making this some kind of crazy game show in which heroes from different worlds were pitted against each other for the sake of the entertainment of observers.

The whole thing stunk. It was like the coliseum in Zeltoble or some form of public execution. Now I understood why

Holn had said she wasn't interested in research into eternal life. She didn't like following in others' footsteps, for one thing, but if this was what it led to, then it already made me feel like throwing up. Was it possible for such desires to exist? Desires that could only be fulfilled by doing something like this? Even with all their advances in culture, did it still take something as lurid as this to entertain them?

But I didn't care about any of that.

"Of course, the heroes who please them, the ones they like, are rewarded with all sorts of bonuses and can have their wishes granted too. That gives them further advantages in future battles," Mamoru explained. This was all totally crazy. S'yne's sworn enemies had said something about a reward for destroying worlds. Maybe this was what they meant. I wasn't about to take part in this inter-world death match for these losers with a divinity complex though! "I admit, there was a time when I considered trying to win favor with them myself . . . to get my own wish granted," Mamoru said, each word heavy on his lips. It must have seemed like an appealing way to get Filolia back.

"You were right not to. Who knows what would actually happen if one of them granted you a wish? They're like kids with a bug under a magnifying glass," I replied. They also tended to give the resurrected—the vanguards of the waves—some pretty strange abilities too. Seya had been a great example of that, with his ability to instantly create food. Even if they could bring the dead back to life, there was a question of whether the content of that body was the actual soul of the departed person.

In any case, if one of our ultimate enemies was here, then we needed to kill them. This might even help to quell the waves in the future. There was also the possibility that the origin of the waves was here in the past, and in the future, we couldn't do anything but suppress them. From a gaming perspective, Mamoru and his allies might be fighting the main battle here in the past, and in the future, we were nothing but background mobs.

I wasn't going to let this chance slip away. If we could kill the ones who set up this insane game, we might be able to bring it to an end.

"That's the one causing the waves?!" someone muttered before I could even give the order to attack the one who assumed the name of god. It was Ren, and he was already rushing into battle.

"Wait! Hold on! Ren!" I shouted. He crouched down, then sprang forward.

"Yeah, we've got to stop these attackers!" Mamoru shouted at me.

"Mamoru is right! If we don't put a stop to this, we'll all be wiped out! They started all these crazy events after showing us that we can't possibly defeat them," Holn said.

"They started by killing the first hero that attacked them, to set an example, and let us know that this was really a fight to the death. Then they wiped out all the heroes from that world before destroying that entire world itself," Mamoru replied. He pointed at the rings. They were likely showing us other worlds on the other side. I shook my head, wondering if there was anything this scum wouldn't do.

"We've been stuck waiting to uncover a technique to kill a god or for someone who can kill a god to arrive and help us," Holn said. I dashed forward, trying to stop Ren, but he was already inside the strange wave area, leaping high into the air to slash down at the one who assumed the name of god.

"Huh?" Cathead suddenly created a barrier out of nothing, blocking Ren's attack. I'd seen something like that before. Minions from S'yne's sworn enemies had deployed similar protection. But Ren took out his sword in his other hand and imbued it with life force. With a splintering crash, a crack appeared in the barrier of the one who assumed the name of god. "What's this now? I don't think we've met before. We don't have a full understanding of all the worlds we're connected to here, but it seems you don't understand the rules," Cathead said.

"You're the one causing the waves? Stop it right now!" Ren shouted.

"What an energetic challenger we have here. Ooh, this could be good for our ratings! Throwing some spice into the

normal routine!" Cathead dropped back in the instant that Ren
shattered his barrier. "Before we get into the main event, then,
let's have an exhibition game!" Cathead suggested. I clicked
my tongue in annoyance. We'd caught his notice already. I had
wanted to try and hit him with a surprise attack, but Cathead
was already looking over at Raphtalia, Fohl, and me. "Well, well,
look at this. Lots of new faces. I'm here, so come and get me.
Just one on one wouldn't be much fun. We seem to have some
powerful participants gathering here in the world of the Shield
and Bow holy weapons. Where did you wander in from, little
lost ones? Huh? I can't seem to track you yet." It sounded like
this one who assumed the name of god didn't know where
we'd come from. So much for the all-knowing part of divinity.
"Hmmm. I'd better thin you out a little, or things might not be
stimulating enough," Cathead said.

"Naofumi!" said Mamoru and Melty together, but we had
already been moved away—Raphtalia, Fohl, and I were tele-
ported instantly over in front of the one who assumed the
name of god. S'yne was left behind. She was swinging her scissors around wildly to try and get some attention. Her weapon
was close to ceasing to function completely, so we didn't need
her getting involved in this. I did think for a moment about
why S'yne might have been ignored, however. She'd likely be
dismissed as being able to do little better than the holy weapon
copies that Holn had created. Cathead had been able to tell

the difference between Mamoru and me, but maybe S'yne's weapon really was on its last legs.

In any case, she could leave this to us.

"Where are we?" I asked.

"No need to worry. This space is set up to match the Shield and Bow world that you were already in," Cathead replied.

"And only heroes will participate, I guess," I noted.

"Would anyone else have enough strength?" Cathead mocked. It sounded like he didn't think much of our chances. I looked around to see those who were displayed in the rings were all watching what was going to happen to us, even as they fought. I signaled Mamoru as best as I could that he should concentrate on wiping out the monsters from the waves. Mamoru snapped back to himself, and the villagers rushed in to join the battle.

That was the way. They just had to leave the battle with the one who assumed the name of god to us and minimize the damage outside as much as possible.

"I see you are all heroes. We have the Sword and the Shield, but then the Katana and Fists . . . are those Gauntlets? You two are vassal weapon holders from the look of it. Where did you wander in from? Or were you called here? What means are you using to block us being able to trace your origins? These silly spirits just won't give up, will they?" Cathead said. He seemed to have a good handle on certain aspects of us, but it also sounded like the weapons were a thorn in his side. If we could kill this guy here . . . it really might end the waves.

"Ren," I called out. I needed to caution him for dashing in like that. It came from his anger and the pressure from his sense of duty. I needed to help him calm down. Realizing what he had done upon hearing my voice, Ren turned to look back at me and then averted his gaze apologetically.

"I'm sorry," he finally managed. "When I heard this is the one behind everything . . ."

"It doesn't matter how it happened. If we had stood out during the fight, I think we would have ended up here anyway. This Cathead sounds like he places his emphasis on entertainment," I said. His comment about thinning us out made it clear he didn't want any side to be overly strong compared to the others. If we ended this battle smoothly with almost no damage, you could be sure he would be back next time with some kind of super-extreme challenge for us to take on. It really did feel like the Zeltoble coliseum. The primary motivation for everything he did was to entertain his audience. "He's making a game of this, trying to toy with us. We can use that to kill him outright as quickly as possible," I said. Time to teach him that when you play with fire, you burn the whole bloody house down. We needed to wipe him out with the rest of these scumbags who were causing the waves. None of this changed our plans.

The role of the heroes might just be to buy some time until

the one who could kill the gods came along—just to survive until that happened. To win, however we could, and get away. He did look like an extension of the kind of enemies we had been fighting all along. That meant we might have a chance against him.

"Okay. Naofumi, just give me the word," Ren replied.

"I will. Bearing in mind who we're fighting here, I expect better than your best effort," I told him.

"You bet," he replied, gripping his swords tightly. "We're taking this guy down!"

Chapter Thirteen: How to Kill a God

"Mr. Naofumi," Raphtalia called, so I turned to look at her. I wondered if she was going to say this was all too dangerous and we should run away, but from the look on her face . . . she was ready to fight too. Fohl, at her side, looked the same. He gave a shout to pump himself up, already in therianthrope form and ready to fight.

"Oh my, you have some interesting little friends. Not that they will do you much good! Attacking a god is the height of foolishness, and you must be made to see this," Cathead jibed. He quickly shifted back away from us but looked ready to attack.

"Access . . . Sword Illusion . . . actualize," Cathead said. Countless swords all appeared floating in the air around him. He looked like a float weapon user. I activated my own two float shields and stepped forward. "Ready to rumble? Let's get this exhibition match started!" Cathead shouted. Before he had even finished, however, Ren and I were running forward. I'd completed my magic ahead of time too.

"My turn!" said the Demon Dragon in my head. The way she could shorten magic casting for me was so convenient, even if I hated the way she sometimes talked inside my head.

"All Liberation Aura!" I shouted. I placed the aura across

myself and all of my allies, seeking to boost our stats as much as possible.

"I'm going in! Instant Blade! Mist!" Raphtalia exclaimed, leading the way. She snatched her sword out from its scabbard and unleashed her skill right at the one who assumed the name of god while in haikuikku. She was using life force too, so I had no doubts her attack would smash the same kind of barrier that S'yne's sworn enemies had used . . . until it didn't! With a crash, the strange barrier took the attack head-on but just held firm.

"I've increased the penetration ratio. You can't expect to pierce a Dimension Shield like that," Cathead responded. He was easily keeping up with Raphtalia in haikuikku and used the ridge of one of his floating swords to casually strike her in the stomach. That was all it took to send Raphtalia flying with a grunt.

"Raphtalia!" I shouted, catching her and absorbing the impact. The difference in strength between us was suddenly, starkly clear, however. Even if our power-up methods were being somewhat restricted, this was still extreme. Sending Raphtalia flying like that with a single attack . . . What the hell was going on?!

"We do get complaints about violence against women," Cathead said. "There's some demand for such content too, of course, but moderation is the key." Raphtalia was coughing and spluttering.

"Raphtalia, are you okay?" I asked her, healing her at the same time.

"I'm . . . fine. You've taken the pain away. But . . ." she started.

"Interesting. You can still flap those lips, can you?" Suddenly, the one who assumed the name of god was right next to us, swinging a sword in his hand. I barely managed to get my shield and float shields into place in time; both float shields were shattered instantly, and an incredible shock wave hit me. I grunted myself and was then blown maybe ten meters through the air, still holding onto Raphtalia. I couldn't believe it. This was like no attack I'd ever been hit by before. I'd been sent flying back further than even the Demon Dragon's attack using the full power of the Shield of Wrath.

"Naofumi!" Ren shouted in shock.

"Brother!" Fohl cried out.

"Try not to get distracted!" Cathead said. "This is still a battlefield! Still, I'd better limit my strength to about half of that last one, or you might expire too soon." Faster than the eye could see, the one who assumed the name of god moved over to Ren and Fohl and performed the same casual, minor-looking attack that he had done to Raphtalia and me. That was all it took to send them flying away, roaring in pain too. They both managed to recover, however, and land ready for whatever might happen next.

"Oh dear. I think I still used too much strength. If I don't hold back a little more, this isn't going to be much fun," Cathead moaned, looking down on us. This guy really was crazy. He'd nullified one of Raphtalia's life-force–imbued attacks. If we didn't even have a way to cause damage, then things weren't going to go well for us.

"Shooting Star Sword X! Hundred Swords X!" Ren wasn't giving up, launching his own ranged attacks at the one who assumed the name of god. In response, Cathead didn't even try to avoid them, just stood there thinking while the attacks came for him. Ren's skills reached him moments later but vanished completely inside his barrier. I had to do a double take. It was like he had just erased them from existence. When we fought S'yne's sworn enemies in the past, and they had used similar barriers against us, Filo had said something about it being like "kicking the ocean." There was a possibility that what we were considering a barrier was actually something like the skill Transport Mirror, sending incoming attacks away somewhere else. That might explain the way that they seemed to just vanish. If he could deploy that in every direction around himself . . . it would be pointless to attack at all. Putting such defenses aside, I had to wonder if there was anything we could really do against someone who could hit me as hard as this.

The strength gap was just too big. What was worse, the terrain here didn't offer any way to hide or escape. We were inside the wave, meaning portals were off the table. I cursed under my breath; we seemed completely cornered—and faster than ever before. I felt the urge to berate Ren to vent my anger, but complaining about the situation wasn't going to change it.

I wondered if there was room to talk my way out of this.

"Hey, I bet your audience is getting bored watching you beat on us," I said, taunting him a little while standing in front of Raphtalia to protect her.

"Some might, but completely one-sided slaughter is pretty popular too. I'm sure primitives like you understand that appeal. I've no intention of listening to anything you have to say, anyway, and I don't need to hear you groveling for your life. It will only make you look more pathetic," Cathead said, totally showboating for his audience rather than speaking to me. He clearly wasn't interested in anything I might have to say—or he might pretend to, to build tension, and then change his mind.

Something entertaining, then . . . maybe if I ordered Fohl to kill Ren, make them fight . . . I was sure his audience would like that. They sounded like a bunch who would enjoy seeing the ugly side of humans on display. That might buy us some time, but it wasn't a definitive answer and it probably wouldn't go well for Ren or Fohl. All something like that would do is please the one who assumed the name of god, playing right into his hands. Even if I survived, I wouldn't have a leg to stand on as a hero after pulling something like that. I might have done it in the past, but not now.

As I desperately tried to think of something to do, I realized that the shield was pulsing.

"What's this?" I said. Raphtalia, Ren, and Fohl were also all looking at their weapons. They were responding to something, but I couldn't tell what. Then my weapon book opened up, displaying the weapon and skill that was causing the reaction.

—Shield 0

Nope, that really didn't seem like a good idea . . . but there had to be a reason that name was popping up at this point in time. I thought back. Kizuna, the Hunting Tool Hero, had used a weapon with the same skills as this shield to overcome various hardships and even delay the arrival of the waves. That proved it had some kind of power beyond what the stats showed. I also recalled what had happened at the filolial sanctuary just prior to our little trip to this world—the text Rishia had read there. "This weapon is highly effective against those who possess eternity . . . for defense against those who would take the name of a god." That sounded like it definitely had some technique for opposing the ones who assumed the name of gods. Considering the hand we had been dealt, I decided it had to be worth a try.

In order to maximize whatever chance this was going to give us, we needed to launch a surprise attack. If he avoided us at the kind of speed he had shown us, it didn't matter if we had an attack that could defeat him—we'd never even land it.

"Ren, Raphtalia, Fohl!" I called out, signaling them with my eyes to not let on what we had all clearly worked out at the same time. They all nodded in return, waiting for my order. I looked at Fohl first and shouted the name of a skill I could use.

"Beast Transformation Support!" At my shout, Fohl started transforming into his second stage. Then I signaled Raphtalia with my eyes to tell her to stick with Fohl. She nodded her understanding.

"You seem to have obtained some understanding of the strength gap between us, but I still need to put on a good show. We've had more people dropping out than expected recently, which is putting everyone on the defensive. That's not much fun to watch. Now, if you'll just play along . . ." The one who assumed the name of god moved almost instantly over in front of me, swinging with his floating swords and thrusting with the sword at my chest. He was likely thinking that taking me out, the specialist at defense, would make the others easy pickings— a bold display of force. His attack provided an opening for me, however. "There's nothing you can do," Cathead continued. "You need to learn that all of this is pointless!" I quickly lifted my shield and unleashed my own skills.

"Air Strike Shield! Second Shield! Change Shield!" I shouted. Of course, every shield I deployed was a Shield 0. It was do or die at this point. This Shield 0 had no defense at all. It was basically garbage, but the Hunting Tool 0 Kizuna used had reflected the power of the cursed accessory and the power that had bound the spirits. My shield had to have similar abilities.

My shields blocked all of the attacks from the one who assumed the name of god. He grunted in surprise as they did so. A moment later, a brilliant light illuminated from Shield 0, and power started to swell inside it.

This was it! I celebrated silently. It seemed to be working. I just needed to hold on. I proceeded to also change the shield I was equipped with to Shield 0. This one was completely different from normal too, shining as though it had regained some kind of original power.

"What is this?" Cathead froze for a moment as I stopped his attacks.

"You're completely exposing yourself!" I replied. I used my shield hand to grab the clothing at the chest of the one who assumed the name of god. He grunted again. His flying blades came in around me, but I caught them on all my refreshed float shields and sent them all flying away. The strength of his attacks was completely different from before I changed to the Shield 0, like feathers brushing my shield.

Ren was closing in at incredible speed, roaring as he came. The swords gripped tightly in his hands were sparkling with the same light as my shield.

"I don't know what tricks you are using, but you'd better not think you've won just because of this," Cathead said. He took my hand and seemed to be attempting to break it, but it didn't even tickle. He sent his floating blades after Ren, who was still rapidly closing in. They struck at Ren from every direction, likely to cause death even if a single one of them landed. But Ren used both of his swords, one in each hand, to knock the incoming blades away, and then directed his weapons at the one who assumed the name of god, who I was still holding onto.

"Sword 0! My mastery is much lower than Naofumi, but here we go!" He changed one of his swords to the blade from the Phoenix materials and the other to Sword 0, preparing a skill as he came in. With a highly satisfying sound, Cathead's barrier was sliced apart. Ren slashed into his back. Then he sliced the arm off of our enemy. I'd been training with Ren in preparation for fighting enemies with floating weapons recently, but I hadn't expected it to pay off so soon.

Cathead gasped and screamed as he looked down to see the severed arm and spraying blood.

"What's going on? What? What? How? This is insane! Impossible!" Cathead raged. He was looking around, clearly in shock at the sudden pain. He didn't seem to have much combat experience, based on this reaction—but if they really did have close to absolute power, it might make sense he'd never been in a real battle.

This sudden pain seemed like a good lesson for him. While he was still shaken, we needed to finish him off.

"No! The god hunters! Is that you?" Cathead asked.

"It does look like these weapons work," I commented. We'd never encountered anyone calling themselves "god hunters." I wondered if this was the thing from Fitoria's wall. The coloring, height, everything looked different, but maybe those were just changes that happened as the description was passed down over time. But I seemed to recall Fitoria also saying the creature on the wall wasn't our enemy. That didn't mean Fitoria was on the side of the ones who assumed the name of gods, surely. There were lots of fishy things going on, but Fitoria had also provided the materials for these weapons. It was too soon to say anything definitive.

"Brother!" Fohl shouted.

"Mr. Naofumi!" Raphtalia was still with him. Fohl had finished his beast transformation and was glowing blue, rushing in with Raphtalia on his back.

"Do it! Give him everything you've got!" I shouted. I gathered all the strength I had and hurled the injured Cathead toward them. Ren unleashed a follow-up attack as well, swinging his Sword 0 powerfully.

"If we end you, we end all of this! Phoenix Gale Blade X!" Ren shouted, charging forward like a flaming bird.

"We're ending this here! Eight Trigrams Blade of Destiny

Thrust!" Raphtalia yelled, unleashing a special attack as Heavenly Emperor.

"Shaking Quaking Fist X!" Fohl roared, smashing his fists down with enough force to crack and split the ground beneath us. All of their training was paying off in the unleashing of these skills, and the power of the 0 weapons was surely compounding the effects. All their incoming attacks proceeded to smash into the completely defenseless one who assumed the name of god. He spluttered and cried out, barely legible, something about "murderers," even as he was mangled by the meeting of the attacks.

"That's right! We're doing this to kill you!" I told him. We continued to encounter enemies who considered everything to be a game. I wondered for a moment if they were treating it like a game by sending in the resurrected. All this talk of an audience . . . I could imagine them enjoying these things like different shows or documentaries.

"Eat this!" The massive fist of the beast transformed Fohl came down in full force combined with the Gauntlet 0. The one who assumed the name of god made a final cry and was then squished with a nasty wet sound.

It was too soon to drop our guard though—not like we'd done with Bitch!

"We're not finished yet! Fohl, Raphtalia, Ren! We have to destroy the soul too!" I shouted. They all shouted back in

agreement, activating the 0 skill on weapons that were powerful against soul-type enemies and then attacking again at full
strength. All that remained after we were finished was a cracked
crater punched into the translucent ground and the pulped
corpse of the one who assumed the name of god.

"We got him," I said. He was dead, dead as a doornail. Even
as I muttered these words, the power faded from the Shield 0.
That seemed to confirm that it was only effective against specific enemies. Even so, I couldn't get over how easy this seemed
to have been. We'd been in real danger for a moment there, but
in the end, we'd won pretty easily. It also told us that we could
defeat the ones who assumed the name of gods. That was good
news. We'd also learned there was a whole bunch of them. This
would be important information going forward.

As I was thinking, the heroes who were fighting to quell
the wave itself and their allies all realized what was going on.
Shouts like "they won!" along with many wordless roars all
filled the air. Some of them were even howling.

In the next moment, the ground vanished below us and we
all started to fall.

"Brother! I can help us land! Let me handle this!" Fohl said.

"Okay. Air Strike Shield, Second Shield, Dritte Shield!" I
shouted, creating multiple shields to act as platforms for Fohl.
He remained in his beast transformation and moved between
the platforms, collecting us up before landing back down on

the ground. We could hear shouts of celebration coming from each of the floating rings too. The wave crack was also clearly shrinking down on its own. We weren't going to have to do anything else; it was just closing. The mood was one of complete celebration—so much so that the fighting had basically stopped.

"We can celebrate once the wave has safely ended!" I shouted. That snapped the revelers back to themselves, and they returned to focusing on the battle to prevent more damage from the waves. The Bow Hero from this time and his party, who had been taking part in the event created by the one who assumed the name of god, also seemed to be prioritizing escape. With cracking sounds as the entire space gave way, the Bow Hero and all the others vanished. I guessed that meant they had escaped.

"Mr. Naofumi, we did it!" Raphtalia celebrated.

"I felt that one," Ren agreed. Both of them looked happy. We'd been in trouble for a moment, but we'd defeated him in the end.

Epilogue: The Fear of Those Who are Eternal

"Brother, is that the end of our fight?" Fohl asked.

"I don't know. If this ends the waves, that would be perfect . . . but we still need to find a way to get back to our time," I said. Mamoru, R'yne, Keel, and the others were dashing over and defeating monsters along the way. Keel and Eclair were wiping out the monsters that had emerged from the waves by simply swinging the modified ancient weapons that Holn had provided. They had certainly received quite the upgrade. They might not be able to match a hero, but putting sufficient magic into these weapons allowed them to really pull their weight.

"Bubba, that was amazing! I wanted to help out too!" Keel said.

"Raph, raph, raph," said Raph-chan.

"Dafu, dafu," said Dafu-chan.

"That would be very dangerous," Natalia said, joining the Raph-chans in cautioning Keel.

"Indeed. Your eagerness is worthy of praise, but if you don't understand your own limits, then you'll simply be killed," the Water Dragon added. Their voices were pitched a little higher than normal though. That just showed what a powerful enemy we had defeated, even from their perspective.

"He only allowed heroes to take part, anyway," I told her.

"I'm amazed you defeated one who assumes the name of god," Natalia said. "When you were all called up there, I prayed that maybe one of you would survive."

"He was pretty powerful," I admitted. We'd basically defeated him using a sucker punch. If we had to fight him when he was prepared, at full strength, I wasn't sure we would win.

"You were amazing up there, Naofumi," Ruft said, riding up on the head of Rat's monster Mikey. "We didn't get to do much this time."

"Raph," said Mikey.

"I think you did well for your first battle, Mikey," Rat said.

"Raph!" said Mikey. I hadn't seen much, but Mikey had basically been a giant Raph species smashing through the enemy. Rat was also standing next to Ruft.

"I'm happy for him, but . . . I also miss Gaelion," Wyndia said, moving over toward Ren and holding the former caterpilland Raph species.

"You'll see him again once we get back to the future," Ren assured her.

"Yeah. You did well today, Ren," Wyndia said.

"It was great," Ren said. "We're going to take down the enemies in the future too, just like this." He looked pretty pleased with himself. I hoped we could keep this momentum going.

"You really know how to worry me, Naofumi," Melty said with a sigh.

"We didn't really have a choice this time, in case you didn't notice. However. . . we're always fighting on a knife-edge, pretty much," I admitted.

"You said it. I need to fight. That way I can help out more in this kind of situation." Melty sighed.

"Why not use one of the weapons Holn just gave us?" I suggested. Melty was pretty enhanced, so she'd attained considerable strength. She had plenty of innate magic too. She'd be well-matched with a weapon that could turn that magic into strength.

"I know, but I just don't like the look of them. Even if Fitoria gave them to us . . ." Melty admitted.

"I understand that. But we can't really be picky, can we?" I reminded her. The fact the high priest had used them was probably why Melty didn't like them. I could also tell that with Melty's magic behind them they would be powerful weapons. She was more in a command position, but being able to fight when she needed to made a big difference. That said, we weren't going to have her fight any of the ones who assumed the name of god. Then Eclair made a thoughtful noise.

"If I'm going to continue to be involved in this fighting, I'm really starting to think that I want a vassal weapon of my own, Ren," she said.

"Eclair . . ." Ren replied a little awkwardly.

"I know. I need to work with you, Hero Iwatani, and the

others, and wait for a weapon like the ones you just used. I'll keep training until that happens," Eclair said.

"That's right! Let's make some weapons, all together . . . weapons that can kill gods!" Ren replied. Everyone was in pretty high spirits, and conviction had definitely been renewed.

"Wow! World peace, baby!" R'yne said. They were making it sound like we had completely won. If it meant the end of the waves, of course, I would be fine with that. If we'd changed the future and ended the waves there too, so be it.

Maybe that was all a pipe dream though.

"I can't believe this."

A pipe dream that was short-lived.

"This is bad. This is really, really bad." The voice was coming from behind me, and it sounded a lot like the voice of the one who assumed the name of god that we already killed. I turned to look and saw someone similar to the dead one but with a dog mascot head. It looked at the crushed body and muttered to himself. "You scum! Primeval pond scum! How dare you do this! Murderers!"

There was another one of them here. This could be a problem.

"Huh? You call yourselves gods, don't you? You haven't heard the stories about heroes who kill gods? That's like half the job of a hero," I taunted him, gauging the situation.

"Watch your mouth, primate!" Doghead raged. Even as we

talked, Ren, Raphtalia, Fohl, and S'yne all changed to their 0 weapons and deployed their skills. That was when I noticed Doghead looked like he was about to crap himself.

"You aren't going to come for us? If you don't, we're coming for you," I warned him. He made a frightened gasp. From that noise, and from the look in his eyes, I could tell what he was afraid of. The one we just killed had talked about not being able to work out where we had come from. It was clicking into place now. They were scared of us having the ability to kill them. Which meant it wouldn't hurt to threaten them some more. "Oh, and don't think taking care of us will end this. Do you know what we have behind us?" I asked. I deployed the Shield 0 and really amped up the pressure.

"Pond . . . scum . . . getting full of yourselves, just because you've found a way to kill a god," Doghead said.

"You're free to think whatever you want. But you still understand the position you're in, right?" I replied, pressing the point and pointing directly at him. "You're next. Not just you alone, all of you. You're all going to take responsibility for this crazy bullshit you've been putting us through!" That was my declaration, not just to the new one who assumed the name of god, but everyone who had to be watching.

"This humiliation!" Doghead retorted. "I won't forget this! You'll suffer the true wrath of the gods now!" I could tell from his voice he was pushing down his anger and his fear.

"What's happening among your audience now?" I taunted. "Are they crying out that they don't want to die? Crying out to be saved?" The new one who assumed the name of god seemed to have realized he was at a disadvantage, because he deployed what looked like a cape and simply vanished, right along with the body of his dead friend. It had to be some kind of instant transmission skill, like a portal. Then the crack vanished too, and the rings with the other worlds vanished, and everything returned to silence.

"Looks like we drove them off," I said.

"You were talking a big game back there," Holn commented.

"That's how I roll," I replied.

"Pretty much what I'd expect from you, Naofumi," Mamoru said.

"Your personality and the things you can actually do don't really match up, do they?" R'yne said. Those two seemed to understand us now. There was no need to play along with this shitty game they were running on us.

"You guys agree with me, right?" I asked. Raphtalia, Ren, Fohl, S'yne, and everyone else from the village nodded.

"You can't surprise me anymore," Ruft replied.

"You were using the limited information we have to lead them to the worst possible conclusions, weren't you?" Raphtalia said. "They did sound pretty scared of these 'god hunters,' that's for sure."

"I spotted that too," I said sardonically. "If they have something they're so afraid of, they shouldn't be pulling stuff like this." It was like the mafia sitting around worrying about the police. They were scared of being punished but desired stimulation, a terrible combination.

In any case, we had dealt with them for now. They had been pretty strong, but if our weapons had been fully upgraded, I wasn't so sure. They had felt like a challenging extra boss beyond the normal end of a game—something tough, but possible to defeat. Right now, our weapons weren't quite at the right level.

"That was a surprise. What were those weapons you heroes from the future were using?" Holn asked. I kept an eye out for the ones who assumed the name of gods coming back.

"The 0 series. We obtained them from what looked like some kind of medicine of eternal life found in some ancient ruins. They are normally just trash, unable to do anything, but if you use them to attack a wave crack, it can delay the arrival of the next wave. They can also resist the binding of the holy weapons," I explained.

"The quelling of irregular power . . . I've theorized about the existence of such a thing," Holn said.

"I'm sure you have. That's why when I saw the one who assumes the name of god using that illegitimate power, I thought it was worth trying them out," I said.

"Your past, in the future . . . maybe the god hunters came

to that time and left that power for future generations," Holn said.

"Maybe," I replied. Once we got home, we were going to be having words with Fitoria. "No matter how that turns out, it's a fact that we took out one of those causing the waves. That means our counterattack has truly started." Everyone nodded in agreement. "Okay! Let's gather together even more tightly and take the fight to these sons of bitches who assumed the name of god!" That was met with a roar of general approval.

And so ended our first killing of a god. We still didn't have a way to get back to our own time, but we'd likely resolved the issues with the waves here in this time period. At least the ones behind them were afraid for their lives now. I hoped the frequency of the waves would decrease.

We finished up the last of the wave monsters and then returned to the village and the castle.

The Rising of the Shield Hero Vol. 21
(TATE NO YUUSHA NO NARIAGARI Vol.21)
© Aneko Yusagi 2019
First published in Japan in 2019 by KADOKAWA CORPORATION, Tokyo.
English translation rights arranged with KADOKAWA CORPORATION, Tokyo.

ISBN: 978-1-64273-132-3

Written by Aneko Yusagi
Character Design Minami Seira
English Edition Published by One Peace Books 2021

Printed in Canada
1 2 3 4 5 6 7 8 9 10

One Peace Books
43-32 22nd Street STE 204 Long Island City New York 11101
www.onepeacebooks.com